MILLIONS OF YEARS HENCE . . .

The Earth was desolated. Fiery winds wrapped it. The polar caps had melted, and earthquakes, exploding volcanoes, and crumbling coastal masses had changed the face of what land was left.

There was no explanation for what had happened or for what had caused the global holocaust. Possibly, the huge luminous teardrops that tore through the smoke covering the seared earth were the cause. But there was no one to explain. . . .

The teardrops appeared again and hovered . . . for a while. None took any action, except one: it loosed energy bolts that burned out the little tree containing the forty survivors of *homo sapiens*.

PHILIP JOSÉ FARMER

has also written:

BEHIND THE WALLS OF TERRA

LORD OF THE TREES

THE MAD GOBLIN

THE WIND WHALES OF ISHMAEL

Philip José Farmer
The Stone God Awakens

ace books

A Division of Charter Communications Inc.
1120 Avenue of the Americas
New York, N.Y. 10036

First Ace printing: November 1970
Second Ace printing: July 1973

Printed in U.S.A.

HE AWOKE AND DID NOT KNOW WHERE HE WAS.

Flames were crackling fifty feet away. Woodsmoke stung his nose and brought tears. Somewhere, men were shouting and screaming.

Just as his eyes had opened, he had seen a piece of plastic falling from under his arms, which had been extended before him. Something struck his knees lightly, slid down his legs, and fell onto a stone disk beneath him.

He was sitting on a chair—his desk chair. The chair was on the seat of a huge throne carved out of granite, and the throne was on a round stone platform. There were dark brown-red stains on the stone. The thing that had fallen was a section of the desk on which he had been leaning when he had passed out.

He was in one end of a large building of gigantic logs, wooden pillars, and huge overhead beams. Flames leaped along the wall toward him. The roof at the other end had just caved in, and the smoke was carried away by a vagary of the wind. He could see the sky outside. It was black, and then, far off, lightning flashed. About fifty yards away, lit by the flames, was a hill. On top of the hill were the silhouettes of trees. Fully leaved trees.

A moment ago, it had been winter. The deep snows had been piled around the buildings of the research center outside Syracuse, New York.

The smoke curled back and blocked off his view. The flames leaped higher and outward toward the many long tables and benches and the thick pillars supporting the roof. These looked like totem poles with their weird carved heads, one on top of the other. The tables held dishes, beakers and some simple utensils. A pitcher, turned over, had spilled a dark liquid onto the nearest table.

He stood up and coughed as smoke tentacled around his head. He got down off the seat of the huge throne, which, now that it was lit by the approaching flames, was revealed as a red and black quartz-shot granite. Bewildered, he looked around. He could see the edge of a partly open door—a two-sectioned door or gate—and outside were more flames and bodies struggling, swaying, falling, and more shouts and screams.

He would have to get out of here before the smoke or the flames overcame him, but he also did not like running out into the battle. He crouched on the stone platform and then stepped down onto the hard earthen floor of the hall.

A weapon. He needed a weapon. He felt in his jacket pocket and came out with the switchblade. He pressed the button, and the six-inch blade shot out. It was illegal to carry a knife of this length in New York of 1985, but if a man wanted to defend himself in 1985, he had to do some illegal things.

He walked swiftly through the smoke, still coughing, and reached the two swinging batwing doors. He got down on his knees and looked underneath, since the top of the gate was over his head.

The flames from the burning hall and from other buildings combined to illuminate the scene. Furry legs and tails, white and black and brown, danced around. The legs were human and yet not human. They bent queerly; they looked like the hind legs of four-footed animals that had decided to stand upright, like men, and so had evolved half-human, half-beast legs.

The owner of a pair of legs fell flat on his back, a spear stuck in his belly. The man became even more confused and shocked. The creature looked like a cross between a human being and a sealpoint Siamese cat. The body fur was white; the face below the forehead was black; the lower parts of the arms, legs and the tail were black. The face was as flat as any human's, but the nose was round and black, like a cat's, and the ears were black and pointed. The mouth, open in death, revealed sharp feline teeth.

The spear was jerked out by a creature which also had crooked legs and a long tail but fur of a uniform brown. And then there was a scream, and the legs staggered forward and fell over the sealpoint-Siamese-human creature, and the man could see most of the details of the spearman's body. Spear*man* was not quite the correct word, since he was not a man. He, too, looked as if he had evolved from quadruped into biped, gaining a number of human features along the way, such as a flat face, forward-placed eyes, a chin, humanoid hands and a broad chest. But if

6

the other creature had resembled a Siamese cat, this resembled a raccoon. He was brown everywhere except across the eyes and cheeks, which were covered by a black bar of fur.

The man could not see what had killed him.

There was no inducement to go outside until the flames would force him. He crouched by the gate and looked through it. He felt dislocated from reality. Or was he in reality, and that hellish scene a fantasy that had somehow come to life in his mind?

Flame licked at his back. A part of the roof crashed down at the other end of the building. He scrambled out beneath the gate on his hands and knees, hoping to crawl away unnoticed.

He stayed along the side of the building as smoke poured out around him. It helped conceal him, but it also made him cough and filled his eyes with tears. That explained why he did not see the raccoon-faced thing that reeled out of the smoke toward him, his tomahawk lifted. Nor did the man realize until it was too late that the thing was not attacking him. He had just been blundering around, blind because of the loss of one eye, which hung by a thread of nerves, and from the smoke. The creature had probably not been aware of the man until just before he almost fell over him.

The man stabbed upward, and the blade went into the furry belly. Blood welled out as the creature staggered backward and thus freed himself of the blade. His tomahawk dropped by the man's head. The man watched the thing reel back, clutching at his belly, then half-turn and fall over on his side. Only then did the man realize that the raccoon-face had not been intent on attacking him. He picked up the tomahawk in his right hand after shifting the knife to his left hand. He crawled on, coughing as more smoke encoiled him.

He felt frozen, yet he was capable of acting. The mind was only beginning to warm up; the body cracked its own ice and broke through the shell in a flash of heat. Another raccoon-face approached him; this one evidently saw him but not clearly. He squinted through the smoke as he trotted toward the man. He held a short heavy spear with a stone tip in both hands across his belly, and he crouched as if he was not sure of what he was seeing.

The man stood up then, the tomahawk and knife ready. He felt that he did not have much chance. Although the furry biped was only about five feet two inches high and

7

weighed maybe a hundred and thirty-five pounds, and he was six feet three and weighed two hundred and forty-five pounds, he did not know how to throw a tomahawk efficiently. And that was ironic, since he was part-Iroquois.

The raccoon-face slowed down as he came closer. About thirty feet away, he stopped. Then his eyes got even bigger, and he yelled. His yelling would have been unnoticed in the general bedlam, but six others—three catmen, as he thought of them, and three raccoon-faces—also saw him. They stopped their fighting to stare, and several called to nearby warriors. These also quit stabbing or chopping at each other, and from this silence a cone of motionlessness and noiselessness spread.

The man edged toward the ladder. The only one who was close enough to be in the way was the raccoon-face who had first noticed him. The others could throw their assegais or tomahawks at him, but he would take his chances on that. So far, he had seen no evidence of bows and arrows.

The raccoon-face moved away as the man came closer, but he was going sideways and so still could get between him and the ladder if he wished. Then the raccoon-face moved closer and raised the spear, and the man had to defend himself. He hated to let loose of the tomahawk, but if he kept it, it would not be much of a weapon against the spear. His sole chance was in getting the creature before he came close enough to stab him with the assegai. He threw the tomahawk with all the force he could summon up in his frozen body. And, as luck, not skill, had it, the edge of the tomahawk hit the raccoon-face in his neck. He fell backward and lay on his back.

There was a yell from the spectators, which by now included almost all the warriors. Even the man could tell that the catpeople were yelling with triumph and the raccoon-people with despair. The raccoon-faces raced for the ladders in a body, throwing their spears and tomahawks to one side. A few made it over the palisades, but most were stabbed or hatcheted in the back before they got to the ladders or while on the ladders. A few prisoners were taken.

It was only then that the man realized that this raccoon-face had not intended to use the spear against him either. He had raised the spear merely to cast it to one side, as if in submission. But the tomahawk had been on its way then. Reality was no tape recorder to be played over again, spliced, or demagnetized.

The Siamese-catpeople crowded around him, though they
8

did not come close enough to touch him. They got down on their knees and waddled toward the man, their hands held out. Their weapons lay on the ground behind them. Their faces held strange expressions; the fur and the round black wet noses and the widely separated, long sharp teeth and the eyes, exactly like those of a cat's, made their expressions unreadable. But their attitudes expressed awe, fear and adoration. Whatever their expressions, they evidently did not mean harm to him.

The flames behind him grew brighter, and he saw the eyes of some of them glow. The irises were shaped like narrow leaves against the glare behind him.

One came closer and reached out a hand to touch him. The hand was, apart from being furry, human-like. It had four fingers and nails, not claws. The thumb was opposable.

He felt the tips of the fingers on his thigh, and that touch seemed to poke a hole through his defenses. The night sky, the burning buildings, the log palisades, the bodies of brown and white-and-black tailed creatures, and, now, the glowing eyes and small faces of children and females looking out of huts. Everything whirled. Around and around. The creature on his knees before the man shouted with terror and tried to scramble backward on his knees. The man fell, striking his shoulder, and lay on the ground while everything galloped by. The one fixed object was the black tip of the thing's tail, which lay before his eyes. It twitched and twitched, and then it grew big and black, and everything was black and silent.

Light and sound returned. He was on his back on soft furs and some soft substance beneath the furs. Above him was a low ceiling with smoke-blackened beams and dark figurines in wood, tasseled with fur, hanging from strips of leather attached to the ceiling. The room, about twenty feet by thirty, was crowded with the Siamese-cat creatures. Those nearest his bed were males, but a moment later a female came through an aisle opened for her by the males. She was about five feet tall and had fully rounded breasts beneath the fur and small hairless areas around the nipples. She wore triple-looped beads of large blue stones around the neck and furry wristbands from which dangled little stone figurines. Her enormous eyes were a deep blue that reminded him of the eyes of a beautiful sealpoint Siamese his sister had once owned.

The males wore beads and breastplates made out of bone,

and wristlets and anklets with little figurines or geometric figures, and several had feathered bonnets which could have been worn by chiefs in a Western movie. Only a few were armed, and these seemed to be more ceremonial than utilitarian, judging from their decorations and their lightness.

The female bent over him and said something. He had not expected to understand her, nor did he. The language was not even identifiable as belonging to any of the great language families. There was nothing Germanic or Slavic or Semitic or Chinese or Bantu about it. If it reminded him of anything, it was of the soft voweled Polynesian language but without glottal stops. Later, when his ear became finer tuned, he heard glottal stops, but these did not mean anything, as they would have in Polynesian. They were as functionless as stops in English.

Her teeth were those of a carnivore, but her breath was sweet. The tongue looked as if it would be as rough as a cat's. Despite her genuinely alien appearance, he found himself thinking of her as beautiful. But then he had always thought that the Siamese cat was a weird and beautiful creature.

He got up on his elbow and started to sit up. His knife, caked with blood, was by his side. The female backed away and the males behind her pressed into each other to draw away also. They murmured in awed tones.

He sat for a moment, his hands gripping the edges of the bed. Actually, he was not on a bed but on a pile of furs inside a niche in the wall. There were no windows, but light came from two open doors at the far wall and from several torches burning in stands fixed to the walls. Outside the door was a mob of males and some females and children. The babies—cubs? kittens?—were very "cute" with their big black pointed ears, round heads, and great eyes. Their tails were not as dark as the adults.

He got to his feet and for a second was dizzy and then became clear-headed. At that moment, a new aisle opened, and another female came through it. She carried a big clay bowl with painted geometric symbols on its side and a soup of meat and vegetables inside. The odor was very appetizing, although not identifiable. He accepted the bowl and the wooden utensil, which was a spoon on one end and a two-tined fork on the other. The soup was rich and delicious, and the chunks of meat tasted like deer or antelope. For a second, he had a vision of a raccoon-man having provided the meat, but he decided that he was too hungry to think about that. Despite the somewhat unnerving silence and the intent gazes of the assembly, he ate all the soup. The female then took the bowl away, and everybody stood around as if they were waiting for him to make the next move.

He walked to the nearest door, an aisle opening for him. The sun had just cleared the hills to the east. He had been out for a long time, especially when he considered that it must have been just from the shock of finding himself in such frightening and unfamiliar surroundings.

Now that he was thinking more clearly . . . where was he? Where in hell was he?

The hills and the trees that he could see in the distance looked as if they belonged to the region around Syracuse. But that was all that was familiar.

The great hall was only half-burned, and the other buildings that he had expected to be nothing but ashes were only half-burned, too. The ground around them was still wet from the rain which had put the flames out.

Aside from the tremendous log hall, the interior of the palisaded village looked like a seventeenth century Onondaga settlement with its long houses. The ladders and the corpses were gone. A few wooden cages near the hall held about a dozen raccoonpeople.

The gates to the palisade were open, showing fields of corn and other plants outside. Females were working in them while younger children ran about and the older worked with their mothers. Armed males stood guard by the fields; others were on high watchtowers placed well outside the fields and also within the palisade.

The sun and the blue sky were those that he had known all his life.

The catmen evidently expected him to do something. He hoped that he was not going to do something that would change their awe into hostility. He was completely bewildered, and he might have gone mad if he had not had a thick bedrock of pragmatism in his nature.

The only way would be to learn the language.

He indicated the female whom he had first seen, the one who reminded him of his sister's Siamese cat. He pointed to himself and said, "Ulysses Singing Bear."

She looked at him. The others murmured and shifted uneasily.

"Ulysses Singing Bear," he said.

She smiled or at least opened her mouth widely. A scary smile. Those teeth could take a big chunk out of him with one bite. Not that they were as relatively large as those of a house cat. They were small, really, and the canines were only slightly longer than the other teeth. But they were so sharp.

She said something, and he repeated his name. It was evident that she was trying to repeat the words, though she may not have guessed that he was saying his name.

After a while, she was able to say, "Wurisa Asiingagna Wapiira."

That was as close as she could come to mastering English sounds.

He shrugged. It was up to him to adapt. He would learn their language.

"Wurisa," he said, and he smiled.

Most of them looked puzzled, and only much later did he find out why. After all, one expects one's god to be able to speak the language of his worshipers. But here was their god and savior, the one for whom they had been waiting for hundreds of years, no more able than a new-born to speak the tongue of the gods.

Fortunately, the Wufea were as able to rationalize as human beings. Their chief priest and his daughter, Awina, advanced the explanation that he had been put under a spell by Wurutana, the Great Devourer, when Wuwiso, the god of the Wufea, had been turned to stone. Wuwiso had forgotten his language, but he would quickly relearn it.

Awina was his chief instructor. She stayed by him almost all the time, and since she loved to talk, even with a god who half-terrified her, she taught him swiftly. She was intelligent—sometimes he thought she was more intelligent than he—and she conceived of many ways to speed up his learning.

She also had a sense of humor, and when Ulysses understood a pun she made he knew that he was advancing swiftly. He was so pleased with himself, and with her, that he almost kissed her. And then he caught himself, as it were, by the back of the neck and pulled himself back. He had been growing very fond of this delicate sinuous laughing creature. But he did not intend to get that fond. Nevertheless, she was the focal point, an island in an unknown universe and a shifting sea, and she was very pleasant to be with. When she was gone, he felt unease ooze in, like lava beneath an iron door.

By the time he recognized her first pun, he had become acquainted with the interior of the village and the area a few miles around it. A dozen young warriors and a priest

12

always accompanied him. They walked in any direction for several miles, but after a certain distance, they stopped him. He wanted to go on, but on the other hand he did not feel ready to force any issues with those who were, after all, his wardens.

North and west, the country was high rolling hills, lakes, and several small rivers and many creeks. It was like that around Syracuse. East, after a few miles of hills, was a large forest of evergreens. South, the country was hilly for two miles and then suddenly a plain began. It ran for as far as he could see from the top of a hill approximately eight hundred feet high. On the horizon was a great dark bulk that he thought might be a mountain range. Then, the second trip, he decided it was a cloudbank. The third trip, he concluded that he did not know what it could be.

He asked Awina about it, and she looked at him strangely and said, "Wurutana!" She sounded as if she did not understand why he would have to ask her about it.

Wurutana, he knew by then, meant the Great Devourer. It also meant something else, but he did not know the language well enough yet to catch certain subtleties.

According to Awina, there were other Wufea villages to the north and east. Their enemies, who called themselves Wagarondit, lived to the west and the north. There were about two hundred people in this village and about three thousand Wufea altogether.

The Wagarondit had their own language, unrelated to Wufea, but both groups used a third language, a trade language, for communication. This speech was called Ayrata.

The Wufea neither had metal of their own, nor had they heard of it. Singing Bear's knife was the first they had seen of steel.

Moreover, they did not know about the bow. He could not understand this. They might not know metal because there might not be any in this area. But even Old Stone Age peoples should have the bow and arrow. Then he remembered the Australian aborigine, who had been so technologically backward that he had not discovered the principles of archery. There was no reason why he should not have done so. He was intelligent enough. But he had not invented the bow. And then there was the Amerindian, some of whom had made wheels for the toys of their children. Yet they had never applied the principle to making big wagons or wheelbarrows or carts.

On his trips, especially to the east, he looked around for suitable wood and found a tree that resembled the

13

yew. He had his guards chop off branches with their stone axes, and they brought the wood back. There he got the gut and the feathers he needed and, after suitable experimentation, produced a number of bows and arrows.

The Wufea were amazed, but they caught on to the uses of the bow quickly enough. After a little practice on the grass targets he put up, they brought out a Wagarondit prisoner. They marched him to beyond the fields and there told him to get going.

Ulysses had hesitated, because he did not know how far he could extend his authority. He knew by then that he was some sort of a god. They had told him that and even if they had not, he could have guessed from their attitude. He had even taken part in several ceremonies in the not-as-yet-rebuilt temple. But just what kind of a god and how powerful he was, he did not know. Now seemed as good a time as any to find out. He had no reason to intercede for the Wagarondit, but he found himself unable not to. He could not stand by while the young warriors tried out their markmanship on the raccoon-man.

At first, some of the Wufea seemed inclined to argue. They looked hard at him and a few even muttered something. But nobody openly opposed him, and when the chief priest, Awina's father, Aytheera, stormed at them, waving his wand with its serpent and big bird heads and rattling pebbles in a gourd, he succeeded in scaring them. The gist of his speech was that they were under a new regime. Their ideas of what a god should be did not necessarily coincide with the god's own ideas. If they did not straighten out quickly, they might find themselves turned to stone by lightning thrown by the god. This would reverse the procedure by which the stone god had awakened, become fleshed, and once again walked among them.

This was the first time that Singing Bear had any hint of what had happened to him. He asked Awina about it later, couching his questions so that she would not know how deep his ignorance was. She smiled slyly and looked at him out of the corner of her huge, slit-irised eyes. Perhaps she had caught on to the fact that he did not know what had happened. But if she were intelligent enough to comprehend this, she was also intelligent enough to know that she should keep her mouth shut.

He had been stone. He was found on the bottom of a lake that had been emptied by a great earthquake. He was attached to a stone chair, and his elbows were on a piece of stone. He was sitting in the stone chair and leaning forward. He was so heavy that it took the efforts of all the males of two villages to lift him out of the mud and drag him on rollers to the larger of the villages. There he had been set up on the granite throne which had been prepared for him many generations before.

Ulysses Singing Bear asked her about the throne. Who had prepared it? He had seen nothing to indicate that the Wufea carved stone.

The throne had been found in the ruins of a mighty city of the Ancients, she said. She was very vague about the identity of the Ancients or the location of the city. Somewhere to the south. In those days, twenty generations ago, the Wufea had been located many marches to the south. It was a plain then, with thousands of game animals roaming it. Then Wurutana had grown over the site of the villages and the city of the Ancients, and the Wufea had been forced to move northward to escape the shadow of Wurutana. Just as they would have had to move again in another generation if Wuwiso had not been hit by lightning and been unstoned, become fleshed.

The lightning stroke, it seemed, had hit him during the storm that occurred when the Wagarondit attacked. It had also set fire to the temple. The other fires were set by the Wagarondit.

That night, Ulysses went outside his new quarters in the temple. He looked up at the sky and wondered if he could be on Earth. He did not know how he could be elsewhere. But if he was on Earth, what was the year?

The stars formed unfamiliar constellations, and the moon seemed to be larger, as if it were nearer to Earth. Nor was it the naked, silver body he had known in 1985. It was blue and green with white masses drifting over it. In fact, it looked much like Earth as seen from a satellite. If it were the Moon, it had been *terrafied*. Its rocks had been treated to give it air, form soil and yield water. In history, there had been articles speculating on the possibility of terrafication, but the chances for even beginning the process would not occur until several centuries from then.

If he was certain of one thing, other than that he was alive, it was that far more than a few centuries, or a few millennia, had passed since 1985.

For one thing, it would take millions of years for a humanoid sentient to evolve from felines. In fact, the evolution should be, theoretically, impossible. The felines of his day were too specialized to change into these creatures. They were in a blind alley.

It was, however, possible that the Wufea were not descended from felines. The Siamese cat appearance might be misleading. Perhaps they were descended from some other genus. Bipedal sentients might evolve from raccoons. They were generalized enough. But human-handed bipedal sentients from the pussycat of his day?

Maybe the cat-like Wufea and the raccoon-like (but also cat-like) Wagarondit were descended from a raccoon or maybe even a primate, a lemur, for instance. It did not seem likely, considering the eyes. In fact, it seemed impossible. And why the retention of the tails? They served no useful purpose of which he knew. Evolution had cut off the tails of the great apes of the hominids. Why had it not done so with these creatures?

Also, there was the other animal life to consider. There were horses, smaller versions of the thoroughbreds of his day, which ranged the plains to the south. Another species, or variety, roamed the forest. They provided food for the Wufea, who had not as yet thought about riding them. The horses were unchanged in any significant features. But there was an animal with a delicate face and a giraffe-like neck that fed on the leaves of trees. He would swear that that animal was evolved from the horse.

There was a flying squirrel, although not the gliding animal of his time; this had bat-like wings and flew like a bat. But it was a rodent, and it must have evolved from the gliding squirrel.

There was also a bird, standing twelve feet high on very thick legs, which looked very much as if its ancestor had been the tiny roadrunner of the southwest.

And there were other animals whose existence meant many millions of years of evolution from the forms he had known.

Awina had been curious about his life before he was turned into stone. He thought it better to say little about it until he found out what she expected his life to have been. She told him the few religious stories about Wuwiso. Essentially, he was one of the ancient gods, the only one to have survived a terrifying battle between them and Wurutana, the Great Devourer. Wurutana had conquered, and the other gods were destroyed. All except Wuwiso. He had escaped, but to trick his enemy, who was tracking him down, he had turned himself into stone. Wurutana had not been able to damage the stone god, but he had taken the god and buried him under a mountain where

16

nobody would ever find him. Then Wurutana had started to grow, to cover the Earth.

In the meantime, Wuwiso lay at the heart of the mountain, unfeeling, unknowing, uncaring. And Wurutana was happy about this. But even Wurutana was not as great as the greatest of all gods, Time. Time washed away the mountain, and eventually a river carried the stone god down a canyon and deposited him at the bottom of a deep lake. And then an earthquake tilted the lake and dumped out the waters and the Wufea found the stone god, as was prophesied. And the Wufea had been waiting for many generations, waiting for the prophesied stroke of lightning which would bring their deliverer back to life. And, finally, at the hour of the Wufea's greatest peril, as had been foretold, the storm had covered the land and the lightning stroke had freed Wuwiso from the bonds of stone.

Ulysses Singing Bear did not doubt that there were some elements of truth in this myth.

In 1985—how many epochs ago?—he was a biophysicist working on *Project Niobe*. He was halfway through getting his Ph.D. at nearby Syracuse University. The goal of the project was the development of a "matter-freezer," as it was referred to by the project workers. The device was capable of stopping for an indeterminate time all atomic movement in a piece of matter. The molecules and the atoms, and the parts that made up the atoms—the protons, neutrons and so forth—would cease all motion. A bacterium subjected to the energy complex rayed out by the matter-freezer would become a microscopic statue. It would be as if made of stone but of an indestructible stone. Nothing—acids, explosives, atomic radiation, great heat—could destroy it.

The device had possibilities both as a preserving agent and as a "death ray," or a "life ray," if one preferred that term. But, so far, it was impractical because of its extreme short range and its demand for enormous power. Also, there was not even a theory as to how the "petrified" matter could be "depetrified."

Bacteria, a sea urchin egg, an earthworm and a rat had been "petrified." The morning that Ulysses fell into his long sleep, he was working on an experiment in which a pygmy laboratory pig would be rayed. If the experiment was successful, the next step would be to petrify a pony.

Everything had gone as before—up to a point. Ulysses was seated at his desk but was almost ready to get up

17

and walk across the room to the control console he supervised. The power had been turned on, and the matter-freezer was warming up. Across his desk he could see the panel which held the power indicators and a number of other meters and gauges.

Suddenly, the needle of the big power meter had swung around to the red. The operators had cried out, and one had jumped up. Ulysses had looked up just as the needle swung around. And that was all he remembered. There was nothing between then and the time he had opened his eyes in the burning temple.

It was simple enough to figure out what had happened, in a general fashion. Something had given way in the complicated device; the device had blown up or shot out a thin and concentrated ray which, theoretically, it was not yet capable of producing. And he, Ulysses Singing Bear, had been caught. "Petrified." Whether the others had escaped or had also been turned into "stone," he did not know. He might never know.

And so aeons had passed while he existed as a statue of matter harder than anything in the universe. He could have been in that form when the sun blew up and shattered the Earth and sent him tumbling among the great fragments outward through space and toward the stars. For all he knew, that very event had happened, and he had drifted for millions, maybe trillions and trillions of years, while galaxies died and new ones formed. Or all matter in the oscillating universe rushed back to form a primal atom and then blew again and he was hurled at speeds half the speed of light out, and then was caught in newly forming matter, perhaps was the nucleus of a planet. Perhaps he was inside a new star and was ejected during an unimaginably vast eruption into space and was caught by the gravity field of a planet and was sucked down and had burned up tons of air in his fall and smashed deep into the earth. And there he lay while the primeval fresh-water oceans changed to saltier matter. And the continents split and floated away from each other, drifting on the face of the earth. And he was lifted up with the formation of new mountain ranges and was exposed by earthquakes, by volcanic eruptions casting him out, by erosion of wind and water many, many times. And after innumerable burials and exposures, he at last came into the hands of the Wufea. And they set him up on a granite throne. And, at last, whether due to the action of the lightning stroke only, or its combination with the naturally decaying effects of the matter-freezer, he had turned from "stone" into flesh in a microsecond. So swiftly that his heart, interrupted in its beat for God knew how many aeons, had continued the systole or diastole, not even knowing that it had been silent and frozen for ages.

His fantasy, he thought, was a vivid one, and contained certain truths, but he did not think that he was in a new universe. He thought that he was still on Earth, no matter how ancient it was. It was too much of a coincidence that this planet had a moon so much like the moon he had known or that it had horses and rabbits and many insects exactly like those he had known.

Being born from stone was enough of a shock. It could have unhinged the minds of many men, and Singing Bear was not sure that he would be able to stay in one mental piece. But after the shock wore off, the loneliness began to hurt.

It was painful enough to know that all your contemporaries and their grandchildren for hundreds of thousands of generations were dust. But to know that you were the only human being alive was almost unendurable.

He could not be sure that he was the only human being on Earth, and this uncertainty kept him from plunging into despair. There was always hope.

At least, he was not the only sentient alive. He did have many people to talk to, even if the speakers were so alien that they often repelled him, and the language contained concepts he could not quite understand, and their attitudes were sometimes puzzling or infuriating.

Their attitude toward his supposed godhood made any intimacy or warmth difficult. Awina was the only exception. She regarded him with awe, but she also had an overwhelming warmth and humor. Not even a god could be immune to that nor could Awina overcome it. She was continually saying that she should not have said such and such and would Wuwiso forgive her? She did not mean to be so nosy or so chummy and so forth. Ulysses would then assure her that he found nothing in her attitude that needed forgiving.

Awina was seventeen years old and should have been married a year ago. But her mother had died, and her father, forty years old and the chief priest, had put off forcing a marriage. He was exerting his authority close to the breaking point, because the unwritten law was that all healthy females should be mated by sixteen at the latest. Aytheera was a pleasant enough man when he got his way and was well-liked for a priest, and he succeeded in keeping his daughter in his house. Nevertheless, he could not have done so for much longer. She would have had to accept a mate and then have moved out to his longhouse. Though the chief priest had many privileges, he could not marry again. Why, no one knew. That was the custom, and custom was not often broken without immediate punishment.

Now, though he could not keep his daughter close to him all the time, Aytheera had another excuse for objecting to her marriage. She was the stone god's handmaiden, and as long as the god wanted her to serve him, she would. Did anyone in the tribe object?

No one did openly. So Awina stayed with the god until bedtime and then returned to her father's house. She sometimes complained that her father kept her up late talking and that she did not get enough sleep. When Ulysses said he would put a stop to that, she begged that he not say anything. After all, what was a little loss of sleep compared to keeping her old father happy?

Meanwhile, Ulysses became more proficient in the Wufea speech. Its sound combinations were easy for him to master except for certain slight vowel variations used to indicate tenses and attitudes toward tenses. He also took lessons from the Wagarondit captives in their language. This was entirely unrelated to Wufea as far as he could determine, though a scholar with access to written records (which did not exist, of course) might have traced them back to a common ancestor. After all, what tyro would suspect that Hawaiian and Indonesian and Thai were descended from the same parent? But Wagarondit contained a number of difficult phones for him. Its structure reminded him of the Algonquian languages, although of course this was only a superficial resemblance.

The trade language, Ayrata, seemed to be unrelated to either of the other two. Its sounds were simple for him, and its syntax was as uncomplicated and as regular as Esperanto. He asked Awina where it came from, and she said that the Thululiki had introduced it. Gutapa was the Wufea pronunciation of the word used by the Thululiki; she could not pronounce this. The Thululiki's own speech was beyond her; they had introduced Ayrata "all over the world." Everybody could speak some Ayrata, and trade and war councils and peace treaties were all conducted in Ayrata.

Ulysses listened to her description of the Thululiki and decided that they were beings out of her mythology. Such things could not exist.

He had also found out by then that the Wagarondit were being saved for the great annual festival of the confederacy of the Wufea. Then the prisoners would be tortured and finally sacrified to him. For the first time, he learned where the blood on the disc below his throne had come from.

"How many days until the festival of the stone god?" he said.

"One moon exactly," she replied.

He hesitated and then said, "And what if I forbid the torture and the killings? What if I said that the Wagarondit should be let loose?"

Awina's eyes opened widely. It was noonday, and her pupil was a black slit against the blue iris. She opened her mouth then and ran her pink rough tongue acrosss her black lips.

She said, "Pardon, Lord. But why would you do that, what you said?"

Ulysses did not think she would understand if he tried to define concepts of mercy and compassion. She had those traits; she was very tender and empathetic and compassionate, as far as her own people went. But to her the Wagarondit were not even animals.

He could not despise her for that attitude. His own people, the Onondaga and the Seneca, had felt the same way. And so had his other ancestors, the Irish, the Danes, the French, the Norwegians.

"Tell me," he said. "Is it not true that the Wagarondit also claim me as their god? Were they not making that great raid so they could carry me off to their temple?"

Awina looked slyly at him. She said, "Who should know better than you, Lord?"

He waved his hand impatiently and said, "I've told you more than once that some of my thoughts were changed to stone, too. I do not remember some things as yet, though doubtless it will all come back to me. What I'm getting at is that the Wagarondit are as much my people as the Wufea."

"What?" Awina said, and then, in a lower tone, "My Lord?"

She was shaking.

"When a god finally speaks, he does not always say what his people expect to hear," Ulysses said. "If a god said

21

only what everyone else knows, why have a god? No, a god sees much farther and much more clearly than mortals. He knows what is best for his people, even if they are so blind they can't see what will be good for them in the long run."

There was silence. A fly buzzed in the room, and Ulysses wondered that that pest had survived. If mankind had been intelligent enough, he would . . . and then he thought, well, mankind wasn't intelligent enough. Even in 1985 it looked as if starvation and pollution, mankind's progeny, would kill off man. It looked now as if all of humanity might be dead, except for one accidental survivor, himself. Yet here was the common housefly, as prosperous as his distant cousin, the cockroach, which also infested the village.

Awina said, "I do not understand what my Lord is getting at, or why the ancient sacrifices, which seemed to satisfy my Lord for so many generations, and against which he never once opened his mouth . . ."

"You should pray that you will be able to see, Awina. Blindness can lead to death, you know."

Awina closed her mouth and then ran the tip of her tongue over her lips. He was finding out that cloudy statements threw them into a panic, that they imagined the worst.

"Go tell the chiefs and the priests that I want to hold a conference," he said. "Within the time it would take a man walking slowly to go all the way around the village. And tell the workers to quit hammering away on this building while we are holding the conference."

Awina, shouting, ran out of the temple and inside five minutes every official who was not out hunting was inside the temple. Ulysses sat on the hard, cold granite throne and told them what he wanted. They looked shocked, but none dared object. Aytheera did say, "Lord, may I ask what you eventually intend to do with this alliance?"

"For one thing, I intend to stop this useless warfare. For another, I intend to take both Wufea and Wagarondit, the best warriors of both peoples, on an expedition against Wurutana."

"Wurutana!" they murmured in awe and no little dread.

"Yes, Wurutana! Are you surprised? Did you not expect the ancient prophecies to be fulfilled?"

"Oh, yes, Lord," Aytheera said. "It is just that, now the time is here, we find our knees shaking and our bowels turning to water."

22

(To the Wufea, the seat of courage was in the bowels.)

"I will be leading you against Wurutana," Singing Bear said. He wondered just what Wurutana was and what he was supposed to do to combat it. He had tried to get as much information as he could about it without letting them know how ignorant he was. He did not think that he should be using his excuse of "petrified" thoughts in the case of Wurutana. That was permissible with other, lesser, things, but Wurutana was so important that he would not have forgotten the slightest detail about it. That, at least, seemed to be the attitude of the Wufea.

"You will send a messenger to the nearest Wagarondit village and tell them that I am coming," he said, leaving it up to them to work out the practical method of approaching a deadly enemy. "You will tell them that I am coming to visit and that we will be bringing the Wagarondit prisoners, safe if not exactly unharmed, and will release them there. And the Wagarondit will release any Wufea prisoners they might have. We will hold a big conference and then go to the other Wagarondit villages and hold meetings there. Then I will pick out the Wagarondit warriors I want to accompany us, and we will go across the plains against Wurutana."

There was plenty of light inside the temple. Both big doors were open, and a big hole at one end had not yet been closed. The light showed the expressions beneath the short sleek fur on their faces and their sidewise glancing at each other. Their eyes, blue, green, yellow, orange, looked sinister and cat-like. Their tails thrashed from side to side, additionally betraying their agitation.

They had expected him to lead them in a war of extermination against the Wagarondit. Now he was proposing peace, and, worse, they would have to share their god with their ancient enemy.

Singing Bear said, "Your real enemy is Wurutana, not the Wagarondit. Now go and do as I have ordered."

A week later, he walked out through the northern gates on the hard-packed path between the fields of corn and the gardens. The old people, the younger warriors left behind to guard the village, the females and the cubs followed them, shouting and waving. Behind him were three Wufea musicians—like the spirit of '76, he thought—a drummer, a flutist, and a standard-bearer. The drum was made of wood and hide. The flute was hollowed out from the bone of some great animal. The standard was a tall spear with feathers sticking out at right angles to the shaft and the mounted heads of an eagle-like bird, a big lynx-like cat, a giant rabbit, and a horse. These heads represented the four clans, or phratries, of the Wufea. The clans resided in every village, and it was the clan system which had bound the various Wufea tribes together. As he understood it, the treaties of peace and union were between the clans of the villages, not between each tribe. Thus, for a while, the rabbit clans of each village had not fought against each other, but the lynx and the horse clans had. Then these had made peace, and the eagle clans, which had been neutral, had also agreed to join the others. Only then had the Wufea villages presented a united front against the Wagarondit. Ulysses did not understand the system; it seemed very complicated and actually nonsurvival, but the Wufea thought their system was the only natural one.

Behind the standard-bearer and the musicians, who played atonal music, were the chief priest and two lesser priests. These wore feathered bonnets, massive beads and brandished wands. After them came a group of twenty-five young warriors, also decked out in feathers, beads and with chevrons of green, black, and red painted across their faces and their chests. Behind them was a band of sixty older warriors. All warriors were armed with stone knives, tomahawks and assegais, and carried bows and quivers of arrows. They were aching to try their new weapons on the Wagarondit. That is, the younger warriors were. The older ones only concealed their scorn for the new weapons when Ulysses was within hearing distance. But he heard better than they thought.

To one side, parallel with the younger warriors, were the dozen Wagarondit. They carried weapons too, and looked very sullen for men who should have been happy. They had been assured by Singing Bear that their people would not disgrace them because they had allowed themselves to be taken prisoner. At first, the prisoners had protested. They said that they would not be allowed to go to the Happy Warground (Ulysses' interpretation of a subtle phrase).

Ulysses had told them that they had no choice. Moreover, things were different now. He, the stone god, had decreed that they *could* go to the Happy Warground after they died. That is, unless they persisted in their stupid protests. They shut up but still could not emotionally accept the new order of things.

The procession walked swiftly across the rolling hills, following a path which war parties and hunting parties had used for generations. There were many huge evergreens and birches and oaks along here but not so many that they constituted a forest. There were birds: bluejays, crows, ravens, sparrows, an emerald-and-honey hummingbird; the fox-red or sable-black winged squirrels; a flash of gray which was a fox; the pointed bright-eyed head of a weasel-like creature looking around the trunk of a tree fifty feet above them; a red rat scuttling across a fallen log; and, high on a hill some fifty yards to their right, a brown colossus that sat up and stared. This was a bear that was totally vegetarian and would not both anybody as long as he was left alone. He ate corn and the produce of their gardens if these were left unguarded, but he could be run off easily enough.

Ulysses breathed in the cool blue sky with his eyes and the cool fresh air with his lungs. The great healthy trees, the healthy bird and animal life, the green everywhere, the absence of polluted air, the feeling of having plenty of elbow room, these combined to make him happy for the moment. He could forget the ache of knowing that he might be the only human alive. He could forget . . . and then he stopped. Behind him, the standard-bearer yelled out an order, the drumming and fluting ceased, and the warriors quit their murmuring talk.

He was missing something. What?

Not what. Whom?

He turned and spoke to Aytheera. "Awina, your daughter. Where is she?"

Aytheera's face was expressionless. He said, "Lord?"

"I want Awina to come with me. She is my voice and my eyes. I need her."

"I told her to stay, my Lord, because females do not go on important trips between villages, neither on peace nor war expeditions."

"You will have to get accustomed to change," Ulysses said. "Send someone for her. We wait."

Aytheera looked strangely at him but obeyed. Iisama, the fastest warrior, ran away to the village, a mile away. After a while, he came trotting back with Awina a few paces behind him. She wore a four-cornered cap with three feathers and had a triple loop of massive green beads around her neck. She ran as a human female runs, and when she slowed down to a fast walk a hundred yards away, she swayed as a human female sways. Her black ears and face, tail, lower arms and legs shimmered in the sun with an undercoat of pale red, and her white fur glowed

25

as if it were snow under a bright spring sun. Her great dark blue eyes were on him, and she was smiling, showing the widely separated stiletto teeth.

When she got to him, she went down on her knees and kissed his hand, saying, "My Lord, I wept because you had left me behind."

"Your tears dried fast enough," he said. He liked to think that she had cried, but he could not be sure if she was exaggerating or saying what she thought he would like to hear. These noble savages were as capable of dissimulation as any civilized peoples. Moreover, should he want her to become so emotionally attached to him? Such a bond could lead to a more intimate feeling, the consequences of which he had fantasied. The images both stimulated and repulsed him.

She took her place at his right and was silent for a long time. Then she began to talk hesitantly, and, after a while, she chattered along as amusingly and as informatively as ever. He felt much happier; the sense of loss had evaporated into the clear air and bright sun.

They marched all day, stopping now and then to rest or to eat. There were enough creeks and small rivers to furnish them all the water they needed. The Wufea, though they may have been descended from cats, bathed whenever they got a chance. They also licked themselves all over in true cat fashion. They were a clean people as far as their own bodies were concerned but were indifferent to the pests in their villages, the cockroaches, flies, and other bugs. And, though they buried their refuse, they were not neat about cleaning up after their dogs and pigs and other animals they kept for pets or for food.

In the late evening, Ulysses, hot, sweaty and fatigued, decided they would camp for the night by a creek. The water was fairly cool and was so clear that he could see the fish scooting along its bottom twenty feet deep. He lay on a fallen tree that stuck out over the creek and watched the fish for a long while. Then he took off his clothes and went swimming while the Wufea and Wagarondit watched him closely as they always did when he was nude. He wondered if they were secretly repulsed by his general lack of fur and the distribution of hair elsewhere. Perhaps not. He could not be expected to be as they, since he was, after all, a god.

When he came out, all others, except for posted guards and Awina, bathed. She dried him off with a piece of fur and then asked permission to go in also. When they had all come out, he looked down into the water from the log. The fish were scared away. But a hundred yards up, he found them again. He used a telescoping pole of some unfamiliar lightweight wood, a line composed of gut, and a bone hook with a worm which Awina dug up for him. It was a thick-bodied creature, as long as his hand, blood-red and with four great false eyes composed of three concentric circles of white, blue and green.

He cast twelve times with no success. On the thirteenth, a fish struck. Thereafter, he had to play it by the gut itself, since the line threatened to tear loose from the pole. The fish was only ten inches long, but it was very powerful and fought savagely. It took him at least twenty minutes to tire it out. When he pulled it in and saw the silvery body with scarlet and pale green spots, staring yellow eyes and short cartilaginous "whiskers," he felt even happier. According to Awina, who carried it off to cook it, the iipawafa was delicious. And it was.

That night, lying in his sleeping bag, looking up at the huge green, blue and white moon through the branches of an evergreen, he thought that he lacked only two things to make him completely happy. One was a deep drink of some good dark German or Danish beer or top-rate bourbon. The second was a woman who would love him and whom he could love.

Before he realized what he had done, he found Awina's furry hand in his and coming close to his mouth. He had unconsciously reached over and picked it up and was about to kiss it.

"My Lord!" Awina said in a tremulous voice.

He did not reply. He gently put her hand back on the top of her sleeping bag and turned away.

But she said, "Look!" and he sat up and stared through the branches at the thing at which she was pointing.

Black and winged, a silhouette only, he flapped across the moon and then was gone.

"What was that?"

"I did not know that any were around," she said. "It has been some time since . . . that was an opeawufeapauea."

"A winged thinking person—hairless," he murmured, translating into English.

"The Thululiki," she added.

"Are they dangerous?"

"You do not remember?"

"Would I ask if I did?"

"Forgive me, Lord. I do not mean to anger you. No, they
27

are not generally dangerous. Neither we nor the Wagarondit our enemies kill them. They are of great service to all."

Ulysses questioned her some more and then went to sleep. He dreamed of bats with human faces.

Two days later, they came to the first Wagarondit village. Long before, the drums had announced that they had been seen. Singing Bear occasionally glimpsed the scouts as they ran from tree to tree or peeked out from behind bushes. They followed along a broad and deep creek which held a number of black and white fish about three feet long. He investigated and decided they were not fish but mammals: pygmy porpoises. Awina said that the Wagarondit held them sacred and only killed one once a year at a ceremony. The Wufea did not consider them sacred, but since these were found only in enemy territory, they never bothered them. If a Wufea raiding party killed one, and the Wagarondit came across the body, they would know that there were Wufea in the area.

About five miles afterward, they left the creek and went up a high steep hill. On the other side, in a valley on top of a low hill, was the Wagarondit village.

The clan houses were round. Otherwise, it looked much like the Wufea settlement. The warriors gathered before the open gates, however, were brown-furred and had black bars across the eyes and cheeks. And they carried bolas and swords of some wood in addition to the stone assegais, knives and tomahawks.

Their standard bore the skull of a giant roadrunner. Awina had told him that this was the superclan totem, the chief of all the clans of the Wagarondit. They held the roadrunner, the apuaukauey, sacred, but they initiated their young warriors by setting one against a giant bird. The initiate would be armed only with a bola and a spear, and he had to bring the bird down by throwing the three-stoned bola around its legs and then cutting off its head. There were at least four young braves a year from each village killed in this dangerous ceremony.

Ulysses leading, the procession started down the long steep hill. The Wagarondit beat on the great drums and whirled bullroarers. A priest, bristling with feathers all over, shook a gourd at them and, presumably, was chanting something, though at this distance Ulysses could hear nothing through the din of the instruments.

Halfway down the hill, Awina said, "Lord!" and pointed toward the sky. The great-winged bat-like creature was gliding toward them. Ulysses watched him as he wheeled before them. Awina had not lied or exaggerated. He was a winged human or near-human. His body was about the size of a four-year-old child. The torso was quite human except for the enormous chest. The breastbone had to be very large for attachment of the great wing muscles. The back was also hunched; the mound looked like solid muscle. His arms were very skinny, and the hands had very long fingers with long nails. The legs were short, frail and bowed. The feet were splayed out, and the big toe was almost at right angles to the feet.

The wings were bone and membrane, the ends attached to the mound of muscle on the back. He had six limbs, the first six-limbed mammal Ulysses had ever seen. But it might not be the last. This planet—or this Earth—had to have many strange things in store for him.

The face was triangular. The head was bulging, round and totally bald. The ears were so big they looked like auxiliary wings. The eyes were large for the face and from a distance looked pale.

There did not seem to be a hair on the naked creature.

The man was smiling as he swept down and half-folded his wings and dropped onto his skinny legs and broad feet. He waddled toward them, having lost all grace the moment he touched ground. He lifted a thin arm and spoke in a piping child-like voice in Ayrata.

"Greetings, god of stone! Ghlikh greets you and wishes you a long godhood!"

Ulysses understood him well enough, but he could not speak the trade language with any fluency as yet. He said, "Can you speak Wufea?"

"Easily. One of my favorite languages," Ghlikh said. "We Dhulhulikh speak many tongues, of which Wufea is one of the least difficult."

Ulysses said, "What news do you bring, Ghlikh?"

"Much to amuse and inform. But with your permission, my Lord, we will put that off until later. At the moment, I am empowered by the Wagarondit to speak first with you. They wish you well, which they should, since you are also their god—they think."

The bat-man's tone was slightly sarcastic. Ulysses looked hard at him, but Ghlikh only smiled, exposing long yellowish teeth.

Ulysses said, "They *think*?"

"Well," Ghlikh answered, "they cannot understand why you took the part of the Wufea when they were only intent

29

on bringing you to this village where you could be properly honored, or what they think is such."

Ulysses wanted to push on and ignore the creature, who was making him somewhat queasy. But Awina had told him that the batpeople were the couriers, the representatives, the gossipers, and the functionaries of many things. It was protocol that a bat-man act as arbitrator between two parties who wished to make arrangements for peace, trade or sometimes for a limited war. In addition, the batmen sometimes became traders themselves, flying in with small, lightweight, but much desired goods from some unknown country, perhaps their own.

"You tell them that I was attacked by two of their number. And for this I punished all of them," Ulysses said.

"I will tell them so," Ghlikh said. "And do you plan any more punishment?"

"Not unless they do something to deserve it."

Ghlikh hesitated and swallowed audibly, his craggy Adam's apple jumping like a monkey on a stick. Evidently he was not as superior as he pretended to be. Or perhaps he knew that he was vulnerable while on the ground, however lofty his opinion of himself was.

"The Wagarondit say that it is only fair that they should ask even a god to prove that he is a god."

Awina, standing behind Ulysses, whispered, "Lord, forgive me. But a word of advice might help. These arrogant Wagarondit need a lesson, and if you let them push you around . . ."

Ulysses agreed with her, but he did not want advice unless he asked for it. He held up his hand to indicate that she should be quiet. To Ghlikh he said, "I do not have to prove anything, but I can be petitioned."

Ghlikh smiled as if he had guessed that Ulysses would say that. The sun struck pale flames in his cat-yellow eyes. He said, "The Wagarondit, then, beg you to kill The Old Being With The Long Hand. The monster has been ravaging the fields and even the villages for many years. He has destroyed many crops and storehouses and sometimes puts entire villages close to starvation. The Old Being has killed many warriors sent out against him, crippled others, and always conquered. Or he has run away, eluding whole hunting parties, only to show up elsewhere and tromp down and eat whole fields of corn or crush houses and push over great palisades of heavy logs."

"I will consider their petition," Ulysses said, "and I will

answer in the next few days. Meanwhile, unless there is something else to talk about, let us go on."

"There is only trivia, news and gossip I bring from many villages of many tribes of different peoples," Ghlikh said. "You may find some of it entertaining or even instructive, my Lord."

Ulysses did not know if that last was a sneer at the supposed omniscience of a god, but he decided to let it pass. However, if it became necessary, he would grab hold of the skinny little monster and wring his neck as an object lesson. The batpeople might be sacred, or at least privileged, but if this fellow became too insulting, he could damage Ulysses' image as a god.

They walked down the hill and across the floor of the valley, passing over a wooden bridge over a creek about three hundred feet wide. On the other side were fields of corn and other plants and also meadows on which a red-wooled sheep with three crumpled horns chomped on the long blue-green grass. The number of stone and wooden hoes and scythes left in the fields showed that the women and children had been working up to the last moment.

To the beat of the drums, the Wufea marched up to the gates, and here Ulysses confronted the chiefs and the priests. The bat-man had launched himself from the hillside and had flown above them as they had marched across the valley. Now he glided in and landed a few feet away from Ulysses, running a little distance after coming to earth. He came back, waddling on his bowed legs, his leathery bone-ribbed wings half-open.

There was more talk, conducted with Ghlikh as go-between. Then the overchief, Djiidaumokh, sank to his knees and rubbed Ulysses' hand on his forehead. The other chiefs and priests followed, and Ulysses and his band entered the village.

There were several days of feasting and speach-making before Ulysses continued his march. He visited ten Wagarondit villages in all. Ulysses was curious about what payment Ghlikh got for his services. Ghlikh by now rode with them on the back of a Wagarondit brave, his bandy legs wrapped around the thick furry neck.

"My payment!" he said, waving his hand airily. "Oh, I am fed and lodged and a few other of my needs are taken care of. I am a simple person. I only want to talk to many different peoples, to converse, to satisfy my curiosity and theirs, to be of service. I derive my greatest joy from being of service."

"That is all you ask?"

"Oh, sometimes I accept a few baubles, some gemstones or excellently carved figurines or objects like that. But my main item of trade is information."

Ulysses did not comment, but he felt that there was more to Ghlikh's business than he said.

On the way back to the first Wagarondit village, the chief, Djiidaumokh, asked him what he meant to do about The Old Being With The Long Hand.

"The people of Nisheymanakh, the third village we visited, have sent a messenger saying that The Old Being has ravaged one of their fields again. He killed two warriors who went after him."

Ulysses sighed. *Noblesse oblige* could not be put off.

He said, "Let us go after this creature at once."

He called Ghlikh to him and said, "Have the Wagarondit ever used you to locate The Old Being With The Long Hand?"

"Never," Ghlikh said.

"Why not?"

"They never thought of it, I suppose."

"And you never thought of telling them how valuable you could be?"

"No. I suppose that The Old Being is more valuable to me alive than dead. If he is dead, then I have just that much less exciting news."

"You will locate The Old Being," Ulysses said.

Ghlikh's eyes narrowed, and his thin lips became a thread. But he said, "Of course, my Lord."

Ulysses knew from conversations he had overheard that at least four generations of Wagarondit had known The Old Being. But he was not always in Wagarondit territory. Sometimes he disappeared for years, and he must then be ravaging the unknown peoples to the north, the west and perhaps in the great forest to the east. He was a huge animal and he had a big territory to cover.

From the description he had pieced together, Ulysses knew that The Old Being had to be an elephant of some sort. But what an elephant! He must be twenty feet high at the shoulder and he had four tusks! The upper tusks curved upward and the lower tusks curved down and back. The Long Hand was the proboscis.

The Old Being's wiliness, his avoidance of traps, his deadly ambushes, his ability to disappear, were legendary.

"He has far more intelligence than you would expect

from a nonsentient," Ulysses said to Ghlikh. Awina stood near them.

"Who said he was one who had no speech?" Ghlikh said. Ulysses was surprised. "You mean, he *can* talk?"

Ghlikh's eyelids lowered. He said, "I would not know, of course. I was merely pointing out that no one actually knows whether or not he can talk."

"Is he the only one of his kind?" Ulysses said.

"I would not know. There are those who say that there are many of his kind many marches to the north. I do not know."

"You should," Ulysses said. "You get around a lot. You fly far, and even if you do not go north, surely there are others of your people who do."

"I do not know," Ghlikh said, but Ulysses thought he detected a barely repressed amusement on his face.

He shoved down his anger, however, and said, "Tell me, Ghlikh, have you ever seen . . . ?" and then he halted. There was no word for metal in the Wufea speech. Not as far as he knew, anyway. He proceeded to describe metal. Then, remembering his knife, he brought it out and unfolded it. Ghlikh, his eyes wide, breathing harder than he should, asked permission to handle the blade. Ulysses watched him while the long skinny fingers felt the steel, gently ran the edge of his thumb over the edge, tasted it with his warty tongue, and held it flat against the vellum cheek. Finally, Ghlikh handed the knife back.

The Neshgai, he continued in response to Ulysses' questioning, were a race of giants who lived in a giant village of giant houses made of some strange material. Their city was on the southern coast of this land. On the other side of Wurutana. The Neshgai walked on two legs, and their tusks were only two and very tiny compared to those of The Old Being. But they had big ears and a long nose that fell to their waists. They looked as if they were descended from a creature something like The Old Being.

Ulysses was so full of questions he did not know which to ask first.

"What is your idea of Wurutana?" he said.

His question was phrased thus because he did not want Ghlikh to know how ignorant he was of his ancient enemy.

Ghlikh, startled, said, "What do you mean? *My* idea?"

"What is Wurutana to you?"

"To *me?*"

"Yes. What would you call him?"

"The Great Devourer. The All-Powerful. He Who Grows."

33

"Yes, I know, but what does he look like? To you?"

Ghlikh must have guessed that Ulysses was trying to get a description of something which he did not know. Ghlikh smiled so sarcastically that Ulysses wanted to smash that thin skull.

"Wurutana is so vast that I cannot find words to describe him."

"You chatterbox!" Ulysses said. "You runner-off-at-the-mouth! Winged monkey-face! You cannot find words?"

Ghlikh looked sullen but did not say anything. Ulysses then said, "Very well! Tell me! Are there beings like me anywhere on this land?"

Ghlikh said, "Oh, yes, some!"

"Well, where are they?"

"On the other side of Wurutana. On the seacoast, many marches west of the Neshgai."

"Why didn't you tell me about them?" Ulysses cried.

Ghlikh looked astonished. He said, "Why should I? You did not ask me about them. It is true that they look much like you, but they are no gods. They are just another race of sentients to me."

So now he had the most urgent of reasons to go south. He would have to confront Wurutana, whether he wanted to or not. If the Wufea and Ghlikh were to be believed, Wurutana covered the land except on the north and south seacoasts.

Ghlikh drew a rough map of the land's outlines in the mud of a creek bank.

North was land marked Unknown. Below that was a crude triangle with the northern part forming the broad base. There was ocean or sea on all parts except the northern unknown. Ghlikh said rumors were that the sea was there too.

Ulysses wondered if the land was all that was left of the eastern part of the United States. The level of the ocean could be much higher. Thus, the Midwest and the Atlantic coastal plain would be submerged. This land might be all of what was left of the former Appalachian Mountain Range. Of course, while he was in his "petrified" state, he could have been taken to other continents and this might be all that was left of a certain part of Eurasia. Or he could be on another planet of another star. He did not think so, but it was possible.

If only he could find something that would identify this place. But after many millions of years, everything would be gone. The bones of men would have perished, except for a few fossilized skeletons, and how many humans had a chance to become fossilized? The steel would have rusted away, the plastic would have deteriorated, the cement would have crumbled, the stone of the pyramids and the Sphinx, of the marble statues of the Greeks and the Americans, all would have been eroded to dust long ago. Nothing of man's would remain, except possibly for some flint tools made by Stone Age men. These might survive long after man's history had perished with his books, machines, cities and bones.

Mountain ranges had been born, lifted up and fallen again. Continents had split and the islands drifted away from each other. Ocean beds had been emptied, new lands risen, old lands become oceans. What was rough and elevated was smooth and level. What was smooth and level was crumpled and raised. Great masses of stone ground against each other and rubbed man's remains to dust. Billions of tons of water roared into suddenly opened valleys and swept everything out or buried it in mud.

Nothing except the land and the sea was left, water and earth in new shapes, new containers. Only life had gone on, and life had taken some new shapes, though there were still old forms around.

But—if Ghlikh could be believed—humankind still survived! Man was no longer lord of life, but he still lived.

Ulysses would go south.

First, he had to kill The Old Being With The Long Hand to prove his godhood.

He questioned the bat-man more. Ghlikh became uneasy and even irritated at times, but he did not become openly angry. Finally, Ulysses said, "Then there are volcanoes and hot springs up north which give out a strong and sickening stench?"

"Yes," Ghlikh said.

Ghlikh knew more about the north than he had intended to reveal, but Ulysses did not wish to delve into the reasons for his reticence at this time. All he wanted was information.

"How far to the north?"

"Ten days' march."

About two hundred miles, Ulysses reckoned.

"You will guide us there."

Ghlikh opened his mouth as if to protest but then shut it.

Ulysses called in the chiefs and priests of the Wufea and

the Wagarondit and told them what he wanted done while he was gone.

The officials were puzzled about his instructions for the collection and treatment of excrement and the making of charcoal. He told them that he would reveal the reasons later.

In addition, he wanted as big a war party and as many juvenile males as could be spared to go with him to the north. On the way they would look for The Old Being, although this party was not primarily to track him down. But it was very much involved with the killing of The Old Being.

The chiefs were not happy about his demands, but they went ahead and put them into effect. A week later a big party of a hundred adult warriors, two hundred juvenile males, several priests, Awina and Ulysses set out for the north. Ghlikh was of them, though not always with them. He flew ahead and scouted the territory, and many times spotted game for them and three times hostile scouts. The hostiles were a people who seemed to be a variety of the Wagarondit. Their fur was black and they had auburn bars across their eyes and cheeks but otherwise were the same as their southern cousins.

The Alkunquib gathered a big war party and tried to ambush Ulysses' party. Ghlikh reported on their location, and so the ambushers became ambushees. The surprise, plus the arrows, with which the Alkunquib were totally unfamiliar, plus the appearance of the giant Ulysses, plus the story which the Alkunquib must have heard of his godhood, turned the battle into a massacre. Ulysses did not lead any charges, nor did the chiefs expect him to. He was happy about that. Was a god supposed to be able to be wounded? He did not like to ask anybody, of course. It was possible that they expected even gods to have to endure wounds. After all, the Greeks and other peoples had thought their gods immortal but not invulnerable.

As it was, he stood to one side and used his great bow with deadly effect. He thanked his God that he had taken archery in high school and then continued it as a hobby in his post-graduate days. He was a good shot, and his bow was far stronger than those of the Wufea. Though they were wiry and strong, despite their small size, he was too big for them. His arms pulled the bow—the "mighty bow of Odysseus," that other Ulysses, he thought—and the arrows went true enough to kill twelve of the Alkunquib and severely wound five others.

The enemy broke and ran after six minutes of battle, and many of them were speared or tomahawked in the back. The survivors were brave, however. On reaching their village, where the females, children and old warriors were waiting in terror, all the males able to hold a weapon, including six-year-olds, stood before the gates, which were closed. With a yell, the Wufea and the Wagarondit, blooded brothers, as it were, rushed the defenders. They did so in an unorganized manner and so got beat back with heavy casualties. Ulysses took advantage of a lull to tell them that they were to leave the Alkunquib and march on.

Their bloodlust was so high that they dared to argue with him. He announced that they would do what he said, or he would destroy them. Fortunately, nobody thought of calling his bluff, or if they did, no one dared voice the thought.

Ulysses, looking at the Alkunquib, was struck with an idea. He needed all the carriers he could get for the return journey, and here were at least a hundred more juveniles.

He arranged through Ghlikh for a conference with the enemy's warchief. There was an intense but brief dispute, and then the chief, faced with the extinction of his tribe, gave in. Two days later, the Alkunquib juveniles marched with the war party as hostages and as carriers-to-be. This village, in the meanwhile, had sent messages to the other Alkunquib tribes to lay off the party. Two tribes paid no attention and attacked, and these in turn were ambushed and decimated. And Ulysses ended up with a hundred and fifty more carriers and hostages. He did burn the two villages as an object lesson, but he would not permit the villagers to be massacred.

Ulysses was anything but exhilarated at his conquests. The bloodshed depressed him. Millions of years of sentiency had passed, perhaps four hundred thousand or more generations, perhaps twice that many. Yet the sentients, the users of speech, the lords of the beasts, had learned nothing. Or was that their lesson, that fighting and bloodshed were inevitable and would last as long as life lasted?

The big party went much more slowly now. So many people could not travel swiftly, and the estimated ten days' march took twenty. But they were not attacked again by any great force. Some tribes skulked on the outskirts and tried to pick off warriors here and there. These were only small nuisances. The big problem was feeding his army. The presence of so many men frightened off the game, and small bands had to go out and scour for miles around ahead and on both sides. And these bands became targets for the locals. But, one day, Ulysses organized a hunt at the suggestion of Awina, and a herd of horses was run over a cliff. They ate well for many days, though they had to delay their journey to smoke much meat.

They came finally to Ulysses' goal: the volcanoes and hot springs. Here he found the sulfur which he had hoped for. This was a greenish translucent form which could be mined with the stone tools of his "men." Inside two weeks, he had all he could carry, and the party started back.

At the Alkunquib villages, Ulysses arranged that the juvenile carriers should be sent back, with gifts, after they had dropped off their loads at the Wufea village.

By the time the party got back to the original starting point, Ulysses found that there was a large supply of potassium nitrate. The Wufea had followed his instructions, which included special treatment to force the decomposition of the excrement at a swift rate. A few days later, after the celebrations and ceremonies, Ulysses set his warriors, and the women who could be spared from the fields, to work on the preparation of the black gunpowder. The result was a proper mixture of potassium nitrate, charcoal and sulfur. The first demonstration startled, panicked and awed the Wufea, Wagarondit and Alkunquib. It was a five-pound bomb which he set off inside a hut built for the demonstration.

Ulysses had lectured everybody on the dangers of the new weapon, including the instability of the powder. He also forbade them to use it except with his permission and under his supervision. If he had not applied limits, he would have found his whole supply gone inside a day for their amusement.

The sixth day, he touched off a rocket with a two-pound warhead in a wooden case. It blew up against the face of a stone cliff and provided a fine spectacle.

After this, Ulysses instructed Ghlikh on the carrying and touching off of the fuse of a one-pound bomb. Ghlikh flew above a great dummy made out of wood and straw and modeled after descriptions of The Old Being. He swooped down and then up, almost stalling, and inserted the end of his fuse into a hole in a small tinder box. Then he quickly released the bomb which fell onto the back of the dummy, but it rolled off and exploded ten feet away. After four tries, Ghlikh was able to estimate the time properly, and the bomb blew the dummy apart.

"Very good," Ulysses said when Ghlikh, grinning like a

demon, landed before him. "You did well. Now, the next step will be to locate The Old Being. You should be able to do that."

"He may be many marches north of here! Or east!" Ghlikh said.

"You'll find him," Ulysses said.

The bat-man waddled off sullenly to eat. Awina said, "I wonder why we did not think about using him to find The Old Being. We should have done so. But then we are not gods."

"I wonder why he is so reluctant to do this for me," Ulysses said. "There isn't much danger for him, except for miscalculating the time for the fuse to burn. But he was reluctant before he knew anything about the bombs."

"I do not know," Awina said slowly, as if she did not want to make any accusations—as yet.

He tried to get her to express any suspicions she might have, but she denied having any. He gave up on her; she could be as evasive as any feline when she chose. But he determined to watch Ghlikh even more closely. However, if Ghlikh did not wish to track down The Old Being, he could just fly away. Or he could just not find the colossus.

Three weeks later, they were in the country of the Alkunquib again. A week before, The Old Being had raided the fields of the most northerly of the Wagarondit. A relay of runners had brought the news to Ulysses, who had roused his force and gotten them to marching northward within an hour. His force consisted of twenty warriors, twenty carriers, Awina and himself. They proceeded at a wolf trot, a hundred paces running and a hundred walking. They ate up the miles from dawn to dusk. Ulysses fell into his sleeping bag every night and rocketed into sleep. He awoke in the morning with every muscle protesting. Not until the fourth day did he wake up without pain. By then he had lost even more weight than on the first expedition. Unlike the smaller, lighter and wiry nonhumans, he could not run all day without extending himself. He was too big and too heavily muscled. But he could not let them see their god poop out, so he kept up the pace.

He had worn out the shoes he was wearing when depetrified and now was wearing moccasins. This made his feet hurt for a long time, but he eventually got used to them.

He estimated that he had lost about twenty pounds since the day he awoke. But the exercise was good for him. He had no fat, and his wind was superb. Still, there wasn't a

Wufea, including Awina, who could not run him into blind staggers.

Deep into Alkunquib land, the party stopped one morning when Ghlikh appeared in front of them. He was flying swiftly, skimming above the treetops, and even at a distance his expression told them that he had found The Old Being With The Long Hand.

A moment later he sideslipped into the glade and landed alongside them.

Panting, he said, "He's up ahead! On the other side of that big hill!"

"What is he doing?" Ulysses said.

"Feeding! Stripping a tree of all its leaves!"

Ulysses had not really expected Ghlikh to locate the beast. But he could have wrongly interpreted the bat-man's reactions. Or, maybe something had caused the bat-man to change his attitude. If so, who or what could have done that?

Ghlikh had some difficulty getting off the ground. The open space was not long enough for him to get a proper run even if he was unburdened. Carrying the five-pound bomb, he had no chance at all. Nor was there any possibility of using a steep hillside as a launching place. Trees covered the hills everywhere.

Ulysses hesitated. He could have Ghlikh carried to a point two miles behind them where there was an area for him to take off. Ghlikh could fly back and rendezvous with them. He did not want to wait around for him but he had to do so if Ghlikh's function was not to be wasted. Besides, he had plenty of time. Why worry about wasting it when he had just put in many millennia with no anxiety whatsoever?

He ordered two Wagarondit to carry Ghlikh between them to the open strip. He then ordered the party to proceed slowly and quietly. Ten of the warriors were ready with their bows and arrows, and the other ten, with the carriers, had prepared their rockets and bombs.

They went up the steep hillside through the huge evergreens that leaned out at a slight angle, and then they crawled on hands and knees over the brow of the hill. Down below was a valley with many trees but with a number of open spaces. About fifty of the trees looked as if winter had struck them. The eater of their leaves was a beast, not a season. He was so huge that Ulysses found trouble crediting his senses. He stood higher than some of the young trees. He was as gray as any elephant, but he had an enormous white spot on his right shoulder. His long yellow tusks looked so heavy that Ulysses wondered that the beast could raise his head. His trunk, relatively longer than those of the elephants of Ulysses' day, moved sinuously through the trees, plucking off whole branches, dragging them into the enormous mouth and then snaking out again. Even at this distance, the rumblings of his brobdingnagian belly reached the hunters.

The wind was from the north, so the beast would not be able to smell or hear them, if they were careful. His eyesight might not be as weak as others of the elephantine clan, so Ulysses cautioned them again that they should use every bit of cover they could.

It took the whole party an hour to work down the hillside and among the trees at the bottom of the valley. By then, Ulysses was beginning to worry about Ghlikh. He should have shown up long ago. What could have happened? Maybe some Alkunquib renegades or members of other tribes to the north were scouting around and had killed Ghlikh and his bearers. Maybe . . . why worry about it? If Ghlikh did not show, there was nothing to be done about it. The attack would proceed without him.

Ulysses motioned to the others to stay where they were, which was mainly behind trees. He took the wooden bazooka into which he had loaded the wooden rocket and crept forward. Behind was Awina, holding a small torch she had just lit. Other torches were being lit from boxes of smoldering punk blown into red heat just before shavings were placed on them. Then the torches were applied to the boxes to catch fire. This was the crucial moment as far as Ulysses was concerned. The smoke, even if downwind, might be smelled by the animal or his eyes, even if weak, might see the thick black clouds.

The thunderous belly rumblings, the tearing off of branches, the dragging through the mouth and stripping off of leaves, and the crash of branches thrown aside continued. The whale-like gray bulk shifted back and forth in a continual little dance. The trunk worked busily, and all must have seemed at peace in the world of The Old Being With The Long Hand.

A shadow fell on Ulysses. He looked up. The dark winged form of Ghlikh was flapping over him. Ulysses waved at him to veer off to the right. If his shadow fell on the beast, who was probably as skittish as any African elephant, it would panic or at least alert him.

Ghlikh either did not see him or else misinterpreted his

41

gesture. He flew straight ahead toward the animal at an altitude of about fifty feet. He held the bomb clutched to his belly with one hand and the small torch with the other. The thick smoke roiled out behind him as if he were a demon on fire.

Ulysses swore and ran toward The Old Being. On both sides of him the warriors and carriers, forgetting their caution in their excitement and fear, crashed toward the beast. Their childhood had been filled with scary stories of this monster, and some had even seen him at a distance or in action. The fathers of two of them had been smashed beneath those enormous pads. But they would not hang back because they would be thought cowards, and it was better to be dead than disgraced. However, they had become overbold, too competitive, and so they were betraying themselves.

And betraying me, too, Ulysses thought.

It was too late to do anything but attack and hope for the best. If only Ghlikh didn't get buck fever and miscalculate, miss that animal, though how anybody could miss anything so big would be a wonder.

But Ghlikh did. Apparently, he had gone on by and then banked, intending to make his run downwind to come up from behind the beast. This was not very intelligent. In the first place, he had gone directly over the beast and so cast his shadow on it. But the animal had not noticed. Now, however, the smoke from the torch came to the beast even though Ghlikh was fifty feet up.

The beast stopped tearing at the branches, raised his proboscis, sniffed here and there, and then began to trumpet.

Ghlikh dropped the bomb and then screamed with frustration.

The colossus answered with a scream of his own and a sudden shift from motionlessness into a charge that picked up speed unbelievably fast. The animal may not have seen anything as yet; he may have been just startled and so was running away blindly. Whatever his motive or state, he was turning toward Ulysses, and, suddenly, the rocket seemed very inadequate.

Despite which, he placed the bazooka and its load on his shoulder and yelled at Awina to light the fuse. He could not see her, but she told him calmly what she was doing.

At that moment, Ghlikh's bomb went off about thirty yards behind the gray juggernaut. The Old Being increased his shrillness of trumpeting and his speed. He also changed

42

his direction so that he was not approaching Ulysses and Awina directly. Unless he veered again, he would miss them by about four feet. But he should be able to see them before then and so would likely head toward them.

Heat fanned by Ulysses' cheek; smoke filled his eyes; the rocket hissed as it raced out of the tube and by his head. It flew in a flat arc toward the creature, which was now charging them, having seen them two seconds before. His trunk was coiled high, and his reddish eyes were on them. The dark blur of the rocket struck the juggernaut's left shoulder, and the explosion deafened Ulysses. Smoke billowed out so that he could not even see the beast. He did not wait to notice the effects of the hit but ran off to one side with Awina close behind him. A carrier was running up to him with another rocket, and then other missiles went over him, one went *by* him, and something struck him in the back.

He fell forward on his face while smoke arranged itself like a tent around him. He coughed and then got up from his all-fours position. He was too stunned for several minutes to realize what had happened. Some rocketeer had gotten excited and directed the missile at too low an elevation. It was this rocket that had almost hit him and had struck a tree near him.

Ulysses got to his feet. His clothes were ripped and he was dirty with black smoke. He looked around for Awina, and then gave a cry of relief. She was standing near him and looking dazed and red-eyed and her fur was black with smoke. But she did not seem to have any wounds.

He turned back to The Old Being. He could hear nothing; for all he knew he was right behind him.

The beast was not. He lay on the ground, kicking his columnar legs while blood poured out like springs from several huge holes. One leg, though moving, was half blown off at the shoulder.

And then, as the warriors and the carriers, shouting and screaming triumphantly, moved in on him, he struggled to his feet, and, hobbling, charged again. The bipeds scattered, screaming with terror, and then the beast caught one with his trunk and lifted him up and hurled him spinning over and over into the branches of a tree.

After that, The Old Being collapsed again and died in a lake of mud and blood.

Miraculously, the Wufea thrown into the tree survived with only a few cuts and bruises.

It took Ulysses a long time to recover his hearing and

his nerves. When he quit shaking, he examined the beast. He was, as Awina said, a mountain that walked. Just cutting off the tusks and transporting them back to the Wufea village would be a great labor. But he knew that when the Wufea, Wagarondit and Alkunquib made their pilgrimage to the village and saw those gargantuan tusks set upright into the ground before the temple, they would feel that their stone god was truly a god. They would also, he hoped, feel a stronger sense of union. All three of the hereditary foes had participated in this hunt for their ancient enemy. And all three could share in the glory.

There was one irritant in his triumph. That was Ghlikh. He asked the bat-man what had happened.

"Lord, forgive me!" the bat-man piped. "I was sweating with excitement! My hand slipped, and I dropped the bomb! I am sorry indeed, but I could not help it!"

"Did your excitement also make you scream and so warn The Old Being?"

"Truly, Lord! My only excuse is that, that giant monster strikes terror and panic into the hearts of every mortal! Look at how close a rocket came to hitting you!"

Ulysses said, "No harm was done."

"Now that The Old Being is dead, may I go?" Ghlikh said. "I would like to return home."

"Which is where?" Ulysses said, hoping to catch him off guard.

"As I have said, Lord, to the south. Many many marches."

"You may go," Ulysses said, wondering what Ghlikh had up his nonexistent sleeve. It seemed to him that Ghlikh would be reporting on him, but to whom he could not even begin to guess. There was no sense in trying to keep him.

"Will I see you again soon?"

"I do not know, my Lord," Ghlikh said with that side-long look that irritated Ulysses. "But you may see others of my kind."

"I will see you sooner than you think," Ulysses said.

Ghlikh seemed startled. He said, "What do you mean by that, my Lord?"

"Farewell," Ulysses said. "And my thanks for what you did."

Ghlikh hesitated and then said, "Farewell, my Lord. This has been a most profitable experience for me and the most exciting of all my life."

He left to say goodbye to the chiefs of each of the three bands and Awina. Ulysses watched him until he flapped away and disappeared beyond a high hill.

He said to Awina, "I think he has gone to tell somebody about the results of his spying."

"My Lord?" she said. "Spying?"

"Yes, I'm sure that he is working for somebody other than himself or his people. I cannot put my finger on anything that will hold still. But I feel it."

"Perhaps he works for Wurutana . . . ?" she said.

"He may," he said. "We'll find out. We'll be going south to find Wurutana after we set these tusks up before the temple."

"Will I be coming along?" she said. Her great Siamese-cat-blue eyes were fixed on him, and her posture betrayed tension.

"I understand it will be very dangerous," he said. "But you do not seem to be afraid of danger. Yes, I will be very happy if you will come with me. But I will not order anyone to accompany me. I will take only volunteers."

"I am very happy to be able to go with my Lord," she said. And then she added, "But are you going to face Wurutana or look for your sons and daughters?"

"My what?"

"For those mortals of whom Ghlikh spoke. The beings who look so much like you that they must be your children."

He smiled and said, "You are very intelligent and very perceptive, Awina. I will be going south to do both, of course."

"And will you be looking for a mate among the mortals who are your children?"

"I do not know!" he said, more harshly than he had intended. Why should this question upset him? Of course, he would be looking for a mate. What a question! And then he thought, well, she is a female, and her question is only natural for her.

But Awina was subdued for several days thereafter. Not until he tried hard to get her into conversation and to jolly her up did she come out of her blueness. Even so, many times he caught her looking at him with a strange expression.

They reached the Wufea village after making some detours to villages near their direct route. They set up the tusks to form the corners of a square before the temple gates and then they built a roof supported by the tusks. There were celebrations and ceremonies until the chiefs complained that the Wufea were going bankrupt. Moreover, the crops were not being properly taken care of, and the extensive hunting to feed all the guests had cleaned out the game for far too many miles around.

Ulysses had ordered the making of more bombs and a few rockets. While this was being done, he went on a great hunt into the southern plains. He also wanted to capture some wild horses and to get a closer look at Wurutana.

The main body of the party returned to the villages with great piles of smoked meat dragged on sledges. They also took with them a number of captured horses with instructions to treat them gently and not to slaughter them.

Ulysses pushed on southward with forty warriors and Awina. They passed great herds of elephants about the size of African elephants but with a mound of fat on the haunches and considerably longer hairs. They went by herds of antelopes of many various species and genera, some of which looked like the American and African antelope of his day.

They sighted packs of wolf-like notch-eared dogs with white and red spots all over their bodies. There were prides of a large cheetah-like striped cat and of lion-sized jaguar-like cats. There were many of the twelve-foot high road-runners. Once, Ulysses saw two of the great birds drive off two jaguars from a horse the big cats had just killed.

His people did not seem as worried about the birds and the animals as they did about the Kurieiaumea. These were a tall long-legged people with reddish fur and white faces. A very savage people, Awina said. They were not related to the Wufea, Wagarondit or Alkunquib. They used bolas and atlatls or spear-throwers.

Nobody said anything about turning back, but the deeper they got into Kurieiaumea territory, the more nervous his people became.

Ulysses insisted that they keep going south. But after two more days, and seemingly no closer to the dark mass, he decided to turn back. His indirect questions had, however, revealed one item of information, though he was not sure that he could belive it.

Unless he misinterpreted their comments, Wurutana was a tree. A tree like no other tree that had existed since the dawn of trees.

They returned without seeing any sign of the dread Kurieiaumea, and Ulysses at once began preparations for the big journey. But now the leaves fell; the winds began to blow cold; he decided to wait until spring.

A month later, with the first snows, Ghlikh and his wife, Ghuakh, flew into the village. Wearing lightweight furs,

46

they looked like winged pygmy Eskimos. Ghuakh was even smaller than Ghlikh but much louder. She was a brassy, bigmouthed, nagging and nosy female whom Ulysses immediately disliked. If she had had feathers and bird-feet, she could truly have been called a harpy.

"Did you get tired of waiting for me?" Ulysses said, smiling.

"I, waiting? Truly, my Lord, I do not know what you mean," Ghlikh said.

But he and his wife asked many questions among the villagers after they had passed on their gossip, news and reports on the movements of game to the south. It was not difficult for them to find out that the stone god was planning to march on Wurutana after the spring thaws. Ulysses, meanwhile, questioned Awina and others and found out that the batpeople seldom came by at this time of the year. The chief priest said that one of the "winged mouths" had not come by this late for at least twenty years, maybe more.

Ulysses nodded on hearing this. He suspected that the batpeople had been sent to find out what was holding him up. And he was sure that the two would be coming back much earlier in the spring than they usually did. He said goodbye to them one cold morning and decided that he would set out even earlier than he planned.

In the meantime, he broke his horses and taught the warriors how to ride. The winter snows were not nearly as heavy as those to which he had been accustomed. This might still be Syracuse geographically, but the climate had become milder. The snows fell frequently but not as thickly, and they melted often. He had plenty of space to ride his horses, which he kept inside the temple. That spring, colts were born, and he instructed his people how to take care of them. He was strong in his insistence that the animals be treated humanely.

Spring finally released the frozen soil, and the plains became muddy. He was delayed starting the expedition because of a sickness that appeared among the Wufea. Dozens died within a few weeks, and then Awina went to bed with the fever. He stayed by her side much of the time and nursed her himself. Aytheera came in often to perform cleansing ceremonies. The germ theory of disease was unknown. The ancient theory of possession by spirits and of evil sent by witches had reasserted itself. Ulysses did not argue with this idea. Without microscopes, he could not prove his explanation, and even if he could nothing could be done to cure the disease. The fever and the accompanying boils on the head lasted about a week in each person. Some died, and some recovered; there seemed to be no apparent reason for some having survived and the others succumbing. There were burials almost every day, and then the fever was gone.

Ulysses had speculated on how ironic it would be if he should fall victim to a disease after having ridden out many millions of years. But he was untouched by the illness. This was an advantage in more ways than one. To have suffered the sickness might have made the others doubt his godhood.

The fever took a month to pass through the area. When it had left, about an eighth of the population had been put under the ground. The disease did not respect age; it took babies, children, adults, and old people.

He felt despondent for several reasons. First, he was getting closer to these people, despite their nonhuman features of body and psychology. Some of the deaths genuinely grieved him, especially that of Aytheera. Perhaps Awina's grief for her father touched him more than the old one's death, but he was affected. Second, the Wufea needed every hand they could get for the spring planting and the spring hunts. They really could not spare the warriors he would need for this expedition.

However, the stone god had given them the bow and the arrow and the horse as transportation. They were now far more efficient in hunting than before he had awakened. And so they went on great communal hunts and brought in great quantities of horse and antelope meat. Moreover, the idea of raising the horses for food occurred to them with no word from their god. They separated the stock into two groups for breeding purposes. One would become their transportation and the other would be bred for short legs and big bodies. They knew the principles of genetics, having raised dogs and pigs for various purposes for a long time.

By then it was really too late to set out on the plains, or too early, depending on the point of view. The mud would have to dry out. So Ulysses waited and deepened his preparations and imagined even more obstacles against which he should prepare or which he could not possibly be prepared. His warriors found the waiting hard, too. The longer the expedition was put off, the gloomier and the more horrible became the tales about the always evil deeds of Wurutana.

Three days before the expedition was to set out, Ghlikh and his wife Ghuakh glided out of the blue.

"My Lord, I thought I could be of service to you!" Ghlikh said, his leathery big-toothed face wrinkling into the similitude of a bat's. Or a very ugly fox's, Ulysses thought.

Ulysses said that he could be of great service. And so he could, up to a point. Beyond that, he would not be trusted. Ulysses had had time to dwell much on the incident with The Old Being and on reports about the bat-people.

Ghlikh's eyes opened when he saw the four wagons that Ulysses had had built. He said, "My Lord, you have given your people many new and serviceable things. With the bows and arrows and the gunpowder and the use of horses, your people could sweep out all the peoples to the north of here."

"True, but I am interested in the conquest of only one being," Ulysses said.

"Ah, yes, Wurutana!"

Ghlikh did not sound surprised. If anything, he seemed satisfied.

The third morning, the caravan started out. Ulysses Singing Bear was mounted on the biggest pony he could find. By his side Awina rode a mare, and then Ghlikh and Ghuakh rode behind two warriors. Forty warriors rode behind them and then came the four horse-drawn wagons and sixty more warriors. On the flanks, ahead and behind, scouts rode. The party was composed in almost equal part of Wufea, Wagarondit and Alkunquib. Ulysses would have preferred that the fighting men all be of one race, because he was tired of preventing or settling quarrels or outright bloodshed between the old enemies. But he wanted to preserve the union and to have taken along only one race would have insulted the other two.

They certainly made a strange and colorful assembly. By then he had decided that all three were feline and had a common ancestor. The resemblance of the Wagarondit and Alkunquib to raccoons was superficial.

The parade wound across the plains, stopping before dusk, or earlier, near a waterhole or creek. They killed much meat and all ate well. Day after day, the huge mass to the south became slightly larger and then, suddenly, it began to grow swiftly. Once, a small war party of the Kurieiaumea came close, but they were equaled in numbers by the invaders. Moreover, they seemed amazed by the fact that these people were riding horses. They kept a respectable distance and tried to keep up with them, but after the second day they lost them. Then, two days later, they were confronted by an army of almost a thousand feathered and beaded Kurieiaumea. Ulysses was not surprised by them. The Dhulhulikh had spotted them half a day before.

Ulysses stopped the caravan and studied them. They were almost as tall as he but as slim as greyhounds. Their fur was reddish, and their ears were set more forward on their heads. Though their faces were as human as those of the Wufea, their teeth were also those of carnivores. They were definitely not feline. There was something doggy about them. They even stank like dogs, and they sweat from their tongues.

Kdanguwing, the chief of the Alkunquib, said, "Lord, shall we charge them?"

The other chiefs scowled at him for presuming to talk. Ulysses held up his hand for him to wait and regarded the enemy even more closely. Their big war drums were beating, and they were all doing a little dance while their chiefs harangued them. They were strung out in a crescent which would enfold the caravan.

He gave orders and the war party spread out in a wedge with himself at the head and the wagons in the center of the mass. It was a formation that had taken a long time for the undisciplined savages to adhere to.

Most of the warriors were armed with bows and arrows, but a number carried bazookas. These would have to dismount, however, to be effective, since the bazooka handler could not touch off the rocket himself. The tops of the wagons were platforms on which rocket tubes were mounted on swiveling columns.

Ulysses gave the order to advance, and the wedge started at a trot toward the canines. That a numerically inferior force would dare attack them on their home grounds seemed to paralyze the canines for a few minutes. But the chiefs finally got them going, and they came running at Ulysses' party. Their ranks got progressively less organized the nearer they came to the horsemen, and by the time the two had almost met, the canines were in a state of chaos. Every man—or every dog-like man—for himself.

Ulysses stopped the cavalry, the bazooka men dismounted, and the archers fired a volley. This was followed by six more volleys, each under the direction of sergeants who watched Ulysses for signals. It was an excellent exercise.

The training paid off, and about two hundred Kurieiaumea went down with arrows in them.

Then, as they broke and ran, rockets struck among them and exploded. Though the warheads carried stone chips as shrapnel, the main effect of the missiles was panic. They threw away their weapons and fled. The cavalry advanced slowly and then stopped while a number retrieved the arrows and cut the ears off the dead and the wounded for trophies.

Two hours later, the dog-men, reorganized, their courage renewed by the scorn of the chiefs, attacked. And again they were cut down and sent running.

It was a great day for the felines, who had usually lost whenever they encountered the canines on their own grounds. They wanted to push on, burn the dog-men's villages, and massacre the females and children, but Ulysses forbade this.

Two days later, the blackish mass ahead became a dark green. Later, they saw blooms of many colors and hues. Gray streaks appeared in the green. These hardened into immense trunks and branches and roots.

Wurutana *was* a tree, the mightiest that had ever existed. Ulysses, thinking of Yggdrasil, the world tree of Norse religion, thought that here was one to match it. It was a world tree if he were to believe Ghlikh's and Ghuakh's description. It was like a banyan tree ten thousand feet high in many places and spreading out for thousands of square miles. It extended branches which eventually dropped to the earth, dived into the earth, and reemerged as new trunks and new branches. It was a solid mass, all continuity. Somewhere in that vast octopus of tree the original trunk and branches were still living.

When they came to the first branch, which plunged from a great distance into the ground before them, they paused in awe. Then they rode around the gray corrugated-bark pillar and estimated that this branch was at least five hundred yards in diameter. The bark was so thick and fissured and indented, it looked like a heavily eroded cliffside.

They were all silent. Wurutana was overwhelming, like the sea, a great earthquake, a flood, a hurricane, a cyclone or a huge meteorite falling.

"Look!" Awina said, pointing. "There are trees growing on The Tree!"

Dirt had collected in many of the deep fissures, and seeds had blown or been dropped by birds, and trees had taken root in the earth in the fissures. Some of them were over a hundred feet tall.

Ulysses looked inside the gloom at the bottom. So thick was the vegetation above, very little sun penetrated down here. But Ghlikh had said that it was easier to travel in the upper terraces than on the bottom. So much water dripped from the tree onto the ground that it formed vast swamps. There were also quicksand and poisonous growths that did not seem to need the sun, and snakes that were venomous and cared not at all for the light. The caravan would disappear in the bogs and marshes within a few days.

Ulysses did not trust the bat-man, but he could believe this account. A dank unwholesome odor was breathed out from the roots. It stank of decay and pale furtive things and soil under water that would suck up anybody who was foolish enough to venture on it.

He looked up along the nearest branch. It came down at a forty-five degree angle from somewhere in that green and multicolored welter several miles away.

"We'll ride on to the next one," he said, "and look around."

It was already evident that they would have to leave the horses behind. It was too bad they were not domesticated goats. He had seen goats bounding from the edge of one bark-ledge to another. They were orange-haired creatures with doubly curved horns and little black chin whiskers.

There were other animals, too. Black-bodied, yellow-faced monkeys with long ringed tails. A baboonish monkey with a green posterior and a scarlet coat. A tiny deer with knobby horns. A coatimundi-type animal. Something hog-like and grunting. And birds, birds, birds!

They rode for a half-mile until they came to the next branch—or root—entering the earth. Water flowed down a channel, a deep groove, on its back and into a creek bed. Ghlikh had said that there were many springs, creeks and even small rivers in the grooves on the tops of the branches. Now Ulysses could believe it. What a mighty pump this tree was! It must send its roots deep into the earth, driving through stone, and it sucked up the water contained in the rock and tapped domes of water far underground. It might even tap the ocean and turn its water into fresh liquid, rejecting the salts. Then it exuded the water at various places, and springs, creeks and riverlets ran.

"This is as good a place as any," he said. "Unpack the horses. And let them go."

"All that good meat!" Awina said.

"I know. But I don't like to kill them. They've been of service to us; they have a right to live."

52

"They'll get eaten up before the week's over," Awina grumbled, but she relayed the order.

Ulysses watched the two batpeople while the unloading was taking place. They sat by themselves under the shade of a projection of bark and talked in low tones. They had been allowed to come this far because they were useful as scouts and they talked so much that they provided information even when they were trying to conceal it. They had warned the party about the dog-men, and they had given Ulysses enough data to piece together some partial pictures of what lay ahead.

But they also were probably detailed to spy on the invaders, and they would betray the party at the best time. At least, Ulysses had to proceed on that assumption.

He paced back and forth for several minutes and then decided that he would allow them to accompany them for a few more days. The Tree was an environment with which everybody except the two batpeople was totally unfamiliar. The party needed all the advice it could get. And although The Tree did not have so many open places, it had enough for the two to fly through. They could make scouting trips ahead of the party. The only trouble was, what if they went ahead to notify somebody that Ulysses and party were coming?

He would take a chance on that for a few days.

He went back to the pile of material and picked out what they should take. Climbing around on this tree would be like climbing a mountain most of the time; they could take only the most essential things. At the moment there did not seem to be much use for the heavy bazookas and rockets. He hesitated for a few minutes and then decided to get rid of them. He would, however, keep a number of the bombs.

He did not want the batpeople to come here and pick up the rockets, so he emptied them and set fire to powder. The resultant explosions shook up The Tree for miles. Hours passed before the monkeys and birds quit squawking and chattering.

After making sure that everything was properly bundled and strapped on, he signaled for them to follow him. He went up alongside the stream, leaping from projection to projection of the bark as if he were crossing a creek on stones. He was glad that he carried four extra pairs of moccasins. The rough bark would wear out the toughest leather in a short time. The others had calluses on their soles like iron. The two batpeople, however, had to be carried. Their weak bandy legs could not get them far along the branch. When he heard their carriers complain, he decided that the bat-men should not be burdens. He made them fly on ahead and wait for them. But he used the excuse that he needed scouts. This was an environment where ambush was fearfully easy.

They spent the rest of the afternoon toiling alongside the stream. The groove running down the spine of the branch was about fifty feet wide and ten deep in the middle. Coming down at a forty-five degree angle, its force was too much for anyone to wade in it. But Ghlikh said that higher up, where the branch was horizontal, the flow was slow enough for bathing. There were also fish, frogs, insects and plants in the stream and, of course, the creatures that ate these. And nearby would be the creatures that ate those predators.

A half hour before dusk, they came to the horizontal part. Here they rested while Ulysses studied the situation. They were partly in a gloom here, and when the sun was directly overhead they would be in complete duskiness. There were branches overhead that were just as big or larger, and these were covered by vegetation, including big trees. Moreover, at places between the branches, on horizontal and vertical planes, lianas and vines grew in an intertwining complex that looked solid enough to hold a herd of elephants.

There was a curtain of solid lianas and flowers that held strange seashell-shaped structures in which lived little shrew-like animals. These apparently made the nests with saliva which dried out to become hard as cardboard. Ghlikh advised against approaching the tiny beasts, because they had a painfully poisonous bite.

There were other dangers, all of which he described to Ulysses. Or at least he claimed to have covered everything.

Ulysses tried not to look appalled. But Awina and some others who had heard Ghlikh seemed depressed. They were a quiet bunch that night as they cooked their meat over small "smokeless" fires. Ulysses did not try to cheer them up; silence was to be desired. If they continued to be gloomy, however, he would have to do something to raise their morale.

He put together a fishing pole and, using a piece of deer meat as bait, went fishing. He caught a shell-less turtle and was going to throw it back when he decided he would try it for breakfast. His second cast got him a small fish which he did throw back. After about five minutes, he hooked a fish a foot and a half long. It had sturdy forefins and little feelers along the side of its body. It finally came in and then he discovered that it could also breathe air. It made a croaking noise and tried to scratch him with the tiny claws on the edge of its fins. He put it in a basket, where it continued to croak so loudly that he released it. He would catch it or its brother in the morning for his breakfast.

The problem of sleeping was solved easily enough, although not to his satisfaction. There were enough smaller fissures so that the entire party could be hidden, but, on the other hand, they could not sleep close enough together. An enemy could approach them and knock them off one by one without a guard even seeing him.

There was nothing he could do about it except to double the guards he would normally have stationed. He took second watch himself, and then lay down in a fissure near Awina. He closed his eyes but soon opened them. The hooting, screaming, moaning, croaking, booming, strumming and whooping made sleep impossible and plucked at his nerves. He sat up, then lay down, sat up again, rolled over and whispered to Awina. When he was tapped on the shoulder to take his turn, he had not slept at all.

The moon had come up then, but its light would not penetrate into this vegetable cavern. Its rays shone brightly several miles away on the plains, where Ulysses wished he were at that moment.

The morning saw all of them as red-eyed as the rising sun. Ulysses drank some water from the stream and then determinedly went fishing. He caught five of the amphibians, three trout-like fish, two frogs and another turtle. He gave these to Awina and she and several of the Wufea cooked them.

Ulysses talked cheerily, though not loudly, and after everybody had eaten the fish (they loved fish) they all felt better. Nevertheless, when they shouldered their packs, they were still tired. The shadows fell on them as they passed from the few spots where the sun penetrated to the lengthy stretches beneath the canopies of branch and liana and they fell silent. There were places where the vegetation was so thick that the batpeople could not fly, and then they had to be carried on the backs of two warriors.

The second day, they were in better condition. The noises of the night were more familiar, and they had gotten more sleep. They were eating well. The fish were still being caught. A Wagarondit shot a big scarlet boar with triple sets of curved tusks, and they roasted and ate it. Also, there were many trees and bushes with berries and fruits and nuts. Ghlikh said that none was poisonous, and so Ulysses ordered him or his wife to sample each before the others ate. Ghlikh did not like the order, but he smiled grimly, and he obeyed.

The third day, at Ghlikh's recommendation, they went up a trunk. He said that if they climbed to the upper terraces, they would find the going easier. Ulysses thought that flying creatures, such as other bat-men, might also spot them far easier, but he decided to go along with the bat-man for a while.

The party had been forced to travel on trunks before, of course. To get from one branch to another was quite easily done if the branches happened to be linked with a complex of lianas and other vegetation. Usually, this was the condition. But now and then they had to travel around a trunk to get to another branch. This was slow but reasonably safe, if one did not look down. The bark was like a very rough cliffside, and climbing up was as easy as going up a chimney with one open side. Ulysses managed the ascent well enough, though his hands and back were torn and bloody. Here the lesser weight, the wiriness and the fur of the nonhumans were to their advantage.

Breathing heavily, Ulysses finally pulled up over the last ledge and was on a branch. He had started climbing early that morning, and it was almost dusk. Below, it was already nightfall; the depths looked cavernously gloomy. The yowl of a leopard-like cat rose past them, sounding far away. A monkey pack whooped about a thousand feet down. He estimated that they were at least eight thousand feet above the ground. Yet they were not at the top of The Tree. The trunk rose at least another two thousand feet, and there were a dozen great branches between the one on which they stood and the tip of this trunk.

It got cold up here after dusk. Twigs, branches and logs from dead trees were collected and piled at the bottom of those fissures which were not filled with dirt. Up here, the dust was not as thick as below and there was more naked bark. The sun went down, and then clouds moved around them. Shivering and damp, they moved in closer to the fires.

Ulysses spoke to Ghlikh, who was sitting near him by the flames.

"I am not so sure that your idea was a good one. It is

true that there is less vegetation here, and so we can move more swiftly. But the cold and the wet may make us sick."

The bat-man and his wife were pale demon figures in the fog and the flickering light of the fire. They were enfolded in blankets out of which their naked heads and the leathery wings projected. Ghlikh's teeth chattered as he said, "Tomorrow, my Lord, we will build a raft and go sailing down a stream. Then you will see the wisdom of my advice. We will cover so much more territory so much more swiftly. You will see then that the discomfort of the nights are more than offset by the ease of travel of the days."

"We shall see," Ulysses said, and he got into his sleeping bag.

The cloud moved over his face like a wet breath and covered it with droplets of water. But the rest of him was warm. He closed his eyes, then opened them to check on Awina. She was in her bag, but sitting up with her back against the wall of the gray fissure. Her large eyes were fixed on him. He shut his eyes then but still saw hers, and when he slept he dreamed of them.

He woke with a shock, his heart hammering, his breath coming hard. The scream was still ringing in his ears.

For a minute, he thought he had dreamed. Then he heard the exclamations of the others and the noise as they fought to get out of their bags. The fire had gotten low, and the figures scrambling around in the dark looked like monkeys at the bottom of a pit.

He stood up, an assegai held ready. Ready for what? His question got a volley of babble; everybody was as uncertain as he. The party was separated into three groups, each of which was around a fire at the bottom of a canyon-like fissure, the top of which was several feet above even Ulysses' head. Then a round object appeared in the fog near him, and a voice said, "My Lord! Two of our people are dead!"

It was Edjauwando, a Wagarondit from another group. Ulysses hoisted himself out of the fissure and others followed him. Edjauwando said, "Two have been killed with spears."

Ulysses examined the dead by the light of the fire, which had been increased with a pile of branches and twigs. The throat wounds could have been made with spears, but Edjauwando was just guessing about the weapons used.

The guards said that they had seen nothing. They had been stationed outside the fissures but had sat at their posts half in their bags and half-wrapped in blankets. They said that the screams had come from out there—pointing into the cloud—and not from the victims.

Ulysses increased the guards and then returned to his fissure. He said, "Ghlikh, what kind of sentients are in this area?"

Ghlikh blinked at him and then said, "Two, Lord. There are the Wuggrud, the giants, and there are the Khrauszmiddum, a people like the Wufea but taller and spotted like the leopard. But neither live this high up. Or, at least, very few do."

"Whoever they are," Ulysses said, "they can't be many. Otherwise, they would have rushed the whole gorup."

"That is likely," Ghlikh said. "On the other hand, the Khrauszmiddum like to play with their enemies as a leopard plays with a young goat or a cat with a mouse."

There was little sleep the rest of the night. Ulysses did doze off, only to be awakened with a hand shaking him by the shoulder. An Alkunquib, Wassundee, was saying, "My Lord! Wake up! Two of my people are dead!"

Ulysses followed him to the crevice in which the Alkunquib had slept. This time, the two dead were guards. They had been strangled and their bodies rolled over into the crevice on top of their fellows. The other three guards, only a few feet away, had heard nothing until the bodies struck the bottom of the fissure.

"If the enemy has any force at all, he lost a good chance to kill many more of us," Ulysses muttered.

Nobody slept the rest of the night. The sun came up and began to burn away the cloud. Ulysses looked around the area for signs of the attackers but could find nothing. He ordered the corpses to be wrapped up in their sleeping bags and tossed over the side of the branch. After the priests had said their little ceremonies, of course. It would have been more fitting, according to their religions, if the bodies could have been buried. But on this branch, any dirt that had collected in the crevices was occupied by a tangle of roots of trees or bushes. So the bodies went over the side in the closest approximation of a burial that could be arranged. They turned over and over, narrowly missing a great branch a thousand feet below and then disappeared into a liana complex.

After a silent breakfast, Ulysses gave the word to march. He led them along the branch for half the day. Shortly after noon, he decided to transfer to a slightly lower one which had been running parallel to theirs for several miles. Its vegetation was much thicker; the reason for this was the riverlet which filled a third of the area on its top. He was interested in building a raft according to Ghlikh's suggestion.

The transfer took place on an almost horizontal liana complex. Ulysses sent the party over in three groups. While the first crawled over, the rest stood guard with bows and arrows. This was a good time for their enemies to try a surprise attack, because those on the complex were too occupied in hanging onto the lianas and making sure their footing would not be on a deceptively firm, but actually insecure, plant. Those staying behind scanned the thick growths for possible ambushers. A thousand enemies could have been easily concealed at a very close range.

When the first party reached the other side, they stationed themselves to cover the next, while a third group remained as rear guard. Ulysses had gone with the first group. He watched the next party crawl over the complex, which sagged just a little under the weight of the Alkunquib and the supplies and bombs they carried. He had already explored the immediate area and made certain that there were no ambushers there.

When the first Alkunquib was about twenty feet from the branch, the third group raised a great shout. Ulysses, startled, saw that they were pointing upward. He raised his eyes just in time to see a log about ten feet long falling toward the Alkunquib warrior. It did not hit him, but it plunged through the tangle, ripping lianas and vines and creepers apart. The warrior suddenly found himself dangling at the end of a liana. Those behind him had frozen at the first impact, and then they scrambled forward recklessly as other missiles, logs, branches and clods of dirt, crashed through the tangle.

Screaming, the first Alkunquib lost his grip and fell into the abyss. Another was hit on the back with a log about two feet long, and he disappeared. A third leaped out to escape a chunk of bark as big as his head and fell through. A fourth tripped and hurtled through an opening which closed up after him. But he reappeared a moment later and reached the dubious safety of the branch.

By then the logs were falling closer to the first party and forcing them to retreat deeper onto the branch. Ulysses also had to step back, but he had ascertained that the missile-throwers were on the branch directly above. On the sides, rather, since they would have been forced to climb down the sides on the rough bark in order to deliver their fire. They were about six hundred feet up and so within range of the bowmen on the other branch. These were Wagarondit under the chieftainship of Edjauwando. He remained cool and barked out orders, and presently the arrows were flying in volleys at the side of the branch above.

The enemies were leopard-spotted felines with hairy tufts on their ears and goat-like chin whiskers. Six, arrows sticking out of them, hurtled through the complex. One struck an Alkunquib squarely, and both went through. The rest of the Alkunquib gained the other side and tore through the bushes to get underneath the branch where the Khrauszmiddum could not hit them. The Wagarondit had stopped firing by then, and Ulysses yelled to them across the two-hundred foot gap. After determining that the leopard-men had climbed back up the sides to get away from the arrows, he ordered the Wagarondit to come across. They did so as swiftly as possible, but before the last had reached safety, they were bombarded from above. This time, the logs and dirt missed all the targets.

Ulysses finally found the two batpeople cowering under a big bush with huge scarlet six-pointed leaves. They had been the first to come across, having launched themselves from the trunk and flapped across. He wished that he had sent them to the higher branch to scout around. From now on, he would do so. In fact, he had a job for them at this moment.

"I want you to fly around until you find where the Khrauszmiddum live," he said.

Ghlikh's skin became even grayer. He said, "Why? What do you plan on doing?"

"I'll wipe them out," he said. "We can't just let them pick us off by twos and threes."

Neither of the two wanted to venture out into the open, but Ulysses said that he would cut their wings off and leave them behind if they did not obey orders. Then he decided to keep Ghuakh as a hostage while her husband went away. He did not use the word hostage or say why he wanted just one to do the scouting, but they understood him. Ghlikh reluctantly launched himself from a cliff-like projection of bark on the side of the branch, glided swiftly downward, began flapping, and then was spiraling upward. No missiles were thrown at him by the enemy.

While waiting, Ulysses had his people use their stone axes to build six large rafts. In about an hour the bat-man swooped down and made a landing on another liana complex. He crawled onto the branch and reported that he had seen a number of the leopard-men but no sign of their village.

Ulysses then told the bat-man that he wanted him to fly on down the riverlet and scout. He did not want to be ambushed while they were on the rafts; they were especially vulnerable on these. Ghuakh would remain with him. Ghlikh did not comment. He took off and was gone a half hour. He had seen nothing in the dense vegetation.

The plant life was not the only plentiful life here. There were scores of butterflies of many colors, bearing intricate designs on their wings and backs. A dragonfly with a four-foot wingspread zoomed over the water, dipping now and then to seize large waterspiders that skated on pontoon feet on the surface. Sometimes, a leaf rustled, and Ulysses glimpsed cockroaches as big as his hand. A flying lizard coasted by; its ribs extended far out on either side and a thin membrane grew between the ribs. Once, on the opposite bank, an otter dashed out and dived into the water. This time, it was not hunting, it was escaping a hunter. A bird about three feet high, a smaller variety of the giant plains roadrunner, came after the otter. It dived in after the animal, and neither appeared again.

Ulysses sat for a while, thinking, while the others either stood guard or sprawled on the mossy vegetation that overgrew much of the branch. The source of the riverlet was a large hole at the juncture of the trunk and the branch. According to Ghlikh, the tree pumped up water and poured it out at various spots like this. The water either ran through the channel, which inclined imperceptibly until it cascaded when the branch took an abrupt declination, or, often, when the branch ran horizontally, additional springs on the way kept the water flowing, sometimes even up slight inclines.

This riverlet apparently ran for many many miles. Ghlikh estimated about thirty-five miles, though he was not sure. The branch, like so many, zigzagged. There were even branches that looped in on themselves.

At last, Ulysses rose to his feet. Awina, who had been lying by him, also stood up. He gave the order, and he stepped onto the first raft. Some Wufea got onto the raft with him, and they shoved off with long poles they had cut from a bamboo-like plant.

The current ran at a sluggish five miles an hour at this point. The water was about twenty feet deep at the center of the channel and was clear for the first six feet. After that, it became murky. Ghlikh said that that was due to plants which grew from the bottom and released a brown liquid from time to time. He did not know what purpose the brown liquid served, but it doubtless had its use in the ecology of The Tree. Nor did he know why the liquid did not rise to the top and so discolor the entire stream.

There were fish in this stream. There were several varieties and sizes, but the largest was about two and a half feet long and looked like a red-and-black-spotted jewfish. They seemed to be plant eaters. A smaller, much more active fish with a pike's long underjaw fed off the water-skating spiders and also dashed after the frogs. But these usually escaped or else turned and gave battle. They had no teeth, but they clung to the side of the fish and scraped at the eyes. Once, a pike sheared off a frog's hind leg, and then the others closed in and tore the wounded animal to bits.

The raftmen kept the rafts close enough to the banks so that they could reach the bottom or even the banks and shove with their poles. They worked together at the low commands of the chiefs, shoving with a grunt as the chiefs counted. Others stood with bows and arrows ready.

The water level was almost up to the top of the banks, and the plants grew thickly along the banks. Sometimes, they reached out and into the waters. And there were trees which had grown at a slant over the stream. These were alive with birds and monkeys and other creatures. The monkeys had thicker fur than their fellows at a lower altitude.

If it were not for the threat of the leopardpeople, Ulysses would have enjoyed this trip. It would have been nice to have sat down and just drifted, like Huck Finn in a stream that Mark Twain would not have imagined.

But this was not to be. Everyone had to be alert, ready to go into action on a moment's notice. And all, he supposed, expected a spear to fly out from behind the dense green and scarlet plants at any moment.

Two tense hours went by and then the rafts came out onto a widening of the stream almost large enough to be called a lake. Ulysses had seen other branches which sometimes spread out, but he had never been on one before. The water also became deeper, and the lakelet was four hundred feet wide. To get across, the rafts could either be pushed by the current, which had become very sluggish, or they could stay close to the banks, where the bottom was shallow enough for the poles to be used. Ulysses elected to stay in the middle where, at least, they could relax for a moment, since they would be beyond the reach of Khrausz-middum javelins.

A moment later, he regretted his choice. A herd of beasts that looked from a distance like hippos waddled from the vegetation on shore and plunged into the water. Snorting and blowing, they cavorted around, coming closer to the rafts but seemingly not on purpose.

Ten yards away, they could be seen to be giant rodents which had apparently adapted to aquatic life. Their nostrils and eyes were on top of their heads, and their ears were provided with flaps of skin. They had lost all their hair except for a brush like a horse's mane on the back of their massive necks.

At this moment, on cue as if they were in a jungle movie, three large canoes appeared in the lake. Two came from behind them and one from the exit to the lake. Both canoes were of painted wood with snake heads projecting from the bow, and each held nineteen leopard-men, eighteen paddlers and a chief in the bow.

A few seconds later, Ulysses saw several huge creatures slither out of the plants on the banks and into the water. They looked like short-snouted, legless crocodiles.

Ulysses opened a waterproofed leather bag on the floor of his raft and took out a bomb. Piaumiiwu, a warrior whose duty it was to keep a lighted cigar in his mouth at all times, except when a fire was handy, handed him the cigar. Ulysses puffed on it until its end was a glow and then touched it to the fuse. It sputtered and then began to emit a thick black smoke which the wind took toward the two pursuing canoes. He held it until the fuse was about ready to disappear, and then tossed it in the middle of the hipporats.

The bomb exploded just before it struck the water. The beasts dived, and most of them did not come up at once, but one emerged just on the other side of Ulysses' raft. Its body, boiling out of the lake, sent water washing around the ankles of those on the raft. It snorted and dived again, and this time came up under the last raft, which tipped over. Yelling, a number of Wagarondit slid into the water, and some bags of supplies and bombs went into the lake, too. Then the behemoth dived once more, and Ulysses' second bomb blew up in the air just as it came up once again.

The leopard-men had been yelling at their quarry, but with the first bomb they fell silent. They also quit paddling and did not resume immediately, even though their chiefs screamed orders at them. By then, Awina had passed out several more bombs, and the best throwers had lit up their bombs. Four went out at the same time, one landing near three great hipporats. Three fell short of the two war canoes, but the explosions scared the Khrauszmiddum. They began to veer away, probably intending to stay out of range of the bombs but hoping to be close enough to cast spears.

The archers got into action then, and a number of paddlers and one chief fell with arrows in them. At the same time three archers fell, run through by spears thrown from the bank.

And a hipporat came up out of the water as if ejected by a catapult, seized the side of a war canoe with its two huge front paws, and pulled the canoe over on its side. The entire complement, screaming, went into the water.

There was a furious boiling here and there. Ulysses saw one of the limbless crocodiles rolling over and over with the leg of a leopard-man in its short jaws. The reptiles were also among his own men, those who had fallen into the water when the hipporat had tilted the raft up.

There was so much going on, Ulysses could not keep track of it all. He concentrated on the bank, where the greatest danger was. The ambushers were only evident now and then, seen through breaks in the vegetation as they threw spears. Ulysses directed the archers to fire into the thick green walls along the bank. Then he got the attention of the chiefs on the other rafts and told them to fire into the vegetation also. These transmitted the orders as soon as the men in the water had been pulled out.

The third war canoe, the one which had come in from the exit, was commanded by a chief brave to the point of foolishness. He stood in the prow of the canoe, shaking his spear and urging his paddlers to greater efforts. Evidently he meant to ram the first raft or to ride the canoe right up on over it and then board it.

The Wufea archers put an arrow through his thigh and six arrows through as many paddlers. But he knelt behind the snakeheads and shouted at his men to go on. The canoe came on, a little slower but still too swiftly to suit Ulysses. He lit another bomb and threw it just as a number of paddlers cast their paddles away and stood up to throw their spears. The canoe cut the water on a collision course with the raft. Nothing, apparently, could stop it.

Ulysses' bomb blew the front part of the canoe off and the chief with it. Water rushed in and flooded the rest of the hull, and it dived at an angle and disappeared momentarily just short of the raft.

The bomb had gone off so close that it deafened and blinded everybody on the raft. But Ulysses, his eyes streaming, saw what was happening a moment later. Most of the shattered vessel's crew were floating stunned or dead on the water, and then they began to go under as many-toothed jaws grabbed them.

The leopard-men on shore were still taking a heavy toll with their spears. Ulysses lit another bomb and threw it. It fell into the water, exploding just after landing. A great gout of water was thrown up on the bank, but it could not have done any injury. However, it must have panicked the spearmen, because their fire ceased. Ulysses ordered the rafts poled ashore. To stay in the lake was too dangerous. The legless crocodiles were making the lake seethe; he did not know where they had all come from. And the hippo-rats were attacking the men in the water.

The other two canoes, filled with dead or dying leopard-men, were drifting away. The arrow fire had been deadly. It was a tribute to the courage of his people, and also to his discipline, that they had kept up a very effective barrage.

Now they turned their undivided attention to the foliage, and the resulting screams told of unseeen hits. When the rafts hit the bank, Ulysses and his men piled out, grabbing the bags and quivers, and then plunged a few yards into the jungle. Here they stopped to reorganize.

Ulysses sent some men back to the rafts with orders to pole them down, close to the bank, until they reached the far end of the lake. He counted his men. Twenty had died. There were a hundred left, of whom ten were wounded. And their journey was, in effect, just begun.

They marched back along the bank without suffering any more casualties. At the end of the lake, they caught the drifting rafts, got back onto them, and resumed their downstream trip. From there the channel narrowed, and the current picked up speed. After a while, there must have been a definitely steeper incline to the branch, because they started to move at an estimated fifteen miles an hour.

Ulysses asked Ghlikh if it was safe to continue on the raft. Ghlikh assured him it was safe for another ten miles. Then they should put ashore, because the riverlet became falls in another three miles.

Ulysses thanked him, though he disliked even talking

to the two batpeople. During the battle, they had cowered behind the archers and held each other in their arms. Ulysses acknowledged that he had no right to expect them to take part in the battle. This was not their fight. But he could not avoid a suspicion that Ghlikh must have seen the ambushers. He had flown close above the river level and so should have seen the one war canoe, anyway. Still, it was possible that he had not. Also, if he was leading them into a trap, why had he stayed with them? He had been in almost as much danger as the rest.

On reflection, Ulysses decided that he was not being fair. He was letting his distaste influence his judgment. Not that he trusted them. He still felt that they were working for whoever Wurutana really was, or possibly for their own people.

The rafts continued at about the same speed. After a while, they heard the soft thunder of the cascades. He let the rafts speed along for another three minutes and then gave the order to abandon them. As instructed, those on the edge of the rafts leaped ashore first. The ranks behind them moved up and jumped. Two fell into the water when the rafts bumped into the bank. One was caught and smashed between raft and bank; the other was swept away.

Those remaining on the rafts threw all supplies except the bombs onto the banks. Ulysses did not trust the stability of the powder to last under the impact of hitting the ground. The bombs were tossed into the hands of those ashore.

He was the last one off. He watched the six rafts being carried along, bump-bumping into the moss-covered wood of the bank. Then the channel curved away, and the rafts were hidden by the thick foliage. A few miles on, the party came to the falls. The riverlet was raging through the narrowing channel, and it arced out over the trunk of The Tree and fell into the abyss. Ulysses calculated that it was eight thousand feet to the ground, which made this waterfall about twice as high as the highest of his day, the Angel cataract in Venezuela.

The party transferred to another branch which had only a small stream, about ten feet wide and three deep, in its channel. They went along the bank, though they could have gone faster if they had waded. But there were beautifully-colored, very poisonous snakes in the water and a few of the legless crocodiles. Ulysses decided to call these snoligosters, after a similar animal of the Paul Bunyan legends.

Before dusk, they made another transfer via a liana complex. They proceeded along this branch until Ghlikh saw a huge hole at the juncture of a trunk and a branch on a nearby trunk. He said that they could lodge in this hole, although they might have to drive out whatever animals were using it for a home.

"There are many such holes, quite large, in The Tree," he said. "Uusually where a branch starts out from the trunk."

"I've never seen any before," Ulysses said.

"You didn't know where to look," Ghlikh said, smiling.

Ulysses was silent for a while. He could not get over his suspicions of this creature. Yet he might be doing him an injustice. And Ghlikh was probably even more eager than he to find a comfortable, easily defended place. On the other hand, a good defensive place could be a good place for an enemy to bottle you up in. What if the leopard-men followed them here and then surrounded it?

At last, he made up his mind. His people needed a place where they could relax, relatively speaking. Also, his wounded needed tending, and some of them would have to be carried if they pushed on right now.

"Very well," he said. "We'll camp in that hole for tonight."

He did not say that he planned to stay there for a few days. He did not want Ghlikh to know anything of what he was planning.

There was no occupant to be driven out, though cracked bones and fresh droppings indicated that the owner, a large animal, might be coming back soon. He ordered the excrement carried out and thrown over the side, and the party moved in. The entrance was about twenty feet wide and seven high; the cave was a hemisphere about forty feet across. The walls were so smooth and polished, they looked as if they had been carved out. Ghlikh assured him that this was a natural phenomenon.

Dead wood was brought in and piled up to block off most of the entrance, and a fire was built. The wind carried some smoke inside but not enough to make it too uncomfortable.

Ulysses sat with his back against the glossy wall, and, after a while, Awina sat down next to him. She licked her arms and legs and belly for a while and then applied the cleansing saliva to her hands and wiped them over her face and ears. It was amazing what the saliva could do. In a few minutes, her fur, which had reeked of sweat and blood, was odorless. The Wufea paid for this with hair balls in the stomach, but they took a medicine of various herbs to get rid of the balls.

Ulysses liked the results of the cleansing, but he disliked seeing them do it. The actions were too animal-like

"The warriors are disheartened," she said after sitting by him in silence for many minutes.

"Indeed?" he said. "They do seem quiet. But I had thought that was because they are very tired."

"There is that. But they are also gloomy. They whisper among themselves. They say that you, of course, are a great god, being the stone god. But here we are on the very body of Wurutana himself. And you are a tiny god compared to Wurutana. You have not been able to keep all of us alive. We are only a little way on our expedition, and we have lost many."

"I made it clear before we started that some would die," Ulysses said.

"You did not say all would die."

"Not all have died."

"Not yet," she said.

Then, seeing him frown, she continued, "I do not say that, Lord! *They* say that! And not all of them, by any means! But enough so that even those who have spoken are pondering the words of fear. And some have spoken of the Wuggrud."

She used the word Ugorto, her pronunciation of the—to her—difficult sounds and difficult combinations thereof.

"The Wuggrud? Ah, yes, Ghlikh spoke of them. They are supposed to be giants who eat strangers. Huge ill-smelling creatures. Tell me, Awina, have you or any of our people ever seen a Wuggrud?"

Awina turned her dark-blue eyes toward him. She licked her black lips as if they had suddenly become dry.

"No, Lord. None of us have seen them. But we have heard of them. Our mothers have told us stories about them. Our ancestors knew them when we lived closer to Wurutana. And Ghlikh has seen them."

"So Ghlikh has been talking?"

He stood up and stretched and then sat down again. He had been about to walk across the cave but remembered that it was the mortal who came to see the god, not the god the mortal. He called, "Ghlikh! On the double!"

The tiny man scrambled to his feet and waddled across the floor. He stood before Ulysses and said, "What is it, my Lord!"

"Why do you spread stories about the Wuggrud? Are you trying to dishearten my warriors?"

Ghlikh's face was expressionless. He said, "Never would I do that, my Lord. No, I have not spread stories. I have merely answered, truthfully, the questions your warriors put to me about the Wuggrud."

"Are they as monstrous as the tales have it?"

Ghlikh smiled and said, "Nobody could be that monstrous, my Lord. But they are bad enough."

"Are we in their territory?"

"If you are in Wurutana, you are in their territory."

"I wish we could see a few and get our arrows into them. Then we'd shake this fear out of my men."

"The thing about a Wuggrud," Ghlikh said, "is that you will see them, sooner or later. But by then it may be too late."

"Now you're trying to scare me."

Ghlikh raised his brows. "I, Lord? Try to scare a god? Not I, Lord!"

Then he said, "It is Wurutana, not the Wuggrud, that have thrown your brave warriors into such a blue funk."

"They are brave!"

He thought, *I will tell them that there is nothing to be done about Wurutana itself. It is just a tree. A mighty big one. But it is a mindless plant which can do nothing to them. And the others, the Khrauszmiddum and the Wuggrud, are only the lice on the plant.*

He would wait until morning to tell this. Just now, they were too tired and dull. After a night's rest and a good breakfast, he would tell them that they could rest for a few days. And he would give them an inspiring speech.

He walked around, made sure that there was plenty of firewood and that guards had been appointed. Then he sat down again, and while he was thinking about his speech, he fell asleep.

At first, he thought that he was being awakened for the guard duty which he had insisted on standing. Then he realized that he was being rolled over, and his hands were tied beind him.

A voice said something in an unfamiliar tongue. The voice was the deepest basso he had ever heard.

He looked up. Torches were flaring in the dome. Giants held them. Beings seven feet tall, even eight feet tall. They had very short legs, very long trunks and long bulky arms. They were naked, and their hair distribution was much like a man's except for the fur across the belly and the groin.

The skin was as pale as a blond Swede's, and the hair was reddish or brown. Their faces were humanoid, but prognathous, with dark round wet noses. Their ears were pointed and set high on their heads. They stank of sweat, garbage and excrement.

They carried huge knobbed clubs, long-handled wooden mallets and spears with fire-hardened points.

The thing—he must be a Wuggrud—spoke again. His teeth were widely separated and sharp.

There was a piping sound. It took a few seconds to grap that the thin voice was Ghlikh's and that he was speaking to the Wuggrud in his language.

Ulysses felt such rage that he should have been able to tear apart the bonds around his wrists. But they held.

He said, "You foul stinking treacherous animal! I should have killed you!"

Ghlikh, smiling, turned and said, "Yes, you should have, my Lord!"

He spat on Ulysses and then kicked him in the ribs. The kick hurt the man's delicate foot more than it hurt Ulysses. The Wuggrud growled something, and Ghlikh hopped away.

The giant reached down and grabbed Ulysses by the neck with a huge hand and sat him upright. The hand choked him. When his senses returned, he saw that every one of his people were bound. No, not all. About ten lay dead, their skulls crushed.

The rear wall had been slid aside, exposing a tunnel. Torches set in stands on the wall flamed inside the tunnel.

So that was how they caught them. But how could so few overcome so many, even if those few were ogres? What had happened to the guards? Why hadn't the noise of the struggle awakened him?

Ghlikh squatted down in front of him. He said, "I got a powder from the Wuggrud. I put it in your water. In everybody's drinking water. It takes effect slowly and subtly. But very powerfully."

It was subtle. The water had tasted pure, and he had no headache or bad taste.

He looked around. Awina was sitting near him with her hands also tied behind her. The thought of something happening to her made him frantic.

His intention to ask Ghlikh why the ten had been killed was stifled. A Wuggrud leaned down and with a single twisting movement of his enormous hands tore off the leg of an Alkunquib. He began tearing at the flesh, ripping off

70

big chunks, and gobbling them with much smacking, chewing, and gulping.

Ulysses thought he would vomit. He was sorry that he could not. Awina had turned her head away. Ghlikh and Ghuakh stood in one corner and looked indifferent.

There were ten of the ogres—that was the best term for them—ten ogres in the dome and each ate upon a corpse. Then they threw the bones down and wiped away some of the blood on their mouths and chins with the back of their hands. They held the uneaten parts against their chests. Their chief growled like thunder at Ghlikh, who pointed at Ulysses and said something. The chief jerked a dirty bloody thumb at Ulysses, and another giant walked over and set him up on his feet, lifting him by the back of his neck. The fingers dug into his neck so severely that he was sure blood would pop out of his veins. The giant got behind him and prodded him toward the tunnel entrance with the point of his spear against his back.

Ulysses tried to give Awina a look that would tell her that he did not think all was lost, but she still kept her head turned away. He walked into the tunnel with the shuffle of huge feet and the sputter of the torches the only sounds. The tunnel curved gently to the right, straightened out, curved to the left, straightened out, and suddenly he was in an immense room in the heart of the trunk.

There were torches all around, set in the walls. Their smoke rose to the darkness-veiled ceiling and disappeared, apparently through vents. There was a slight draft of air, also going toward the ceiling. The stench was overpowering; the odors of garbage and excrement were so strong they seemed almost solid. They stuck in his throat and threatened to strangle him.

Behind him Ghlikh said, "Shau," his equivalent of "Phew!"

There were about ten adult females and thirty juveniles and children scattered around the room. The females were almost as big as the males and much fatter. Their breasts, hips, thighs and stomachs were huge and sagging. On seeing the meat in the males' hands, they set up a cry. The males threw the mangled remains to them, and women and children began to eat.

The room was divided into two parts. The smaller was set in a high niche at the other end and held a disk-shaped object placed vertically in the wall. A set of steps cut out of the wood gave access to it. Ulysses climbed it while the sharp wooden point of the spear dug into his back. Ghlikh and the chief followed him.

The disk was actually a membrane set in a ring of living wood, which was flush against the wall. Near it were two sticks of wood with slightly knobbed ends. Ghlikh picked these up and began tapping on the membrane. Ulysses listened and counted. The taps consisted of some sort of code, he was sure of that. Perhaps it was a primitive Morse code.

Ghlikh stopped tapping. The membrane vibrated. Its surface changed shape, and sounds came out. Pulses. Dots and dashes.

Ghlikh stood there with his head cocked to one side and his huge ears wiggling. When the membrane quit vibrating, he began tapping on it. After a while, he stopped to listen to some more pulses of unequal duration. Ulysses could make out patterns, units with dot-dot-dash-dot, dash, dash-dot-dash-dot, and many more, but these made no sense to him, of course.

The membrane could be likened to an eardrum or the diaphragm in a telephone. Behind it might be the end of a long vegetable nerve-cable, and at the other end, God only knew where, would be an entity transceiving at another membrane.

Ulysses had wondered why they had thought it necessary to bring him here. He found out a minute later when Ghlikh started to ask him questions.

"How did you plan to conquer Wurutana?"

Ulysses did not reply, and Ghlikh said something to the chief, who growled at the giant behind Ulysses. Ulysses jumped when the spear point cut into him, and he kept from yelling only by clamping his lips together.

There was no point, really, in not answering. And he might find out something about Wurutana while giving him information.

"I didn't have the slightest idea of how to conquer Wurutana," he said. "I came here primarily to find out what Wurutana was."

Ghlikh smiled and said, "You forgot to say that you were also going to the south coast to determine if your kind existed there."

He tapped on the membrane and then listened to the reply. He said, "Wurutana has decided that you should be taken to the city of my people. The Wuggrud will escort you there."

He spoke to the chief, who seemed to be protesting. But the tiny Ghlikh spoke firmly to him and then shook his fist and screamed at him. The giant sullenly acquiesced, and

Ulysses was led down the steps and out of the chamber. As soon as they were in the tunnel, he was able to breathe easier. He said, "Ghlikh, what about Awina? And my men?"

"Oh, they will go to make food for the Wuggrud, of course."

He spoke to the giant, who bellowed with laughter.

Ghlikh said, "We'll leave at dawn. Not all your people will be killed. That is, not at once. Some wil be taken along and butchered as needed."

Ulysses hesitated. He wanted to ask that Awina be brought along with him. The idea that he might have to watch her skull being broken and her body torn apart and devoured raw sickened him. It would be easier on him if she were left behind and he was spared that sight. But then there was always a chance of escape, however slight it seemed at the moment. If she were left behind, she had no chance. With him, she might live.

But Ghlikh hated him, and he might do exactly the opposite of what Ulysses wanted. Asking him to take Awina along might ensure that she would be left behind. Or, worse, Ghlikh, knowing Ulysses' fondness for her, might have her butchered before his eyes.

He would have to chance that. He just could not keep his mouth shut.

"Ghlikh," he said. "You seem to have great authority here, as the representative of Wurutana, whoever he is. Can you see that Awina will be brought along with us?"

Ghlikh smiled and said nothing for a long time. Then, just before they reached the end of the tunnel, he said, "We'll see."

He meant to torture Ulysses with uncertainty. So be it. Ulysses could wait. There was nothing else he could do.

When they entered the dome, Ghlikh directed that Ulysses be placed by Awina. He grinned when he did this, and Ulysses knew that he was taking pleasure at the thought of their agonized conversation.

As soon as he was by her, Ulysses said softly, "The first chance you get, reach into my pocket and get my knife out."

He saw Ghlikh, across the room, talking to his wife, who looked over at them and smiled nastily.

Ulysses said, "I'll snuggle close and appear to be talking to you. You get into my pocket and get the knife and open the blade. You know how. And then saw away at the bonds."

He managed to get closer and leaned his head against

73

her, working his mouth so that he seemed to be whispering. She stank of sweat and fear, and she was trembling.

"Even if they don't see us, and if I can get your hands loose, what can we do against those?" she said, nodding at the giants.

"We'll find out," he said. A giant walked toward them, and Ulysses froze. But the Wuggrud turned his back on them and then sat down in front of them. Ulysses could not have wished for a better wall behind which to hide. Presently, the huge head dropped, and the giant was snoring like distant thunder. The others lay down to sleep with the exception of one who stood in the entrance. He, however, did not seem particularly interested in keeping an eye on the captives. Why should he? They were all tied up, and they were small, and he stood between them and the outside.

Ulysses was worried about Ghlikh and Ghuakh, however. At any moment one of them might think of the knife and come over to take it away from him. He could not see them now, which meant that they could not see him, either. Ghlikh might not like that; he would want to enjoy Ulysses' suffering.

But Ghlikh did not come. Possibly, he and his wife had decided to take a nap, too, before the hard journey began. Ulysses fervently hoped so.

As long as no one was watching them, Awina could work swiftly. She scooted around so her back was to him and then groped into his pocket. In this situation, her feline suppleness and the smallness of her hand and arm also helped. She got her fingers around the end of the knife and slowly pulled it out. She dropped it, and they both went rigid as the knife made a slight sound. The giant garrumphed deep in his throat and raised his head for a moment. The snoring stopped. Ulysses thought his heart would stop. But the head drooped forward again, and the growling and sawing started up.

Awina pressed the button, and the blade snicked out. It took ten minutes of awkward sawing before the leather cords were cut. Ulysses massaged his wrists and worked his hands to get the circulation going. Then, keeping an eye on the guard, who was presenting his brutish profile to them, Ulysses cut Awina's bonds.

The next step was very crucial. If the guard saw them, or if the two batpeople were not sleeping, they would raise an alarm. At this stage, there was not much just two puny captives could do against the aroused giants.

He whispered to Awina to move slowly along the wall. He would slowly follow her until the sleeping giant in front of them blocked him from the guard's view. In the meantime, she was to cut the bonds of the Wufea next to her. Then he was to free the next man. And so on. When ten had gotten free, the knife was to be passed back to Ulysses. It would take too long and be too much in the open to attempt to free everybody.

Awina sent the knife on down the line and also transmitted his instructions. Neither he nor she could see the batpeople, but the Wufea next to her said that they were sitting with their backs near the wall and their heads between their knees. They looked as if they were sleeping.

The torches were almost out, and the fire at the entrance had long ago died. In a short time dawn would be graying the entrance and then the dome. The guard might wake up another to stand his duty at any moment. Or he might have orders to wake everybody up at dawn.

Awina put the knife in his hand, and whispered, "They say they're ready."

He looked around the back of the giant. The guard was scratching his back with the end of a stick and looking out the entrance. The bows, arrows, spears, knives, bombs, and the supplies of the captives were piled up near the entrance. The weapons of the giants were on the floor by their hands.

He rose cautiously and slowly, making sure that he would be hidden by the Wuggrud if the guard should turn. He reached around with the edge of the blade turned inward, and he slashed open the giant's jugular vein. The blood shot out, the snoring became a rattling, his knees opened, and his head fell down between his legs. Ulysses picked up the spear and, the bloody knife in his teeth, ran toward the guard.

Behind him, he hoped, the others were seizing the spears and clubs of their captors and using them to killing effect.

One of the giants cried out as he was struck.

The guard dropped the stick and whirled to face inward. Ulysses drove the spear into the belly, but it did not go far. The fire-hardened point was not sharp enough, and the belly of the Wuggrud was protected by many inches of fat and massive muscles. He weighed probably five hundred and fifty pounds, maybe more. He took the spear with only a backward step, and then he shoved against it and charged Ulysses. The man clung to the spear and ran backward. There was nothing he could do but go along with the Wuggrud. Fortunately, the guard was empty-handed.

But then the guard, bellowing madly, stopped, and he grabbed the spear and shoved it away so violently that Ulysses was knocked off his feet. The guard, blood streaming from the wound, bent down and picked up the spear and raised it to run it through Ulysses. His enormous strength could have driven the end of a telephone pole through the body of a bull.

Ulysses stepped inside the point and pushed the knife through the fat and the muscles and ripped upward. At the same time, a black and white fury leaped upon the shoulders of the giant from behind, and a stone knife stabbed into its right eye.

The giant dropped the spear and staggered backward. Ulysses clung to the knife, which came out of the belly. He leaped in again, because the giant had reached upward to grab Awina. Ulysses cut into the giant's groin, turned the blade, and pulled it out. The giant grabbed for the wound, and Ulysses ran the knife through the back of his hand.

A bow twanged, and the giant fell, an arrow driven through his neck. Awina rolled over to escape being crushed. She had fallen off when he had reached back.

Ulysses whirled. The bellows, shouts and screams had suddenly ceased. Every giant lay dead on the floor. Most of them had died as they slept. Three had wakened in time to fight and had killed three Wufea.

He whirled back toward the entrance to see Ghuakh launch herself off the edge of the branch and Ghlikh close behind her.

Shouting, he ran after them, snatched a bow and arrow from the Wufea who had shot the guard, and ran out. Ghlikh had jumped off a large projection and was falling, his wings flapping. Ulysses fitted the nock of the arrow to the string and, unconsciously estimating the wind, aimed and let the shaft loose. It went all the way through the thin membrane of the right wing.

Ghlikh fell, screaming, but then his wings began flapping again and he descended in controlled flight toward a great branch on another trunk. Here Ghuakh waited for him. Ulysses watched them for a few minutes while his wife inspected the hole in his wing and their mouths worked furiously.

Ulysses returned to the cave and gave the knife to a warrior to cut the bonds of the others. When everybody was up and armed, he told them that they must go into the inner cave. They were eager for revenge. Inside the big cave, they killed all the Wuggrud in a few seconds. They shot the adult women, who could be as dangerous as the males, and then speared the juveniles and the infants.

Ulysses then went into the niche and tapped the membrane. The response this time was swift, understandable, and near-deadly. From a thousand hitherto unseen apertures in the walls, the floor and the ceiling, sprays of high-pressure water struck them, knocked them down, and rolled them over and over. They fought to their feet and were knocked down again. They spun around and around until they had gotten to the tunnel, which by then was half-flooded. Choking, coughing, bumped by the dead bodies of the Wuggruds, they slipped and slid to the outer dome and then out the entrance. Here the sudden rise of water almost swept them off the branch.

After a while, the stream dwindled and then quit. Cautiously, Ulysses went back into the dome, which had been swept clean of all bodies and the supplies. Most of these, fortunately, had been caught outside and stocked out of the way of the flood.

The entrance to the tunnel was sealed with a solid and sticky mass much like a honeycomb.

Ulysses counted noses and tallied the supplies and ammunition. Half of them still had their bows and a quiver-full of arrows. There were ten bombs left. Eighty-four warriors, not counting himself and Awina, were alive. They were a fatigued, beaten and bedraggled bunch. Their bow-strings and feathers on the arrows were wet and thus useless at the moment. The fuses of the bombs were also soaked, and possibly the powder was wet. They had little food.

Aufaieu, who was now the ranking Wufea chief, said, "Lord, we are ready."

He paused and then added, "To follow you back to our villages."

Ulysses tried to look him in the eye, but Aufaieu would not meet his gaze.

"I am going on," Ulysses said. "I am going to the south coast and there find out if mortals who look like me exist."

Aufaieu did not point out that a god should know this. He said, "And what about Wurutana, Lord?"

"There is nothing to be done about Wurutana at this time."

What could he or anybody do? Wurutana was just a tree, and whoever sat in power, whoever controlled the bat-people and the Wuggrud and possibly the leopard-men,

77

could not be located. Not now, anyway. The Tree was just too vast; the controlling entity could be hiding any-place in it. But Ulysses would capture a bat-man someday and force the location of the king of Wurutana out of him.

Or he supposed he would. Now that he thought about it, just why should he search out this hidden ruler? As long as he stayed within The Tree and did not bother those on the land outside The Tree, let him do what he wished. Ulysses had only come this far because he had not known what or who Wurutana was and because the Wufea and the others seemed to think that Wurutana was a danger to them and that the stone god could do something about it.

There was nothing to be done about The Tree itself. It would continue to grow until it covered the land. The Wufea and others could either adapt to it, learn to live on it, or they could build boats and seek out other lands.

"There is nothing to be done about Wurutana at this time," he repeated. "What we will do, what *I* will do, will be to go on and explore the land along the sea to the south. If you wish to desert me, you may. I do not want cowards to accompany me."

He did not like to use such words. These people were not cowards. He did not blame them for feeling down-hearted and eager to give up. He felt that way, too, but he was not going to give up.

Awina said, "*Cowards* is right! Go back to your villages, to the clans you have disgraced! The women and the children will mock you and spit on you! And you will not be buried with the brave men! You will be buried in earth reserved for cowards! The ghosts of your ancestors will spit on you from the Happy Warground!"

Aufaieu jerked as if she had hit him with a whip. He snarled soundlessly at her, and his great dark-blue eyes glared. It was bad enough to be talked to like that by a man. But a woman! Especially a woman who had gone through exactly the same perils and battles as the men.

"I am leaving at once," Ulysses said. He pointed toward the south. "I am going that way. I am not turning back. You may follow me or you may not. I will say no more."

Aufaieu looked panic-stricken. The thought of going back without the stone god to lead and comfort them was a terrifying one. They had only gotten this far because he had extricated them from the difficult positions. And then, even if they made it back without him, they would have to explain to their people why they had deserted their stone god.

Ulysses shouldered a bag containing some food and two bombs, and he said, "Come on, Awina."

He walked past the entrance to the hole and started to work his way around the trunk. When he got to the other side, where another mighty branch began, he paused. He heard noises behind him and said, "Awina! Are they coming?"

She smiled and said, "They are coming."

"Good! Let's push on, then!"

He halted about a hundred yards on, where water welled up from a cavity on top of the branch and ran into a deep groove. Fifty yards down, the groove became a wide channel, and a riverlet started its many-miled course. He waited for the others to climb around the trunk, clinging to projections of bark, and when they had all straggled to the spring, he spoke to them.

"Thank you for staying loyal. I can't promise you anything except more of what you've had. But if we do find anything rich, anything valuable, we will share equally in the profits."

Some were silent; some murmured, "You are welcome, Lord."

"Now," Ulysses said, "we'll build rafts again. But we will put railings on them to keep any legless things or great water rats from snatching us off the rafts."

While a third of the men were cutting down the bamboo-like plants for logs and poles, and lianas for binding the logs, he set another third up as guard. The remainder went hunting. By the time the rafts were ready to be launched, the hunters had returned with three goats, four monkeys, a snoligoster, and a big ostrich-like bird. They started fires, butchered the carcasses and set them up to be roasted. When the odor of the meat filled their nostrils, their hearts filled with cheer. Before long, they were laughing and joking. By then Ulysses and Awina had returned with a string of eight fish.

While Awina prepared the fish, Ulysses pondered on recent events and on what he should do next. Though he had not seen the batpeople since he had gone around the trunk, he knew that there was nothing to keep them from dogging him. All they had to do was stay out of range of their arrows. And when they found more leopardmen or the Wuggrud, whom he was convinced were descended from bears, they could bring them down on the war party.

Moreover, there must be many more of the caves with the diaphragms or membranes. There might be a network that interconnected most of The Tree with some central control. And it was possible that this control was the batpeople's chief. After all, he had nothing but his own hunch that somebody other than Ghlikh's people was the entity known as Wurutana.

If he did get to the south coast, he might find that Ghlikh had lied to him. He may have told him that story about humans living there as an additional lure to get him into The Tree.

He concluded that there was only one thing he could do. That was to go ahead and trust to fate and the skill and courage of himself and his party. But if he did chance across the city of the batpeople, he would invade it if he could. Even if the bat-men were not the controlling force or entity, they were executives for Wurutana. They would have valuable information.

He could not see the sun because of the trunks, branches and vegetation foliage overhead and on both sides, but the strongest part of the light seemed to come from the first quarter of the heavens. He gave the order to launch, and they set out on four rafts. They proceeded without incident for about ten miles, at which point the sun was entering on the last quarter. And then they saw Ghlikh flying parallel with their course. He was about sixty yards to their left and high enough so that he could be seen just above the tops of the trees that filled the space between the riverlet and the side of the branch. He flapped faster when he saw that he had been observed and then disappeared beneath the wall of greenery. A few minutes later they saw him sitting on the branch of a giant redwood-like tree growing out of the larger branch.

Some of the warriors wanted to shoot at him, but Ulysses told them not to waste their arrows. He wondered where Ghuakh was, and then it occurred to him that she may have gone on ahead to notify the Khrauszmiddum or Wuggrud. Or perhaps she was going to the city of the Dhulhulikh and meant to bring them down on the invaders.

The rafts passed the tree on which Ghlikh sat. He watched them until the riverlet took a bend that carried them out of sight. A moment later they saw him flapping along and then he was gone. But he came back and perched on the branch of another redwood. He was close enough this time so that Ulysses could see the hole in the wing where the arrow had gone through.

Ghlikh remained on the branch until the rafts had gone around another slight curve. The moment he was out of sight, Ulysses leaped from the raft and forced his way through the thick vegetation. He was hoping that he could get to the side before Ghlikh took off from the branch. After all, Ghlikh didn't have to be in a hurry. The party he was watching could not get far away.

To get to the side swiftly, he had to make far more noise than he wished. If he were a Tarzan, he could have swung from branch to branch on the parasitical trees, and if he had had more time, he might have tried it. But he did not, and so he rammed through the fronds, the pulpy shafts and the hard many-branched bushes, thorns and lianas that grew from plant to plant. He carried his bow and extended this ahead of or above himself. But when he crawled through a bush or a thorn barrier, the arrows sticking out of his quiver caught, and he had to stop to pull them loose.

Finally, he put the quiver on the ground and took two arrows in his hand. After that he made better time. Twice he scared away the Chihuahua-sized deer and, once, he leaped away from a hissing snake with a triangular head and black, orange and yellow chevrons down its back.

He got to the edge just as Ghlikh leaped out from his tree, extended his wings and then began flapping. Ghlikh went down and then up, coming even with the side of the branch about twenty feet past where Ulysses crouched behind a bush. Ulysses stood up and aimed ahead of Ghlikh and released the shaft. It went through his right ear and on ahead of him.

He screamed and fell off to one side. Ulysses pushed out to the very edge of the branch and fitted another arrow to the string. By then Ghlikh had quit screaming and had checked his fall. He was about fifty feet down and ahead, and this time Ulysses aimed a little less ahead of his target.

The arrow went through Ghlikh's right wing and shoulder. The arrow must have gouged a groove on the top of the right shoulder, because it kept on going. But Ghlikh was hurt, and he dropped, wings trailing into the gloomy abyss. Ulysses tried to follow him all the way but lost him in the duskiness and density of the foliage.

Unless the bat-man struck something, though, he would probably recover and land safely. Ulysses sighed and returned to the raft. He had at least given him the scare of his life.

"Stop around the next bend," he said after he had jumped back onto his raft. He told them what had happened, and though they were disappointed that he had not killed Ghlikh, they did enjoy his description of Ghlikh's terror. They scrambled out after him and pulled the rafts into the vegetation, where they cut the binding lianas and stacked the poles under bushes. After that, they crossed to the other side and here began the difficult, but not impossible, climb down the side. When they were as far as they could go vertically, they moved out horizontally. Before dusk, they were inside one of the large cavities that abounded on the sides of the branches. These quite often held animals: apes, monkeys, baboons, or cats ranging from housecat size to leopard size. The owner of this one happened to be out, and when he came back, he turned out to be an ocelot-sized cat with tiger stripes. He did not dispute the den with them.

"We stay here until our meat and water run out," Ulysses said. "If Ghlikh didn't get killed or badly hurt, he'll be back up here. But he won't find us. Or, if he does, he's likely to get an arrow through his belly."

Ulysses did not like the idea of hiding, because his "men" needed action. But if he could throw off the bat-people and anybody they had summoned, the inactivity and the tension of lying around cooped up would be worth it.

The next morning, he was glad that he had hidden. He was awakened by Awina, who reported hearing strange voices, many voices, from somewhere close. He crawled out to a place near the opening and listened. The high thin voices so far away belonged to the Dhulhulikh. They were calling to each other as they flew above the jungle or waddled through the vegetation. Though small, they had trouble making progress in the jungle because their wings caught and the thin membranes tore so easily.

"We'll stay in here all day," Ulysses said. "But if they're still here tonight, we'll go out and catch us one."

They got as far back into the hole as they could. It was well they did, because about an hour later a batwing flew by. He was going swiftly, but it was evident that he was scanning the fissures and caves on the side.

After the Dhulhulikh had gone by, Ulysses went to the side of the entrance and motioned for the Wufea chief to get on the other side. As he had suspected, the batwing decided to come back for a closer look. The little fellow dropped into the opening without warning, shooting in so swiftly that he had to run a little way in before he could stop. It was a foolish move, and the batwing must not have really thought that there would be anybody in there. He was probably just following orders, and so regarded this entry as routine.

If so, he had the shock of his life. He was grabbed from behind and front before his eyes could get adjusted to the dimness of the cave. A big hand clamped down on his mouth, and the edge of a hard palm chopped his skinny neck.

Ulysses had the unconscious bat-man bound and his mouth gagged. When he saw the man's eyes open, he told him, in Ayrata, what he had to do if he wanted to live. The bat-man nodded that he would obey, and the gag was removed. But a knife was held at his throat.

His name was Khyuks, and he was in a special attack force.

And who had called them here?

Khyuks did not answer that. Ulysses twisted the fragile foot a little bit while Aufaieu held his hand over the man's mouth. Khyuks still would not talk, so Ulysses punched several holes in a wing. After some more treatment, Khyuks began talking. It was Ghuakh, Ghlikh's wife, who had reported to them.

If that were so, then the city of the bat-men could not be far from here, Ulysses thought. He was in luck.

Not so, Khyuks said. The place was only a small settlement, an outpost.

How many Dhulhulikh were in this attack force?

About fifty.

Ulysses had no way of checking on this at the moment.

How did they plan to fight the invaders?

As he asked this, he studied the finned and stone-pointed wood darts in the belt around Khyuks' waist.

The Dhulhulikh would drop the darts on the warriors, of course. And Khrauszmiddum would be coming to attack on land.

At that moment, another batwing landed. He came up and stalled just outside the entrance and landed only a few feet inside. The Alkunquib stationed by the sides of the entrance leaped for him, but the batwing did a backflip through the hole and escaped them. A Wufea, however, sent an arrow through him, and the batwing dropped without a sound. They crouched inside the hole, waiting for a cry to arise announcing that the arrowed man had been seen. But no cry came.

"They'll be counting noses sometime later," Ulysses said. "And they'll start looking for the missing soldiers, you can bet on that."

"What do we do?" Awina said.

"If they don't start looking until dusk, then we get out of here. We go back into the jungle above. If they find us before dark, then we've got a hell of a fight on our hands."

He did not add that the batwings could simply starve them out.

Khyuks would answer some questions. Others he just would not. He was such a frail creature, he could not endure much pain. When the pain got too much for him, he fainted. And when he was revived and tortured again, he fainted once more.

He would not tell them where the city of the Dhulhulikh was. He did tell them that the city held the spirit of Wurutana. But he would not say what the "spirit" of Wurutana was. He insisted that he did not know. He had never seen Wurutana. Only the chiefs of the Dhulhulikh had. At least, he presumed they had. He had never heard any chief say that he had seen Wurutana. Wurutana's spirit, rather. This Tree was the body of Wurutana.

Wurutana was the god of the Dhulhulikh. Also of the leopard-men and the bear-men, though the simple Wuggrud had a number of other gods, too.

Ulysses was curious about the depth of control by Wurutana. He asked if the Khrauszmiddum and Wuggrud ever fought among themselves.

"Oh, yes," Khyuks said. "Every tribe fights his neighbor. But none fight us; all obey the voice of Wurutana."

And how many Dhulhulikh were there in all?

Khyuks did not know. He insisted, even after fainting several times, that he just did not know. He did know that there were many. Very many. And why not? They were the favored of Wurutana.

Were there any people like Ulysses on the south coast?

Khyuks did not know, but he had heard that there were. After all, the coast was many flights away, and only a few of the batwings ranged far and wide.

Dusk eventually came. Khyuks was unconscious again. The batwings had ceased to fly by. Ulysses thought that they must be searching farther down the riverlet. By the time they discovered that two were missing, they would not know when they had dropped out. And it was next to impossible to search in the dark here.

As soon as he thought it dark enough, he gave the order to move out. Khyuks was tied to Ulysses' back and gagged. Ulysses had given his word that the batwing would not be killed if he gave information. It was true that Khyuks had not answered all the questions, but he had answered most. And Ulysses admired the little man's courage and endurance. He knew it was dangerous to be sentimental to an enemy, but he did not feel like killing the plucky little fellow. Moreover, he might be able to use him later.

They returned to where they had hidden the raft logs and the poles. The rafts were put back together, and the party launched itself out on the dark riverlet. The moonlight did not filter down very far. Occasionally, a ray broke through an avenue of branches. Once, a thin ray lit up great dark round objects in the water ahead of them. There was a snort, and a needle of water shot up from some aperture in the creature. Then the water boiled as bodies disappeared. The rafts pushed on through the roiling as the occupants waited, tensely, for the great hipporats to appear beside the rafts or, worse, underneath them. But the rafts proceeded unmolested.

Several times, Ulysses saw the seemingly endless lines of a legless crocodile slide out from the silvery-black bushes and into the silvery-black water. He waited for the violent upthrust of a short-jawed, many-toothed head onto the raft and the closing of teeth around the leg of someone—or himself. Or the lash of a mighty tail from the darkness and the smash of bone and pulping of flesh and the body flying into the riverlet.

More miles passed without incident. Birds and unknown animals gave their weird cries. Then the current picked up and they were going so swiftly that the polers had no need to shove against the bottom. Now they were busy pushing against the bank so that the rafts would not bump against them.

The great branch was leaning downward at a steeper rate, although the inclination was not noticeable in the dark by the raftmen. If it had not been for the pickup in the current's speed, they would have thought they were on a level.

Ulysses liked but also worried about the speed. He crouched down by the bound Khyuks and splashed water from the riverlet onto the little face. The water made the unconscious bat-man open his eyes.

85

He croaked, "I am thirsty."

Ulysses dipped more water with his gourd and lifted Khyuks' head so he could drink. Then he said, "I think the water is rushing toward some fall. Do you know anything about it?"

"No," Khyuks said sullenly. "I know nothing of any waterfall."

"That means what?" Ulysses said. "That you are ignorant of this area or that there is no waterfall at the riverlet's end?"

"I didn't fly over the end of this branch when I came in," Khyuks said.

Ulysses said, "Well, we'll find out the hard way whether or not there is a cataract. I want to get out of here with all possible speed, and I'll keep us on the rafts until the last possible moment. There might be some difficulty, but not an impossibility, I hope, in getting off the rafts at the last moment."

He did not elaborate. Khyuks was not so deep in pain that he could not visualize what might happen. It could be every man for himself, and Khyuks, his legs and hands tied, would be dependent on someone else to get him ashore. There might not be enough time for anyone to carry him or throw him ashore, even if anyone felt so inclined.

After a while, Khyuks spoke again. It was evident that he loathed himself. He wanted to keep his mouth shut and take whatever was coming. But he was unable to face the death at the end of the branch. Perhaps, Ulysses thought, there was something especially horrifying about death in water to him.

"Judging by the current," he said slowly, "we must be about three miles from the end. Where the first cataract is."

Ulysses considered the possibility that Khyuks was not frightened. He might be lying so that he could trap them all, send them all to a falling watery death, including himself.

"We'll go another mile or so," Ulysses said. "Then we'll get off the rafts."

There was enough light so that he could see Khyuks' face Now and then, the light strengthened as the moon's rays shot through openings between leaves and branches and trunks thousands of feet above them. The bat-man's face was as unreadable as a piece of leather.

At that moment, a cry brought Ulysses upright and raised

a chill on the back of his neck. He turned around to see what Awina was pointing at. There was a big tree growing out of a dirt-filled crack about fifty yards away. It was only about fifty feet high, but it spread out horizontally to eighty feet or so on either side of the massive trunk. The cry had come from something on one of its branches. A moment later, he saw its origin. A number of dark bodies launched themselves from the dark mushroom shape out into the abyss below the great branch on the rim of which the tree grew. Great leathery wings spread out, and the little bat-man disappeared behind the vegetation. Within a minute, the first of them reappeared again, flapping strongly to carry himself up and over the rafts. And in another minute there were many more.

There was only one thing for Ulysses to do. If his people stayed on the rafts, they would be open to attack from above. Worse, they would have to quit the rafts later on while under attack and under conditions which would make it difficult to defend themselves.

He shouted an order, and the polers on the outside of the rafts shoved against the bottom. The rafts moved in toward the banks, and those on the bankward edges leaped out and grabbed the bushes. Meanwhile, Ulysses had begun tossing the heaviest boxes through the air and onto the banks. He hoped that the impact would not trigger the unstable black gunpowder. The boxes of bombs fell onto the bushes without reacting.

Then he lifted up Khyuks and heaved him with an effort that dipped the raft on his side. The little fellow, squawking, crashed face-down onto a thick growth. Wulka, a Wagarondit, picked him up.

By that time, the first of the batpeople was swooping down on the raft, his little hands holding a short spear. He never got above them; an arrow thudded into his chest and he fell with a loud splash. A great legless length launched itself from the bushes on the opposite bank, roaring as it went through the air.

Ulysses shot once, noted that his arrow had driven into the shoulder of a bat-man, and then turned and leaped onto the bank without waiting to see the man's fall. He held his bow out with his right hand and clutched at a branch with his left. His hand closed around a thorny length, and he exclaimed with the pain. But he did not let loose.

Something hit the dirt just beside his right foot. A missile cast, or dropped, by one of the flying men. Then he had dived over the bush, pulling himself over, and never mind possible damage to the quiver or the bow. When he was behind the bush, he crawled on through the vegetation until he was covered by a large and heavy bush. He roared at his chiefs and at Awina until they had all answered. In response to more of his orders, they made their way through the tangles until they were close to him. During this time, the bat-men had been swooping over the jungle and dropping or hurling assegais, darts, and shooting small arrows. No one was hit, and after a while the bat-men quit their blind bombardment. They were losing too many weapons.

In the meantime, the archers had brought down five of the fliers. The batpeople retired to the tree for a conference.

Despite their retreat, they held the upper hand. Their enemy could only go so far in one direction and then they would have to climb down the trunk or up the trunk to get to another branch. If they did this, they would be exposed, and the batpeople could kill off the entire party with little or no casualties to themselves.

If their enemy continued to hide in the dense vegetation of this branch, they would just be putting off the inevitable. The batpeople could send for more fliers and, in time, flush them out. Especially since they would be restricted in their hunting and could be starved out if the winged men did not care for a direct battle.

Ulysses had tried to count his foes while they were zooming over in the moon-speckled darkness. He estimated they numbered about a hundred. At the moment, they were gone except for six sentinels who kept diving and climbing but always just out of effective range of the arrows.

Ulysses crouched under the bush and tried to think of what to do. And while he thought, he became aware of a very faint murmuring sound. He requested quiet from those around him and, within a minute, thought he could identify the noise. It had to be the distance-muted roar of a waterfall.

He gave orders to the nearest, Awina, who relayed them. There was some delay because the party, for the most part, was reluctant to leave their present location. This gave them excellent protection but Ulysses knew his "men" and what they were thinking. He yelled at them and told them what would happen in the future if they did not get going. Once it was explained, they reacted swiftly enough. They just did not live much in the future; they had trouble seeing past their present situation.

The end of the branch, or, rather, the place where it abruptly bent at ninety degrees to the horizontal, was two miles away. The party made slow progress because of the thick vegetation and also because they were under orders to move slowly and quietly.

Ulysses saw the spume of white and black about a quarter of a mile before he got to it. He had climbed a tall tree to get a better look, at the same time making sure that he would not be seen by the bat-men, who were flying overhead now and then. The mists rose up and spread out to some distance, as he had hoped. Up in the tree, the roar of the falling water was unfiltered by the jungle.

He was about to climb back down when he saw a Dhulhulikh flap by. He clung to the tree and tried to make himself look like a barky excrescence. No moonlight hit him directly, though enough sieved through the leaves to make the darkness more silver than black. The bat-man went by once, winging so slowly he was just short of stalling. Then his wings beat faster and he climbed as he banked. He came back toward the tree, moving through patchy areas of blackness and pale yellow, the moon's rays bouncing off his bald head and catching beams off his wings, which were darker than his body. He came down just above the tops of the brush, and then flew upward, beating his wings to keep from a complete stall. Just before he landed on the branch of the tree, on the other side of the trunk from Ulysses, he did stall. And he landed as smoothly as an owl on the branch.

He had no talons with which to grip the branch, but he reached out and grabbed a smaller branch and so kept himself from going ahead. After he had folded his wings, he turned to face away from Ulysses. He wore a belt with a stone knife and carried in one hand a short slender spear. From a cord around his neck hung a coiled instrument. Ulysses guessed that this was a horn of some kind. The fellow was sitting there to watch for the enemy. If he saw them, he would summon the others with his horn.

There was no noise from below loud enough to rise above the soft thunder of the waterfall. His men had seen the bat-man and were waiting for the next development. The jungle looked unpopulated.

Ulysses left his position and worked his way around the trunk. His bow and quiver were at the foot of the trunk. Fortunately, they were on the side of the trunk opposite the bat-man and were also in the shadows. Ulysses had only his switchblade knife, which was held between his teeth. He had to cling with both hands and move very slowly. Even though the waterfall drowned out noise, it was not so loud that the keen-eared bat-man would not be able to hear the rustle of leaves or creak of branch.

The man continued to face away from Ulysses as he moved out on the same branch as the one he sat on. He stood upright, balancing himself easily, because the branch was thick. He slid one foot ahead and then brought the other up, slid his forward foot ahead, brought the other up, and so on. Once, he stopped and took the knife from between his teeth. The bat-man's wings half-spread, flapped slightly and then folded back in. In that moment, Ulysses saw the hole in the membrane of the right wing. And he recognized the silhouette of the man's head and the set of the shoulders. It was Ghlikh.

His intention to kill was gone. He could use Ghlikh.

Killing would be easier than capturing. He had to make sure that he could knock Ghlikh out and at the same time keep him from falling. Though Ghlikh weighed only about forty-five pounds, he could be hurt or even killed by a thirty-foot fall. Ulysses also had to make sure that he didn't rush too swiftly or he might go over along with him.

He approached very slowly, afraid that the little man would detect the bending of the branch under his two hundred and forty-five pounds. But Ghlikh was not out near the slender part of the branch. He was halfway, still on the thick part. And so Ulysses was able to chop him along the side of his neck, not too hard, because he was afraid he would snap the thin, probably hollow-boned, neck. Soundlessly, Ghlikh collapsed and fell forward, and Ulysses had to grab with the other hand and seize his wing. He called to those hidden in the brush, and they came out. A moment later, he dropped the unconscious man into waiting arms. By the time he got down, Ghlikh was tied and gagged. A few minutes afterward, his eyes opened. Ulysses stood in the moonlight so that Ghlikh could see who had captured him. Ghlikh's eyes widened, and he struggled. He was still squirming when he was hoisted on-to Ulysses' back as if he were a backpack. Ulysses told Wulka, the Wagarondit chief who was carrying Khyuks, to hit Ghlikh again, and Wulka gladly obeyed.

The half-mile was covered as swiftly as possible. Ulysses had the honor of being the first to start the climb down. The mists shrouded him, not only from the view of any bat-men who might be coming along soon, but also from view of the others. What with the darkness and the clouds rising from the abyss, he could barely see two feet before, or under, him. The droplets collected over his body and made him cold. They also made the bark and his fingers and toes slippery.

There was nothing to do but go down. If he had been alone, or with people who did not expect him to be a god, he might have stayed outside the mist and taken his chances on being seen by the batpeople. But he could not avoid his obligations or break his word.

"The mist is our protection," he said. "But like all protections, all shields, it has its disadvantages. It exacts a price. It hides us from our enemies, but it also holds its dangers. It will be slippery, and we will be blind."

It was also very slow going, he thought, as he groped with his foot for a projection below him. His hands clung to outthrusts of bark, one foot was half in a fissure, and the other foot moved around for a ledge or crevice. Finally, it found a ledge, and he lowered himself gently, made sure he had a secure hold, and then lowered his foot again. This process went on for an unaccountable time, and then the darkness paled, and he could see just a little more than before.

He had a solid extension beneath him. Carefully, he walked out on it, testing each unseen inch of bark with his toes. The waterfall roared on his left and water swirled against his left foot. He jumped as something touched him, and he whirled with his knife in hand. Dimly, he saw the short, slender, black-and-white figure of Awina. She came closer then, her eyes big round darknesses. He put the knife away, and she clung to him for a moment. Her fur was wet, but after a minute their bodies began to warm each other. He ran his hand over the round top of her head and felt the wet silky ears and then ran his hand down her back. She felt more like a drowned rat than the soft deliciously furry being he had known.

Other figures jelled out of the mists. He moved away from Awina, counting them as they appeared. All were there.

Ghlikh began twitching. He had been as motionless as a bag of meat during the descent, but now he thought it was safe to move and try to get his circulation going again. Ulysses had him removed from his back and the bonds around his legs taken off. The little man hopped around on his skinny legs and huge feet while two Wagarondit stood ready to stab him if he tried to run or fly.

Ulysses walked carefully out of the mists. The top of

the waterfall was about five hundred feet up. There were no batpeople in sight. Only the bushes and sides of leaning trees broke the edge of the upper part of the branch. He turned and saw that the branch continued on a horizontal plane until it was lost to sight. There was nothing to keep them from building more rafts and continuing on the riverlet. But they must hide in the jungle until nightfall again. They could sleep part of the day, although they had to spend some time in hunting. Their food supply was getting low.

Late that evening, no longer sleepy but suffering from hunger pangs, they organized four hunting parties. An hour later, they butchered a legless crocodile, a hipporat, two big red goats and three large monkeys.

They ate well that evening, and everybody felt much better. They cut down poles and bound them together and then set out on the riverlet. Before dawn, they came to another downward bend of the great branch and another cataract. They climbed down but stayed outside the mists, and by dawn they reached the bottom and another riverlet; after sleeping and hunting again, they made more rafts. The bottom of the third waterfall proved to be also the bottom of The Tree, or, as Awina called it, the Feet of Wurutana.

The vast trunks, branches and other vegetation growing overhead to a height of ten thousand feet formed a complex that barred all but a few of the sun's rays. A deep twilight reigned here at noon, and in the mornings and afternoons a near-night like a storm of ravens' feathers filled the spaces between the gigantic columns and buttresses plunging into the swamp. The ground beneath The Tree received the precipitation of the cataracts and the rainfall that was not caught by the branches and the colossal leaves of The Tree and the vegetation that grew on The Tree. A swamp had formed at the base of The Tree, a vast unutterably dismal swamp. The depth of the water varied from one inch to many feet, enough to drown a man. Out of this water, and out of the mud, many strange, foul-smelling, pale and blotched plants grew.

The twilight showed them nightmare forms. Great pieces of bark, many of them bungalow-sized, had fallen off the sides of The Tree and hurtled downward, striking branches and trunks and knocking off other large and decaying crags of bark. The Tree, like the World-Snake of Norse mythology, shed its skin. Bark was always rotting and then breaking off and either falling onto the tops of the mighty branches, there to decay more, or else coming down like cold black falling stars to splash into the water and the mud of the swamp. There, half-sunk, they decayed, and the insects and vermin that infested this dusky world bored into the great masses and made their houses therein.

These were long thin corpse-colored worms with hairy heads; beetles colored a hard blue and armed with huge mandibles; long-nosed shrew-like beasts with saberteeth; pale yellow scorpions; bright scarlet-and-midnight-black snakes with tiny horns on top of their triangular heads; many-legged soft-bodied dozen-antennaed long-bodied centipedish creatures which emitted a stinking gas with a loud explosion when startled; and a host of other repulsive animals. The great broken chunks of bark, lying everywhere in the dimness like boulders left behind by the retreat of a glacier, were crowded with the venomous verminous life.

Around the jagged slabs grew tall slender branchless plants which produced a heart-shaped greenish-yellow berry that sprouted from cracks in the horny shells of the plants. There was also a thick slimy weed that projected a foot or two above the muddy water or the watery mud underfoot. Above this there sometimes flapped a broad-winged insect with body and wings the color of the skin of a man just dead, and its head was white with two round black markings and a down-curving black mark below the two markings, so that its face was that of a skull. It flew by silently, sometimes just touching a member of the party with the tips of its wings and causing that person to jump. But all motion and noise were subdued. The people talked very quietly, often whispering, and they did not laugh. Their feet sank into the water and the mud beneath and were pulled out slowly, almost apologetically, so that sucking sounds were slow and soft. The people huddled together, and no one wanted to step aside into the bushes or behind the tall pale gray-blue stalks to attend to their needs.

Ulysses had thought, at first, that he would keep to the swamp. Though the going was slow and rough, this place seemed more desirable than the area above, where there were too many sentient enemies. But one day and one night among the Feet of Wurutana were enough for him and more than enough for his people. The next morning, when he almost jumped a foot as a blood-colored frog leaped off a slab of bark onto his shoulder and then into the ankle-deep water, he decided that he could not take much more. They had tried to sleep on a piece of bark as big as a small chateau. But all night long they had been disturbed by the creatures which crawled out of the holes in the bark and by the weird sounds of the swamp animals.

He decided that he would lead them back up the nearest inviting branch. They had to skirt a broad area which seemed to be filled with quicksand pools, so it was not until noon that they reached a rough-surfaced column that dived from the heights into the swamp. Thankfully, they began clambering up it, and by dusk they had reached a promising horizontal portion of a branch. This contained a riverlet which, however, looked poisonous. Its water was carmine.

Ulysses examined it and found that the color came from millions of tiny creatures, each of which was so small it was almost invisible when isolated. Ghlikh, who had decided to talk by then, said that these animals spawned once a year. He did not know where they came from or where they went. The waters of the riverlets and the pools would remain red for about a week and then would become clear. In the meantime, they served as food for the fish, birds and beasts in the jungle. He recommended making a soup of them.

Ulysses took his recommendation, but he made Ghlikh drink the soup first. After several hours went by with no bad results to the bat-man, Ulysses gave the go-ahead. He drank a gourdful and found the soup very rich and tasty. For the next few days, as they poled their rafts, they ate merely by scooping up the carmine animals from the water. Not having to stop to hunt made their progress far swifter. They traversed approximately fifty miles, climbing down three cataracts, before they reached the lowest level of the riverlet. By then the carmine animals had disappeared.

When they climbed up again, Ulysses, acting partly on a whim and partly on curiosity, led them as high as they could go. The climb took three days up the gnarled and fissured side of the vertical trunk. At night, they slept on a projection of bark big enough to form a ledge to hold the entire party. The third day, they climbed through the clouds and only broke free of them toward evening. But in the morning the clouds were gone, and they could see into the abyss. They were at least ten thousand feet up. The trunk continued to rise for another two or three thousand feet, but there was no sense in their climbing any higher. This was as high as the branches grew. This branch was a bonanza; it seemed to go on forever, and its downward slope was very gentle.

94

A spring welled out at the junction of branch and trunk, and more springs added to the bulk of the riverlet so that, a mile away, it became navigable.

Every mile or so, the branch extended a vertical part which went all the way to the bottom—as far as they could determine—or else joined with another branch below.

To prevent the bat-men from trying to fly away, Ulysses had punched holes in the membranes of their wings and tied them together with thin strings of gut. He had forced them to climb up the trunk by themselves, since their weight was too much for anyone to bear on that extended climb. They had been in the middle of the line that crawled up the craggy barky cliff so that they could not try to climb off. They were so light, they could climb much faster than even the agile Wufea.

Ulysses ordered camp made. They would rest for several days, hunt and scout around. He hoped that he could find another hole in a trunk and so get a chance to experiment with the communication-membrane inside. Ever since his experience with the Wuggruds, he had looked for other holes. He was sure that these must exist by the many thousands, but he had seen none. They were everywhere, according to the bat-men. It was frustrating to know this and yet be unable to find them. However, he was also sure that each hole would be guarded by the bear-like Wuggrud or leopard-like Khrauszmiddum. He could not really afford another encounter with them if they outnumbered his people. But he chafed. If only he could get to a communication-membrane. By now he knew the code. The language was the trade language, and the code was similar to Morse in that it used a combination of long and short pulses.

He had gotten that out of Ghlikh during the nights when everybody should have been resting from the day's labors. Khyuks had steadfastly refused to tell him the code. In fact, Khyuks refused even to admit that there was such a thing as a code. But Ghlikh was another person. His threshold of pain was lower, or his strength of character was less. Or he was more intelligent than Khyuks and realized that he would have to break sometime. So why not tell now and save himself much pain for nothing?

Khyuks cursed Ghlikh for a traitor and a spineless gutless coward, and Ghlikh said that if he did not shut his mouth he would kill him at the first chance. Khyuks replied that he would kill Ghlikh the first chance *he* got.

Though Ghlikh did reveal the code, he did not—or could not—reveal the location of the central base of his people.

He swore that he had to be high enough above The Tree to see certain navigational checkmarks that would eventually guide him to the base. These marks were high trunks which grew leaves in a pattern that could be determined only by someone about two thousand feet above them. They might even be under one at this moment, but he could not tell from below.

Ulysses shrugged this disappointment off. He had no plans for attacking the base even if he knew its location. He lacked the force for an attack. But he would have liked to know where it was so that when he did have enough force, he could attack it. He would find out, one way or another.

He was sitting with his back against a comparatively smooth slab of loosened bark, a big fire about ten feet in front of him. It was almost night. Below, it *was* night. The sky was still blue, and faraway clouds were touched with pink, light green and a darkening gray. The cries and screams of hunting animals and the hunted wafted up like almost forgotten nightmares, they were so faint. The two bat-men were near him, sitting side by side but not speaking or even looking at each other. The Wufea, Wagarondit and Alkunquib were around six large fires. Guards were posted out on the branch and also out of sight on bark ledges on the sides of the branch. The mouthwatering odor of roasting meat and fish was everywhere. A hunting party had gone out onto the branch earlier and returned with three four-horned, auburn-haired goats, ten large fish (taken from a black-and-gray-spotted cougar-sized cat which had caught them), bags full of ten different types of berries, and three large heavily furred monkeys.

The hunters had reported that the vegetation on top of the branch consisted mainly of short but thick-bodied fir trees, berry bushes, a knee-high grass which grew out of dirt caught in the fissures, and an ankle-deep moss. The riverlet contained an abundance of fish but no snoligosters or hipporats. The main predators seemed to be the black-and-gray puma, a small bear, and several types of otters. The other animals were the goats and monkeys.

They ate well that night and slept as close to the fire as they could get without burning. At this height, it got bitter cold after the sun went down.

In the morning, they ate the remnants of their supper for breakfast and set out to build rafts. They cut down some of the firs, which were only about twenty feet high, and made rafts. And they launched out with good spirits and high hopes.

For once, they were not disappointed or deceived. The riverlet took them at an easy pace for about thirty miles and then ended in a widening of the branch. Here the riverlet did not hurtle over a ninety-degree bend in a cataract. It just spilled over the sides of the wide area, blocked by an upward bend of the branch. The party disassembled the rafts and carried the poles up the incline, which was at a forty-five-degree angle. Once on top, they found another spring which soon grew into another riverlet. They put their rafts together and let the stream take them. This type of portage was repeated ten times. Eventually, the branch took the longest uninterrupted stretch they had so far experienced. It lasted about sixty miles, and the descent was so gradual that the water just ran out into the swamp. Ulysses estimated that they must have covered about two hundred and fifty miles on the one branch. Ghlikh said that they had been fortunate to find this one. Only a few were like this.

They climbed up out of the stinking cold wet swamp until they found a promising branch about six thousand feet up. Ten days later, they came to a waterfall, the foot of which was five thousand feet below them. And here The Tree ended.

Ulysses felt a little dazed and a little unreal. He had gotten so accustomed to the world being one gigantic tree with its many levels of interfused and winding branches, seemingly sky-high trunks and dense vegetation, that he had thought of the world as only—Tree.

Now before him was a plain that stretched out perhaps fifty or sixty miles and beyond were the tops of mountains. On the other side of the range, if he could believe Ghlikh, was the sea.

Awina stood beside him, close enough so that her furred hip rubbed against him. Her long black tail moved back and forth, its tip sometimes tickling the back of his legs.

"Wurutana has spared us," she said. "I do not know why. But he has his reasons."

Ulysses was angered. He said, "Why can't you think of our success as being due to my powers as a god?"

Awina started and looked up at him sidewise. Her eyes were enormous, as always, but the pupils had become slits.

"Your pardon, Lord," she said. "We owe you much. Without you, of course, we would have perished. Still, you are a small god compared with Wurutana."

"Size does not necessarily mean superiority," he said.

He was angry, he thought, not because she denied or depreciated his godhood. He certainly was not that insane. It was just that he wanted to get the proper credit for bringing them through. Credit as a human being, even if he was forced to speak in terms of his godhood.

He wanted Awina, more than anybody, to give him credit. Now, why should he wish that? Why should this beautiful but weird creature, this sentient but nonhuman being, be so important to him?

On the other hand, he thought, why shouldn't she? She had been his mainstay from the first day here, she had taught him his first language (in a manner of speaking), she had served him in many capacities, not the least of which was that of morale upholder. And she was very attractive, in a physical sense. It had been so long since he had seen a human being, he had become accustomed to the nonhuman. Awina was a very beautiful female (he almost thought *woman*).

Yet, though he was often very fond of her, he sometimes felt repulsed by her. This occurred when she got too close physically. He moved away, and she looked at him with an unfathomable expression. Did she know what he was thinking? Did she correctly interpret his moving away?

He hoped not. Because if she did, she was intelligent and sensitive enough to know that the avoidance of physical contact was a defense on his part. And she would know, as he knew, why he had to defend himself.

He shouted at Wulka and the other chiefs. "Let's go! Follow me down off The Tree! We'll be on good solid dry ground soon!"

The descent went well enough, though he had to resist a tendency to hurry. The vast black-gray bulk of The Tree seemed to be even more threatening, now that he was about free of it, than when he had been inside it. But nothing happened; no Wuggrud or Khrauszmiddum boiled out of The Tree to make a final attack.

However, once they were out on the plain, they would be easily detected by the winged men. It would be best to stay inside the shade of The Tree until nightfall and then move out.

Fortunately, the ground at the base of the great Tree here was not so swamp-like. Once they had moved away from the branch down which the riverlet had run, they found dry ground. They made their camp on the northward side of a branch which rammed into the earth at a forty-five-degree angle. Ulysses studied the plain, which was covered by a shin-high green-brown grass and was spotted with small stands of an acacia-like tree. There were great herds of grass and leaf eaters out there: horses, antelopes, buffalo, the giraffe-like animal which he thought had evolved from the horse, the elephant-like beast which could have evolved from the tapir, the giant heavily legged rabbit, and the bluish curving-tusked long-legged swine. There were predators, too, the twelve-foot high roadrunner, the chee-tah-like leopard, and prides of porcupine-haired lions.

That night, the party moved out from The Tree. They did not get far because they spent so much time in hunting. At dawn they made small fires inside a stand of acacia and roasted the meat. Then they slept in the shade of the trees while some stood guard.

The third day, they reached the mountain range. Ghlikh did not even have to be threatened with torture. He vol-unteered the information about a pass, and so they marched along the mountains for two days until they found the gap. It took two days to get through the mountains. Abruptly, just at dusk, they came around the shoulder of the moun-tain and there, sparkling far off, was the sea.

Then the sun was down, and the sky became black. Ulys-ses felt happy without knowing why. Perhaps it was be-cause the mountain shut off the view of The Tree and the night kept him from seeing anything that reminded him that he was not in his own time and on the Earth on which he had been born. It was true that the stars formed unfa-miliar constellations, but he could ignore that. Later, he was unable to ignore the moon. It was too huge and too bluish-green and white-flecked.

They rose at dawn, ate breakfast and then set off down the slope of the mountain. By dusk they had reached its foot, and the next morning they set out across the rela-tively flat land for the sea. This was heavily forested at first, but, the second day, they reached an area of many open fields, houses, barns and fences.

The houses were square buildings, sometimes two-storied, usually built of logs but occasionally of granite blocks, rough-hewn, set in mortar. The barns were part stone, part wood. Ulysses investigated several and found all unoccu-pied by anything except wild animals. There were plenty of wood and stone figures and some paintings, all primi-tive, but there were enough human figures to assure him that the artists had been men.

He used *had been* because there was no sign of any human body, living or dead.

Sometimes, he came across a house or barn which had been burned. Whether this was due to accident or war could not be determined.

The animals that had been in the unburned barns, and in the houses, had either escaped or died of starvation.

Nowhere was there even a human bone.

He spoke to Ghlikh. "What has happened here?"

Ghlikh looked up at him, shrugged his bony shoulders and spread his wings out as far as the string would allow them. "I do not know, Lord! The last time I was here, six years ago, the Vroomaw lived here. Aside from occasional raids by the Vignoom and the Neshgai, they led a peaceful life. Perhaps we will find out what happened here when we get to the main village. Now, if I were to be permitted to fly ahead, I could find out very quickly. . . ."

He cocked his head and smiled painfully. He could not, of course, be serious about his proposal, and Ulysses did not even comment on it. They were passing their first graveyard at that time, and Ulysses halted the column. He wandered through the yard, examining the headpieces of the graves. These were thick poles carved out of some reddish hardwood with the skulls of various birds and animals at the tops. There were no other means of identification on the graves, and Ghlikh and Khyuks did not know what the skulls were supposed to mean.

The column resumed its march down the narrow dirt road. The farms became more numerous, but all were deserted.

"Judging from the state of decay of the buildings and of the growth of vegetation around them, I'd say they were abandoned about a year," Ulysses said. "Maybe two years."

Ghlikh told him that the Vroomaw were the only human beings of whom he knew, except those who were the slaves of the Neshgai, of course. In fact, the Vroomaw may have been descended from the Neshgai's runaway slaves. On the other hand, the Neshgai may have gotten their slaves from captured Vroomaw. In either event, the Vroomaw lived in an area about a hundred miles square and had a population of about forty-five thousand. There were three main villages of about five thousand citizens each, and the rest lived on farms or hunted. They had had some trade with the Dhulhulikh and with the Pauzaydur. The latter were, according to Ghlikh, a people who lived *in* the sea, not *on* it. They were a sort of porpoise-centaur, if Ulysses could believe Ghlikh's descriptions.

Ulysses inquired about the history of the humans, but Ghlikh professed ignorance on this.

Ulysses decided that he knew less about this world than he had when he opened his eyes in the burning hall of the Wufea. Well, not really. But he was far more confused. There were all the many genera and species of sentients, many of whom could not be accounted for by the theory of evolution, and now there were the human beings who had suddenly and mysteriously disappeared. He had been thrilled for days by the prospect of seeing a human face again, of hearing human voices, of touching human skin. And they were gone.

The dirt road wound through the country and eventually led them to a stockaded village by the sea. There was a harbor here with most of the vessels, ranging from dugouts to single-masted ships like Viking craft, wrecked on the shore. Apparently, a storm had swept most from the anchorage and deposited them on the beach.

The village looked as if everybody had decided to get up during the noonday meal and walk out. About a quarter of the houses had been burned down, but this could be attributed to lack of attendance of cooking fires.

There was only one thing to mar the picture of a whole population voluntarily deserting. That was a tall wooden pole in the center of the main square. Its top bore a carved wooden head. The head was hairless and had very big fan-like nonhuman ears, a long snakish nose and an open mouth from which projected elephantine tusks about four inches long. The head was painted a dark gray.

"Neshgai!" Ghlikh said. "That is the head of a Neshgai. They have left this behind as a sign of conquest."

"If they took this country by assault, where are the signs of violence?" Ulysses said. "Where are the skeletons?"

"Obviously, the Neshgai cleaned up afterward," Ghlikh said. "They are a very neat people. They like order and cleanliness."

Ulysses looked for evidences of mass burials and found several large graves. He dug into one and uncovered a pile of about a hundred skeletons. All were human.

"The Neshgai would take their own dead back to their country," Ghlikh said. "All Neshgai are buried in one place, a very sacred place."

"How long have the Vroomaw been here? Surely you know that much about them?"

"Oh, about twenty generations, I would say," Ghlikh said, screwing up his face.

"That would be about four hundred years," Ulysses said.

Why couldn't he have been depetrified a hundred years ago? he thought. Then he could have found his own kind and settled down among them and had children. And with his knowledge of technology, the humans would not have been conquered by the Neshgai. It probably would have been the other way around.

Of course, he would be dead now, buried with a pole above his grave and the skull of some beast on the end of a pole. HERE LIES ULYSSES SINGING BEAR, 1952 A.D.-10,000-000 A.D.

For a little while, he was depressed. Since the grave would be his inevitable end, why concern himself about anything? Why not go back to the Wufea village and settle down there among people who worshiped him? As for the mate he needed so strongly . . .

Inside an hour, he had shucked off the black mood. It was the essence of life to disbelieve in death for one's self, to act as if life would continue forever. And life had to act also as if little issues were big ones. To take a realistic attitude toward life and death meant that one lapsed into unreality. Into insanity. It was ironic that the only way to keep one's sanity was to ignore that one was in an insane world or to act as if the world were sane.

He explored the houses and the temples and then went down to the beach. There was a ship, still riding at anchor, which had not been damaged too badly. Its hull was fouled and several of the boards needed replacing, but it could be fixed up with material from storage sheds in the docks. He explained to his chiefs what he wanted done. They nodded as if they understood, but they also looked doubtful. Scared, perhaps.

It occurred to him then that they knew nothing about sailing. Indeed, for all of them except himself and the batpeople, it was their first sight of the sea.

"Sailing will be strange and perhaps frightening for you at first," he said. "But you can learn. You may even delight in it, once you know what you can and cannot do on the sea."

They still looked dubious, but they hastened to carry out his orders. He studied the masts and the sails available. All the boats and ships used the square rig. Apparently, the Vroomaw did not know about fore-and-aft rigs. Which meant that they probably did not know about tacking or sailing close-hauled. He could not understand this. It was true that man had put out to sea for many thousands of years before he invented sails to enable him to tack back and forth. But, once the fore-and-aft sail had been invented, it should have remained forever in man's technology. It had not, which meant that there had been a catastrophic gap in the continuity of man's knowledge. There must have been a total fall into savagery with no contact with the seas for at least several generations. And no lore handed down, not even by word of mouth.

He picked a large house to live in and moved in Awina and the chiefs, letting the others stay in three separate houses with their subchiefs. Guards were stationed at the main gate and told to beat the huge drums in the house over the gate if they saw anything suspicious.

Three weeks later, the ship was ready. It was launched from its drydock and Ulysses took the entire force out on its maiden cruise. Its sailors had been given verbal instructions. Now they tried to put their hazy knowledge into effect. They almost capsized the boat several times. But, after a week of steady schooling, they were ready for an extended coastwise voyage. Ulysses, besides building and installing a fore-and-aft rig, had also built and installed a rudder. The Vroomaw boats had used big oars or sweeps to steer.

He christened the boat the *New Hope*, and one fine dawn they set out for the land of the Neshgai.

The coast was flat with many good beaches and only a few cliffs here and there. The water was comparatively shallow to about two miles off the coast and free of shoals or large rocks. The trees, large oaks, sycamores, fir, pine and several unknown to the Earth of his time, came down close to the beach. There were plenty of animals: deer, antelope, the long-necked giant horse, which he called a girse when he thought in English (which was not often anymore), buffalo, huge wolf-like animals, seals, and porpoises.

He asked Ghlikh why the land between the Neshgai and the Vroomaw was empty of sentients.

"I can only speculate," the little winged man said. "But I would say that it is because all sentients along the coast had gone to live with The Tree."

Ulysses noted the *with*. Why not *on?* Ghlikh talked as if there had been an invitation, and the sentients had moved into a house with others.

"Living is easier with The Tree," Ghlikh said. "There one can hide from one's enemies. Food is plentiful and easy to get."

"And snoligosters and hipporats to eat the unwary fisher," Ulysses said. "And if The Tree abounds with game, it also abounds with fierce flesh-eaters, a number of which are not averse to eating man. And if a tribe can hide easier, it can also be approached easier after it's found. That thick vegetation has disadvantages as well as advantges."

Ghlikh shrugged and smiled with an air of superiority.

"True. But it is well that a few die now and then, otherwise the tribes would increase to such numbers that there would be no room and all the food would be eaten. Some must suffer for the good of the many. Moreover, there is no war among the peoples of The Tree. Not as you or the peoples of the plains know it. The Tree counts its tribes, and when a tribe has too many people, then The Tree notifies its neighbors that they may war on it. It also warns the tribe to be attacked. Then the young warriors of the two tribes arrange to meet in combat. Or, sometimes, during short periods, attacks on the dwelling places themselves are allowed. And it is permissible to kill the females and the children. But this does not happen too often. And when it does, it is welcome. The little wars add excitement—and value—to life."

"I wonder why the Neshgai and Vroomaw did not go to live with The Tree?" Ulysses said.

"The Neshgai think they are better than The Tree!" Ghlikh said angrily. "Those ponderous big-bellied long-noses were once savages, like the Wuggrud and the Khrauszmiddum. But then they dug up the buried city of Shabawzing and found many things in it that enabled them to go from savagery to civilization in three generations. Also, they are so big and clumsy, they cannot live comfortably in The Tree nor climb very far."

"And the Vroomaw?"

"They did live with The Tree—once. But they left, despite the commands of The Tree to stay where they were. They are a very contrary, troublesome, obnoxious people, as you will find if you come across them. They moved to the seashore and built their houses there. Some say that they first allied themselves with the Neshgai, who treacherously enslaved them. And then a number of Vroomaw escaped and came here to build a nation, planning some day to march against their former masters. But it is evident that the Neshgai struck first."

Ghlikh seemed to be very happy about the fate of the humans.

He added, "The Neshgai's turn is next. But their death

will come from The Tree, which never forgets nor forgives. The Neshgai are beset now with attacks from the Fishnoom, brothers to the Wuggrud, and from the Glassim, brothers to the Khrauszmiddum. The Tree has sent them out from his bosom to bedevil the Neshgai and, eventually, to exterminate them."

He added, even more viciously, "And the same fate will come to the peoples of the plains in the north if they do not go to live with The Tree. Eventually, The Tree will grow over the plains, over all the land except for a narrow strip on the coasts. And The Tree will not endure any sentients on the coast. He will kill them, one way or another."

"The Tree?" Ulysses said. "Or the Dhulhulikh, who use The Tree to bend all the others to their will? Who pretend to be servants of The Tree but are, in reality, its masters?"

"What?" Ghlikh said. He shook his head. "You surely do not believe that? You must be crazy!"

Yet he had such a barely concealed, smiling expression that Ulysses wondered if he had not hit upon the truth.

If his theory was more than a theory, it would explain much. But it would still leave much to be explained. How had The Tree originated? He could not believe that The Tree had naturally evolved from any of the plants living in his day.

And then there was the mystery of the origin of all the unrelated types of sentients.

The boat sailed on along the coast, putting in close to shore and anchoring when the skies were too cloudy to give light for safe navigation. When the moon was visible, the boat sailed all night. Ghlikh and Khyuks provided information from time to time about the Neshgai. Mostly, they sat huddled on a platform before the base of the mast, their wings almost brushing the creaking wood, blankets over their shoulders, and their heads close together. Though they hated each other, they now talked to each other. They were too lonely, miserable and scared not to take refuge in their native speech from time to time.

Ulysses did not know what to do with them. They had given him most of the information he wanted. He was sure that there was other information he could get, if only he knew the right questions. But he was worried that they would escape some day and would bring back a horde of their fellows. Every day that passed increased the probabilities of their getting away.

He did not want to kill them, though that was the only logical thing to do. However, it was true that they still had not revealed the location of their base city. Only in the air, so they claimed, could they find their way back home.

He used this rationalization for not killing them. They might be able someday to point out the way to their base. If they must do it from the air, so be it. Apparently, no one knew about balloons or dirigibles, and so the bat-men were very smug in thinking that their secret was safe.

The sixth day, Ulysses saw his first porpoise-men. He had taken the ship away from the coast because a great rock stood in their way. Before the ship was within two hundred yards of the rock, he saw the curious animals on a shelf of the rock a few feet above the surface of the sea. He took the *New Hope* as close to the rock as he dared—the leadsman was singing out four fathoms—and he and his crew stared at the four creatures sunning themselves on the ledge. They looked more like the legendary mermen of his time than the porpoise-centaurs described by Ghlikh. From the breasts down, they were fish-like. Rather, porpoise-like, since the fins were horizontal, not vertical. The skin of the lower body was the same light bronze as the upper. The genitals of both male and female were hidden within folds of the lower body. The bodies from the breasts up were quite human, and the fingers, contrary to what he had expected, were not webbed. The noses were very thin; Ghlikh said the nostrils could be closed tightly with muscular action. The eyeballs could be covered by a rigid transparent sheath which came down from under the eyelids. The hair on their heads was very short and sleek, looking from this distance more like seal fur than hair. Two had black hair, one was an ash-blond, and the fourth had auburn hair.

Ulysses waved at them and smiled. A woman and a man waved back at him. Ghlikh, who had come upon the poop-deck, said, "That is well done. It is not good to be unfriendly with the Sea-Folk. They can take the bottom right out of a boat if they wish."

"How friendly do they get?"

"They sometimes trade with the Neshgai and the humans. They bring in strange sea stones or fish or goods from sunken ships and exchange these for wine or beer."

Ulysses wondered if they could become allies in his war against the Neshgai, that is, if he *had* a war against the Neshgai. Ghlikh did not think they would take sides, unless one side gravely offended them. But even the arrogant Neshgai treated them with courtesy and occasional gifts. The

Neshgai had a large fleet which they did not want to see on the bottom of the ocean.

The rock and its strange burden dropped behind them. Ghlikh said, "Another day at this rate, and you will be along the coast ruled by the Neshgai. Then what?"

"We shall see," Ulysses said. "You are fluent in their speech?"

"Very fluent," Ghlikh said. "Moreover, many of them can speak Ayrata."

"I hope they're not too astonished when they see me and my crew. I would not want them to attack just because they panicked."

An hour after dawn of the following day, they passed an enormous symbol carved out of stone. It was a great X inside a broken circle. This was the symbol of Nesh, the ancestral eponymous god of the Neshgai, Ghlikh said. This carving, which could be seen for many miles out to sea, marked the western boundary of their country.

"You will see a good harbor soon," Ghlikh said. "And a town and a garrison of troops. And some merchant ships and some swift naval vessels."

"Merchant ships?" Ulysses said, ignoring the threat in his tone. "With whom do they trade?"

"With each other mainly. But some of their great ships sail far around the coast to the north and trade with the peoples there along the coast."

Ulysses began to feel excited. This was not so much from the danger of confronting the unknown as from a new idea. Perhaps the Neshgai did not have to be his enemy. Perhaps they would be friendly, and they would help him. They certainly had a common interest in combating the great Tree or whoever was using The Tree. And possibly they might be working with the humans, not making the humans work for them. Who knew what lies the bat-people had fed him?

Presently the shore curved deeply inward, and then he saw a breakwater to his left. It was composed of huge blocks of stone which extended for several miles. More than just a breakwater, it was a high wall to protect the harbor and the town within from hostile ships. On the tops of the cliff he could see some huge gray buildings and then, as he went by the first of the entrances, a number of ships and a town on the slope of the hill behind.

They had passed a tower on top of the breakwater and seen figures behind some of the narrow slits of windows. Something roared, and he looked back to see a giant form on top of the tower. It was holding an immense trumpet to its great mouth. The elephantine proboscis was lifted above the instrument as if it, not the instrument, were trumpeting.

Ulysses decided that it would look better if he went in to meet them instead of them coming out. Surely they would not believe that this small ship would be entering to attack. He took the ship in between the wide gates of the breakwater, underneath the two towers on each side of the entrance. He waved at the people in the tower and was surprised to see that most of them were humans. They wore leather helmets and carried shields which he supposed were of wood. They brandished spears—stone-tipped, of course—or held bows and arrows on him. Behind them towered the gray-skinned figures of the Neshgai. Presumably, the giants were the officers.

There was no fire from the towers. They must have thought as he did, that one small ship could not be entering with belligerent intent.

He was not so sure a moment later when he saw a large vessel, a long low galley-type craft, moving swiftly toward him. It was manned with many soldiers, two-thirds of them humans, and it was steered by a rudder. It had no sails. It also had no oarsmen.

His eyes widened then, and he had the sickening feeling that he had just stuck his head into a guillotine. He had seen or heard nothing to indicate that the Neshgai were so advanced technologically.

But when the galley swung around behind them and then came partway alongside to ride herd, it emitted no sound other than the hissing of water cut by the sharp bow and the slap of waves on its side. If the craft held an internal combustion motor, it also had excellent noise-repressing devices.

"What drives that?" he said to Ghlikh.

"I do not know, *Lord*," Ghlikh said.

His emphasis of *Lord* indicated that he believed that Ulysses' day as a god was about over. But he did not seem particularly glad. Perhaps the batpeople were in danger of being enslaved also. Yet, this did not seem likely, since Ghlikh had said that the Dhulhulikh traded with the Neshgai.

He stared at the ship. How to reconcile its advanced method of propulsion with the primitive weapons of its personnel?

He shrugged. He would find out in time. If he did not, he would have more important matters to concern him. Patience had always been a virtue of his, and he had strengthened it enormously since awakening. Perhaps his unimaginably long "stonehood" had enabled his psyche to absorb some of the endurance of inert and hard matter.

His ship lowered sail, and the oarsmen back-oared to slow the ship down, then raised them as the ship began to slide in alongside the dock to which an officer on the galley had waved them. Humans clad only in kilts took the ropes thrown out by the furry crew and brought the vessel alongside many rubbery-looking bags. The galley slid in a minute later and then reversed its invisible noiseless engines and stopped an inch from ramming into the structure before it.

Ulysses got a close view of the Neshgai then. They stood ten feet or over and had short heavy columnar legs and big feet that splayed out. Their bodies were long—he would guess that they had much back trouble among them —and their arms were thickly muscled. Their hands had four fingers each.

The heads were much like the carved head he had seen in the Vroomaw village. Their ears were enormous, but much smaller in proportion to the head than an elephant's. The forehead was very broad and knobbed at the temples. They had no eyebrows, but their eyelashes were very long. The eyes were brown, green or blue. The skinny wrinkled proboscis, when dangling, fell to their chests. The mouths were wide and had everted lips—almost negroid lips, in fact. Two tiny tusks protruded at right angles to the plane of the face. Their mouths contained only four molars, and this, of course, would affect their speech. Their Ayrata, the trade language, would have a mushy sound. It was so indistinct that it was almost a new language. But after the ear was tuned to it, the language became intelligible. However, the humans had difficulty reproducing Neshgai sounds and so their Ayrata was a compromise between that which other well-toothed peoples spoke and that which the Neshgai spoke. Fortunately, the Neshgai could understand the particular Ayrata of their slaves.

Their skins were varied from a very light gray to a brownish-gray.

They wore peaked leather helmets with four flaps, much like Sherlock Holmes' deerstalker cap, Ulysses thought. They wore enormous beads, stones of various sorts strung on leather cords, around their thick necks. Heavy breastplates of bone painted in red, black and green covered their relatively narrow chests. Their only clothing—universal among humans and Neshgai alike—was a kilt. The officers' legs were bound in green puttees, and their enormous feet were shod in sandals. Some wore cloaks of a heavy cloth with great white feathers sticking out of the hems.

To Ulysses, these creatures combined a somewhat repulsive alienness with an aura of power and wisdom. This last resulted from his own attitude toward elephants, of course. Then he reminded himself that the Neshgai might be descended from probiscidea but they were not elephants, any more than he was just an ape. And though their giant size and doubtless great strength gave them advantages, they would also give them certain disadvantages. There was a debit side to everything.

A magnificent Neshgai stood apart and ahead of the others on the dock. It was he who spoke to Ulysses while everybody else listened respectfully. He trumpeted shrilly through the long nose—a salutation, as Ulysses would learn—and then delivered a short speech. Though he knew it was in Ayrata, Ulysses could understand little of it because of the strange sounds. He asked Ghlikh to translate, warning him not to lie.

"And what will you do to me, *Lord?*" Ghlikh said, looking sidewise at him with undisguised hate.

"I may kill you here and now," Ulysses said. "Do not start gloating yet."

Ghlikh snarled wordlessly at him and then repeated in more intelligible Ayrata what the official, Gooshgoozh, had said.

The sum of it was that Ulysses should surrender himself and his furry crew to Gooshgoozh. He would be conducted into the city, into the main administration building itself, the home of the ruler and of his chief aid, Shegnif. There he would be interviewed by Shegnif. Unless Ulysses agreed to surrender at once, Gooshgoozh would order his forces to attack them.

"This is the capital?" Ulysses said, waving his hand at the city on the hill. It was the largest habitation he had seen so far, but even so, it could not hold more than thirty thousand, including the humans.

"No," Ghlikh said. "Bruuzhgish is many miles to the east. It is there that the Hand of Nesh and his aid, Shegnif, live."

Ghlikh used a word to indicate Shegnif's position which could be translated as Grand Vizier.

Gooshgoozh spoke again, and Ghlikh said that they must leave the ship and march up the hill to the garrison. There they would all be provided with transportation to the capital. Apparently, he was not worried about the weapons which the party carried.

Ulysses left first to stand beside the towering Gooshgoozh. The giant exuded an odor more like a sweating horse than an elephant. Ulysses found it rather pleasant. The Neshgai's stomach was, however, rumbling, a phenomenon that was to surround Ulysses in this land. Moreover, the Neshgai began to chew on a big stick made of pressed vegetables and chewed as he gave more orders to his soldiers. The Neshgai spent much time eating because of the demands of their big stomachs. But not as much time as an elephant would.

Finally organized, the cavalcade marched up a street which ran straight up the hill. The Neshgai soldiers, human slaves and nonhuman officers, followed the line of new-comers. Wulka carried Khyuks on his back. Ulysses, carrying Ghlikh, followed the enormous Gooshgoozh. He walked very dignifiedly, and very slowly, up the hill. By the time they reached the top, he was panting, and saliva was running out of his mouth. Ulysses remembered a comment by Ghlikh that the Neshgai were prone to heart disease, lung and back trouble, and distress of the feet and legs. They paid for the combination of great size with a bipedal structure.

The street was paved with bricks set in mortar and was about fifty feet wide. The houses were square, had triple domes, and were covered with many figures and geometric designs and painted in a manner that was called "psyche-delic" in Ulysses' time. There were no citizens or slaves in the street because the soldiers cleared them out. But many gray or tanned faces looked out of the windows and doors at them as they passed. According to Ghlikh, the Neshgai had never seen the furry feline beings before.

Gooshgoozh left them standing outside the garrison fort, which was a castle-like structure built of cyclopean blocks of granite. An hour passed and then another hour. It was just like being in the army, Ulysses thought. Hurry and wait, hurry and wait. Ten million years had made a new genus of sentient but had made no difference in military procedure.

Awina had been shifting back and forth from one foot to the other, but she finally came up to Ulysses and leaned against him.

She said, "I am afraid, my Lord. We have put our-selves into the hands of the long-nosed men, and whatever they decide to do with us will be done. We are too few to fight our way out."

Ulysses patted her back and then stroked it, enjoying even in his anxiety the sensuous softness of the fur. He said, "Do not worry. The Neshgai seem to be an intelligent people. They will realize that I have too much to offer for them to dispose of us as if we were a pack of wild dogs."

That had been his original reason for so boldly entering into the Neshgai territory. But now the galley had made him wonder. What if these people were so far advanced that nothing he could offer them could match what they already had? It was true that he had seen no signs of land transportation using motors, and that seemed strange. Perhaps the motors the galley used required too much space and fuel to be used in automobiles. In which case, he could show them how to build steam cars.

Then the gates of the fort opened, and a line of automobiles and trucks drove out. They looked somewhat like the earliest cars of his time, more like modified carriages and wagons. They were built of wood except for the wheels ad tires. The wheels seemed to be of glass or another plastic which looked like glass. (Glass, of course, was a plastic.) The tires looked like white rubber, and they were (as he found out later) made of the specially treated sap of a tree which had not existed in his time.

The vehicles had to be huge to accommodate the gigantic Neshgai. The steering wheels were enormous, more like those of sailing ships. They seemed to require great hands and strength to turn, which may have been why only Neshgai were the chauffeurs, even for the trucks. However, Ghlikh said that the humans were never trusted to operate cars or any advanced technological devices except the voice transmitters.

No sound came from under the hood. Ulysses put his hand on the wooden hood but could feel no vibrations. He asked Ghlikh what drove the cars, and Ghlikh shrugged.

"I do not know," he said. "The Neshgai allowed me a certain amount of freedom as a trader of goods and information. But they would not describe their devices or even let me get close to any unless I was supervised."

This must have been frustrating for Ghlikh, Ulysses thought, since his primary objective here would undoubtedly be to get the secret of Neshgai technology.

Their culture contained many contradictions. There were so many primitive things here, side by side with advanced devices. The Neshgai had bows and arrows and plastic-tipped spears but no gunpowder. Or perhaps they knew about gunpowder but had no firearms because they lacked the metal or a plastic which could be used in the place of metal.

Gooshgoozh sat in the back seat of the foremost vehicle. He stopped eating a huge dish of vegetables and drinking from a pitcher of milk long enough to order food for the humans and the newcomers. Most of this was vegetable, but there was some horse meat. Horses were also used, as he discovered, for drawing wagons and carriages for the human slaves and the rural Neshgai.

After the food was eaten, most of Ulysses' party was herded into the trucks, and the human soldiers piled in with them. Ulysses, his chiefs, Awina and the two bat-men went into the car behind Gooshgoozh's. His car moved out onto a brick road covered with plastic into which was set pieces of brick to afford more traction. Ulysses watched the driver, who controlled his speed and the braking with a single pedal under his right foot. The instrument panel held a number of dials and gauges with various symbols around the faces. Ulysses studied them because they were the first indications of writing he had seen. There were some familiar symbols, a reversed 4, an H on its side, an O, a T, a barred Z, but these were symbols whose simplicity made it probable that they would be independently invented.

The vehicles had windshields but the sides were open. Wind was no problem since the cars never exceeded an estimated twenty miles an hour. And they slowed down to ten when ascending steep hills. There was not even a slight purr from the motors.

After about an hour and a half, the cavalcade drove into the square of a large fort, and the party got out of their vehicles into others. Ulysses did not understand why they should have to exchange cars as if they were riders of the Pony Express. Then it occurred to Ulysses that his simile of the Pony Express might be more appropriate than he had thought. Maybe the motors were not mechanical or electrical but were biological. Could the Neshgai be using some kind of muscle engine?

He saw a slave pouring fuel into the tank through a pipe on the side of the hood, and this strengthened his theory. The stuff was certainly not gasoline or anything like that. It was thick and syrupy and had a vegetable odor. Food for the living motor?

The cavalcade set out again, proceeding through country as before. This was rolling and heavily wooded except for the cleared fields and farmhouses. There were some strange plants growing in these, and once, when they stopped to rest, he walked over to the nearest growth. Nobody tried to stop him, though three archers did stay close. The plants were about seven feet high, green, and made of thin stalks topped by box-like growths of a darker green. He pulled one over to examine it. The stalk bent readily without indications of breaking. He opened the fleshy box by digging his fingers into a slit across its top. Beneath the layers of soft greenish leaves was a thin cartilaginous plate the surface of which was crossed by broad and thin dark lines. At the junction of the lines were little green pulpy nipples. He tried to visualize what the plate would look like when it ripened.

Unless he was using too much imagination, he was looking at a not-yet-matured printed circuit board.

Gooshgoozh said something, and everybody got back into the vehicles. Ulysses looked at the fields with more interest and, inside a mile, he saw another crop which he thought he could identify. Or, at least, he could make a reasonably inspired guess about its nature. These plants were short, squat and bore round cases wrapped in leaves. The cases were about four feet long, three wide and two deep. His theory was that these were the motors for the vehicles. They were of vegetable, not animal origin, though they might be high protein plants.

He considered the implications of his discovery while they drove past more fields with a variety of plants the nature of which he could not even guess. They also drove through a number of villages composed of the larger, more finely carved and painted houses of the Neshgai and the smaller, bare, often unpainted houses of the humans. After a while, he quit trying to theorize about the vegetable technology of the Neshgai and considered the implications of the setups of the villages and the farms. The humans seemed to outnumber the Neshgai about six to one or about three human adults to one Neshgai adult. Huge as the Neshgai were, strong as they seemed to be, one Neshgai should not be a match for three swifter cooperating humans, even if some of the humans were female.

What kept the humans from revolting? A slave mentality? Some weapon which made the Neshgai invincible? Or were the humans actually living in a symbiosis with the

114

Neshgai which was profitable enough for the humans so that they did not mind slavery?

He considered the human soldiers sitting on seats facing him. They were half-bald. Both the men and the women he had seen in the villages were half-bald, though the children had a full head of hair. The hair was very curly, almost kinky. Their skins were a beautiful dark brown. Their eyes were brown or, sometimes, greenish-brown. The faces were mainly narrow with a tendency to aquiline noses, jutting chins, and high cheekbones.

The only nonhuman feature was their lack of a little toe. But this could be accounted for by evolution. After all, some speculators, scientists and laymen alike, had said that man might lose his little toe. And his wisdom teeth.

He leaned forward and spoke in Ayrata to the soldier opposite him. The man looked puzzled, and a little alarmed, at first. Ulysses repeated his request at a slower rate. This time, the soldier understood most of the message. His Ayrata was not quite Ghlikh's or Ulysses', since Ayrata was his native speech, and it had deviated somewhat from the original. But Ghlikh knew the unfamiliar words and translated them.

The soldier looked dubious at first, but Ulysses reassured him that he meant no harm. The soldier turned and asked the giant in the front seat if he should obey. The great elephantine head turned, looked at Ulysses, and then spoke. The soldier opened his mouth wide, and Ulysses looked inside and ran his finger along the teeth. There were no wisdom teeth.

Ulysses thanked him. The Neshgai took out a notebook and wrote something on it with a fountain pen the size of a big flashlight.

The journey took until late at night. They changed vehicles five times. At the end, they came down out of a series of high hills onto a plain set on a cliff above the shore. The city was still well lit with torches and electric light bulbs. Or what looked like bulbs, though Ulysses thought they could be living organisms. They were attached to hard brown cases of living vegetable batteries or fuel cells.

The city itself was walled and looked more like an illustration of Baghdad in a copy of *The Arabian Nights* than anything else. The cavalcade drove through gates which were shut after them and wound through streets toward the center of the city. Here they got out and were marched into a huge building and upstairs into a huge room where the doors were locked on them. However, they found food waiting for them and, after eating, went to sleep on the bunkbeds.

Awina climbed into the bunk above him, but he awoke in the middle of the night to find her clinging to him. She was shaking and sobbing softly. He was startled, but he controlled himself and asked her, in a low voice, what she was doing here.

"I had a terrible dream," she said. "It was so frightening it woke me up. And I was afraid to go back to sleep. Or even to be alone in bed. So I came down here to get strength and courage from you. Did I do wrong, my Lord?"

He rubbed her between the ears and then stroked and fondled the kitten-fur-smooth ears.

"No," he said. He had gotten used to having the felines touch him so that they might draw from him some of his god-like qualities. It was a harmless superstition and it did benefit them psychologically.

He looked around. The bulbs, set in clusters in containers on the wall, were not as bright as when they had come into the room. They gave enough light so that he could see the others near him clearly, however. They were all sleeping. Nobody seemed aware that Awina was in his bed. Not that anybody would have objected. He knew by now that he had the power to do anything with them that he wished, and they would not object. He was their god, even if he was, after all, a small god.

"What was the dream?" he said, continuing to stroke her. Now he ran his fingers along her jaw and then up and over her round wet nose.

She shivered and then said, "I dreamed that I was sleeping in this very place. And then two of the gray-skins came in and lifted me out of my bed and carried me out of this place. They took me down many halls and down many dark staircases and into a deep chamber beneath this city. There they chained me to the wall and then began to hurt me terribly. They rammed their tusks into me and tried to pull my legs off with their trunks and, finally, they unchained me and threw me on the floor and started to crush me with their great feet.

"At that moment, the door to the room opened, and I saw you in the next room. You were standing there with your arm around a human female. She was kissing you and you saw me and laughed at me when I begged you to help me. And then the door clanged shut and the Neshgai began to step on me again, and one said, 'The Lord takes a human mate tonight!'

"And I said, 'Then let me die.' But I did not really want to die. Not away from you, my Lord."

Ulysses considered her dream. He had had enough of his own dreams concerning her to know what his unconscious was trying to tell him, although he was also consciously aware of what his feelings were. An interpretation of her dream was difficult, though. If he used the Freudian dictum that dreams represented wishes, then she wished him to have a human female as a mate. And she also wished to punish herself. But punish herself for what? She would not be guilty about any desire for him. The Wufea culture did have plenty of things about which their people could feel guilty, as did all cultures, human or nonhuman, but this was not one of them.

The trouble was that the Freudian dictum had never been proved to be true and, second, the subconscious of people descended from cats (if they were from cats) might differ from those of people descended from apes.

Whatever the interpretation of her dream, it was evident that she was worried about human females. Yet he had never given her any reason to consider him anything other than a god. Or to consider herself as any more than a good assistant to a god, even if the god was fond of her.

"Are you all right now?" he said. "Do you think you could get back to sleep?"

She nodded.

"Then you had better get back up into your bed."

She was silent for a moment. Her body had stiffened under his hand. She said quietly, "Very well, my Lord. I did not mean to offend you."

"You did not offend me," he said. He thought he should not add anything. He might weaken and ask her to stay with him. He needed some comforting of his own.

She climbed out of his bed and went up the ladder into her own. He lay for what seemed a long while, while the tired and anxious Wufea, Wagarondit and Alkunquib snored, stirred or muttered around him. What would tomorrow bring? Today, rather, since it surely would be dawn soon.

He felt as if he were swinging in the cradle of time. Time. No one understood it, no one could explain it. Time was more mysterious than God. God could be understood, God was thought of as being like a man. But Time was not at all understood, its essence and origin not even lightly touched as it went by.

He was swinging in the cradle of time. He was the ten-million-year-old baby. Maybe the ten-*billion*-year-old baby. Ten million years. No other living creature had endured such a passage of time, whatever time was, and yet ten million or ten billion years were nothing in time. Nothing. He had endured—not lived—ten million years, and he must die soon. And if he did—when he did—he might as well have never lived. He would be no more than some miscarriage that had occurred in some subhuman two million years before he was born. Just as much and no more, and what good was life for him? Or for anybody?

He tried to shunt this train of thought off into oblivion. He was alive, and this sort of philosophizing was useless, even if inevitable for a sentient. Even the less intelligent of human beings must surely think of the futility of individual life and of the incomprehensibility of time at least once in his/her life. But to dwell on such thoughts was neurotic. Life was its own answer, question and answer wrapped up in one skin.

If only he could sleep . . . he awoke with the opening of the great doors and the thumping of the huge feet of entering Neshgai. And then he ate breakfast and took a shower (his people abstaining) and used his knife to scrape off his few whiskers. He only had to shave about every third day and this task took only a minute. He did not know if his Indian genes were responsible for this hairlessness or if there were also other factors.

He shed his clothes, which were too dirty and torn to wear, and gave them to Awina to wash and repair. He stuck his knife into the pocket on the side of the kilt a slave gave him, put on new sandals, and followed Gooshgoozh out of the room. The others were not invited; the big doors closed in their faces.

The interior of the enormous four-story building was as ornately carved and as brightly painted as the exterior. There were many human slaves in the wide and lofty corridors but very few soldiers. Most of the guards were twelve-foot high Neshgai with leather helmets wrapped in brilliant scarlet turbans and holding spears that looked like young pine trees and shields on which were painted *X's* inside broken circles. They came to attention when Gooshgoozh neared them and ground the butts of the spears with a resounding noise into the marble floors.

Gooshgoozh led Ulysses down many halls and up two flights of winding marble stairs with exquisitely carved handrails and then down more corridors which opened onto vast rooms with massive bejeweled furniture and painted bejeweled statuary. He saw a great number of Neshgai females. These were between eight and nine feet tall and totally lacked the little tusks. They wore kilts and long jeweled earrings and, occasionally, a ring or ornament inserted into the skin on the side of their proboscises. Their breasts were below their chests and were, like those of all the sentient females he had seen, fully developed whether the female was nursing or not. They emanated a powerful and pleasing perfume, and the young ones painted their faces.

At last they paused before a door of some rich red color and dense grain. It bore a number of figures and symbols in alto-relief. The guards before it saluted Gooshgoozh. One opened the doors, and Ulysses was led into a cavernous room which had many shelves with books and a few chairs in front of a gigantic desk and chair. A Neshgai, wearing rimless glasses and a conical tall cap of paper painted with a number of symbols, sat behind the desk.

This was Shegnif, the Grand Vizier.

A moment later, Ghlikh was ushered into the room by an officer. He was grinning, and part of this pleasure undoubtedly originated in relief at the unbinding of his wings. Part of his pleasure also came from anticipation of humiliation, and worse, for Ulysses.

Shegnif asked Ulysses some questions in a voice deep even for the thunderous-throated Neshgai. Ulysses answered them without hesitation and truthfully. They were mainly requests for his name, where he came from, were there others like him, and so on. But when he said that he came from another time, perhaps ten million years ago, and that a lightning stroke had "depetrified" him, and that he had come here through The Tree itself, Shegnif seemed to be struck with a lightning bolt himself. Ghlikh did not like this reaction; he lost his grin and began to shift uneasily on his big bony feet.

After a long silence broken only by the stomach rumblings of the three Neshgai, Shegnif removed his great round spectacles and polished them with a cloth the size of a large throw rug. He put them back on and bent over his desk to look at the human standing before him.

"Either you are a liar," he said, "or an agent of The Tree. Or, just possibly, you are telling the truth."

He spoke to Ghlikh. "Tell me, Batwings. Is he telling the truth?"

Ghlikh seemed to shrink within himself. He looked at

Ulysses and then back to Shegnif. It was obvious that he could not make up his mind whether to denouce Ulysses as a liar or to admit that his story was true. He would want to discredit the human, but if he tried and failed, then he would be discredited. Perhaps being discredited among the Neshgai meant death, which would account for the sweat over his body in this cool morning.

"Well?" Shegnif said.

The advantage lay with Ghlikh, since he was known to Shegnif. On the other hand, Shegnif may have had his suspicions about Ghlikh and his kind.

His remark about "an agent of The Tree" must mean that he considered The Tree to be an entity, a hostile one. If this were so, then he must have his ideas about Ghlikh's motives, since he must also know that the bat-people lived in The Tree. Or did he know that? The Dhulhulikh could have told him they came from the other side of The Tree, and he would have had no way of checking up on them. At least not until Ulysses showed up.

"I do not know if he lies or not," Ghlikh said. "He told me that he was the stone god come to life, but I did not see him come to life."

"Have you seen the stone god of the Wufea?"

"Yes."

"And did you see the stone god after this man appeared?"

"No," Ghlikh said hesitantly. "But then I did not look in the temple to see if he was still there. I took his word for it, though I should not have done so."

"I can question the catpeople about him. They will know whether or not he is the stone god," Shegnif said. "Since they acknowledge him as the god come to life, I do not believe that they will call him a liar. Let us assume that his story is true."

"That he is, indeed, a god?" Ghlikh said, unable to suppress all the scorn he felt.

"There is but one god," Shegnif said, eyeing Ghlikh closely. "Only one. Or would you deny that? Those who live on The Tree say that The Tree is the only god. What do you say?"

"Oh, I agree with you that there is only one god," Ghlikh said quickly.

"And that is Nesh," Shegnif said. "Right?"

"Nesh is truly the only god of the Neshgai," Ghlikh said.

"That is not the same thing as saying that there is only one god, the god of the Neshgai," Shegnif said. He smiled, exposing a white-walled mouth, white gums and the four molars. He lifted a big glass of water in which was a glass tube and sucked water through the tube. Ulysses was surprised; he had seen the Neshgai suck water up their prehensile trunks and blow it into their mouths. But this was the first time he had seen one use a straw tube. Later, he saw them drink directly from glasses which had narrow mouths designed to go between their tusks.

Shegnif put the glass down and said, "Never mind. We do not require that non-Neshgai worship Nesh, since his concern is only with the worship of his sons and he would refuse to be worshiped by any but them. I find you to be rather shifty, Ghlikh. Be more direct in the future. Leave it to us slow-moving, slow-thinking Neshgai to be circuitous!"

He smiled again. Ulysses began to think that he could like the Grand Vizier.

Shegnif asked Ulysses more detailed questions. Finally, he told them that they could sit down, and the officers let themselves down gently into the chairs. Ulysses sat on the edge of one, his feet dangling. He did not look as small and pitiful as Ghlikh, however, who resembled a small bird squatting at the entrance to a large cave.

Shegnif put the tips of his banana-sized fingers together and frowned as much as an eyebrowless person could frown.

"I am amazed," he said. "You must be the living source of a myth which originated unguessable millennia ago. Although I should not say myth, since your story seems to be true.

"The Wufea found you at the bottom of a lake which had been in existence for many thousands of years. There is not much doubt that they found a stone statue which looked like you. Even the evasive bat-man here confirms that. But did you know that you have been above ground many times before the Wufea found you? And lost or stolen many times?"

Ulysses shook his head.

The Grand Vizier said, "You have been the god, or the central focus, of more than one religion. You have been the god of a little primitive village of one species or another, and have sat on your chair, petrified, while the little village became the great metropolis, the capital, of a highly civilized empire. And still sat there while the empire was shattered, and the civilization crumbled, and the people died, and there were only ruins inhabited by lizards and owls around you."

"My name is Ozymandias," Ulysses murmured in English. For the first time, his English sounded foreign to him.

"What?" Shegnif said, looking over his spectacles and down his proboscis at him.

"I was only talking to myself in a language that has been dead for millions of years, Your Viziership," Ulysses said.

"Ah, yes?" Shegnif said, his small greenish eyes lighting up. "We'll see that it's recorded by our scholars. In fact, we plan on keeping you very busy for some time. Our scientists have been informed about you, and they cannot restrain their eagerness."

"That is interesting," Ulysses said. Was he going to be nothing but a laboratory specimen to these people? "But I have much more to contribute than recordings of the past. I have a very definite present and future use. I may be the key to the survival of the Neshgai."

Ghlikh looked strangely at him. Shegnif, lifting his trunk, said, "Our survival? Indeed? Tell me more!"

"I would prefer to speak when the Dhulhulikh is not present."

Ghlikh shrilled, "Your Viziership, I protest! I have remained silent, as you wished, while this human told his lying story of his purported adventures in The Tree! But I can keep silent no longer! This is very serious! He is imputing sinister motives to us Dhulhulikh, who only want to live in peace with everybody and to engage in a business profitable for everybody!"

"No judgment has been delivered," Shegnif said. "We will hear the statements of everybody, including your colleague, Khyuks. In fact, the others are being interviewed even now, and I will read summaries of the interviews later today. By the way, and this will interest you, too, batman, we have records which indicate the stone god was once here. He certainly looks like the stone god. And he is just as certainly not one of our humans. You have noticed the full head of straight hair and the five toes, I presume?"

"I did not say he was a slave or a Vroomaw, Your Viziership," Ghlikh said.

"Well for you that you did not," Shegnif said.

He spoke into an orange wooden box before him, and the big doors swung open. Ulysses wondered if they had a form of radio. He had not noticed any antennas when he was in the city, but then it had been night.

Shegnif stood up and said, "We will continue this tomorrow. I have more urgent business to attend to. However, if you can prove what you said about your being the key to our survival, I will listen to every word. I can arrange a special interview with you late this evening. But you had better not be wasting my time, which is very valuable."

"I will speak with you this evening," Ulysses said.

"Am I to have no chance to defend myself?" Ghlikh wailed.

"Every chance, as you well know," Shegnif said. "Don't ask questions which do not need asking. You know I am busy."

Ulysses was led back to the barracks room but Ghlikh was taken to another room where, apparently, Khyuks was also kept. The last of the interviewers, teams of humans and Neshgai, were leaving just as Ulysses returned.

Awina hurried to him, saying, "How did it go, Lord?"

"We are not in the power of altogether unreasonable beings," he answered. "I have hopes that we will become the allies of these people."

The boxes which held the bombs had not been taken away from them. In fact, they still had all their weapons. If they were allowed to keep them because the Neshgai were contemptuous of them, they might yet show the Neshgai that they should not take some things for granted. One bomb should blast open the locked doors to this room, and a few more might kill and shake enough of the elephantine creatures to allow the party to get to the harbor. And there they could seize a galley, which should be relatively easy to operate. Or, if they wanted to get far away, they could seize a sailing ship, of which there were plenty in the harbor. And which, he suspected, had auxiliary vegetable engines.

But there was no sense in doing this except as a last resort. If the Neshgai intended to kill or enslave them, they would surely have seized their weapons. He would issue orders that his men should resist if they were asked to surrender their arms. And he would tell them his plans for escaping if this happened.

In the meantime, he would see what developed with the Neshgai. He needed them as much as they needed him. He had the knowledge and the drive, and they had the materials and the personnel. Together, they could attack The Tree. Or the batpeople, whom he believed were the powers behind The Tree.

That evening, an officer who introduced himself as Tarshkrat came for him. He followed the billowing cloak of the giant into the office of Shegnif. The Grand Vizier asked Ulysses to sit down and offered him a dark winy liquid. Ulysses accepted it with thanks but did not drink much. Even that little made his veins sing.

Shegnif snuffed the stuff up his trunk and squirted it into his mouth while tears of pleasure, or pain, ran down his cheeks. The stone container before him held more than two gallons of the liquor, but he did not drink much. He just tried to give the impression that he did. While listening to Ulysses' speech, he dipped the trunk frequently into the stone vessel. But he was probably just stirring the liquid with the tip of his trunk.

Finally, he held up a hand for Ulysses to stop talking, and he rumbled, "So you think that The Tree is not an intelligent entity?"

"No, I do not think it is," Ulysses said. "I think the Dhulhulikh would like everybody to believe that it is."

"You are probably sincere in your belief," the Grand Vizier thundered. "But I know that you are wrong. I know that The Tree is a single sentient being!"

Ulysses sat even more upright, and said, "How do you know?"

"The Book of Tiznak has told us that," Shegnif said. "Rather, it has told some of us that. I cannot read the Book except here and there. But I believe those who claim they can read about The Tree."

"I do not know what you mean."

"Nor do I expect you to know. But you will know. I'll see to that."

"Whether or not The Tree is sentient, it grows," Ulysses said. "It will cover this land in about fifty years at its present rate of growth. And where will you Neshgai go then?"

"The Tree seems to be limited in its growth near the seacoast," the Grand Vizier said. "Otherwise it would have covered us up long ago. It is growing northward and will eventually shadow all the land to the north. Except near the coast. It is not the growth of The Tree itself that we fear. We fear the peoples of The Tree. The Tree has been sending them against us, and it will not stop until it has exterminated us or forced us to go live with it."

"You really believe that?" Ulysses said.

"I know that!"

"What about the Dhulhulikh?"

"I did not know, until you told me, that they lived in The Tree. They had always claimed they came from the north. If your story is true, then they are our enemy. They are, you might say, the eyes of The Tree. Just as the other peoples, the Vignoom and so forth, are the hands of The Tree."

124

Ulysses said, "If The Tree is an entity with intelligence, then it should have a central brain. And this brain, once located, could be destroyed. If The Tree is just a mindless vegetable entity which the Dhulhulikh control, then the Dhulhulikh can be located and destroyed."

Shegnif pondered this for a few minutes. Ulysses watched him over the top of his tall glass and took a sip of the strong stuff. How strange, he thought, to be sitting in a Brobdingnagian chair and talking to a being descended from elephants, talking about little winged men and a plant that might have a brain or many brains.

Shegnif curled his trunk up and back and rubbed his forehead with its double-tendriled tip. He said, "How would killing the central brain of The Tree or killing all the Dhulhulikh stop The Tree from growing?"

"If you kill the brain of an animal, you kill the entire animal," Ulysses said. "This may hold true for a complex vegetable entity, in which case The Tree will die. And the Neshgai will have enough firewood to last them a thousand years," he added.

Shegnif did not smile. Perhaps the Neshgai sense of humor was not that of humans.

"If the brain is dead but The Tree still lives, The Tree is at least not organizing its people to attack you. They are primitives, relatively few in number, who would be warring against each other if The Tree, or the batpeople, did not prevent it.

"If The Tree is only a means for the Dhulhulikh to control this land, then killing the Dhulhulikh will disorganize the other peoples who live on it. And then we may attack the problem of killing The Tree itself. I would suggest poisoning it."

"That would take much poison," Shegnif said.

"I have much knowledge of poisons."

Shegnif ridged his skin where his eyebrows would have been if he had them. "Indeed? Well, poisons aside, how could you possibly locate the Dhulhulikh? Or attack them? They have all the advantages."

Ulysses told him how he thought it could be done. He talked for more than an hour. Shegnif finally said that he had heard enough. He would have rejected his ideas at once if anyone else had submitted them. But Ulysses had said that the devices he would build had once been commonplace, and he saw no reason to doubt him. He would have to think about the proposal.

Slightly tipsy, Ulysses left the Grand Vizier. He was optimistic, but he also knew that Shegnif would be talking again to the bat-men, and there was no telling how they might influence him.

The officer who conducted him led him to a suite of rooms instead of the barracks. Ulysses asked him why he was separated from his people.

"I do not know," the officer said. "I have my orders, and they are to house you here."

"I would prefer to be with my people."

"No doubt," the officer said, looking down at him along his rigid trunk, extended at a forty-five-degree angle to the plane of his face. "But my orders say otherwise. However, I will convey your request to my superiors."

The suite had been constructed for Neshgai, not for humans. The furniture was enormous and, for him, inconvenient. However, he would not be alone. He had two human women as his attendants.

"I do not need these slaves," Ulysses said. "I can take care of myself."

"No doubt," the officer said. "I will pass on your request to be alone."

And that will be the end of that, Ulysses thought. *The slaves are provided for more than my comfort. They are also spies.*

The Neshgai stopped at the door, his hand on the knob, and said, "If you need anything that the women can't provide, speak into that box on the table. The guards outside will answer."

He opened the door, saluted by touching his right index finger to the tip of his upraised proboscis, and closed the door. The bolt shot home loudly.

Ulysses asked the two women for their names. One was Lusha; the other, Thebi. Both were young and attractive, if he overlooked the half-baldness and the too-prominent chins. Lusha was thin and small-breasted but graceful and swaying-hipped. Thebi was full-breasted, just on the verge of being fat. Her eyes were a bright green and she smiled a lot. She reminded him very much of his wife. It was possible, he told himself, that she might even be descended from his wife, and, of course, from him, since he had three children. But the resemblance to Clara could only be coincidental, because she would not be carrying any genes from ancestors that remote.

Lusha and Thebi had thick, dark, almost kinky hair which started halfway on top of their heads. It fell down to their waists and was decorated with little wooden figur-

126

ines, rings and several tiny brightly colored ribbons. They wore earrings, their everted lips were rouged and their eyes ringed with a bluish kohl. They wore strings of colored stones around their necks, and their stomachs bore painted symbols. These, they explained, were the marks of their owner, Shegnif.

Their kilts were scarlet with green pentangles. A thin black stripe ran down both sides of their legs and ended in circles around the anklebones. Their sandals were painted golden.

They led him to the bathroom, where it was necessary for all three to climb up a portable wooden staircase provided by the majordomo. He sat down in the washbasin which the Neshgai used to wash their hands, and the two women stood on the edge of the basin and gave him a bath.

Later, Thebi ordered food and the dark liquor—*amusa* in the Ayrata tongue—brought in. He climbed into bed on the portable staircase, and he slept at the top of the bed while they curled together on the floor on a blanket.

In the morning, after breakfast, he opened the box on the table and inspected it. It contained hard vegetable plates that looked like printed circuit boards, but the rest of the equipment was solid-state, though nonmetallic. It seemed to be living, and it fed from a vegetable case with three connections. This might be a vegetable fuel cell. There were no controls. Apparently the organism contained some biological mechanism which operated automatically as receiver or transmitter, probably in response to spoken commands.

He again questioned the two women after his examination of the transceiver. They were undoubtedly spies, but he could also gain information from them. They answered him readily enough. Yes, they were slaves and the descendants of a long line of slavery. Yes, they knew about the capture of the Vroomaw. Or some of the Vroomaw, that is. Part of them had surrendered without a fight because of the attractive offers the Neshgai had made. The others had been forced to surrender after an overwhelming force of Neshgai had invaded. The Vroomaw had then been transported, or marched, to the Neshgai borders where they were stationed as garrison troops with their families. They would protect the Neshgai from the invasions from The Tree. They were freemen but restricted to certain areas. They had little contact with the slaves. Thebi did not say so specifically, but she conveyed the idea that there was more communication between the slaves and the border troops than the Neshgai knew about.

Thebi was not as frank about the mental state of the slaves. At least, Ulysses got the idea that she was being far from honest. This migh⁺ be because she was afraid that he would report to the masters or, perhaps, the suite might be bugged. He had searched for listening devices and found none, but his unfamiliarity with the living instruments made it possible for him to look at one and not recognize it as such.

Also, Thebi might not be aware of the general state of contentment, or lack thereof, among the slaves. She might be too isolated from those outside the palace. This, however, did not seem likely, since she seemed to know much about what was happening on the border, although she could have picked this up from listening to the Neshgai.

He would have to find out for himself how happy the slaves were. Not that he had any plans for rousing them to a revolt or joining any underground that might exist. He did not believe in slavery, but he was also not going to upset a status quo without good reason. His primary aim, now that he had found human beings, was to fight The Tree.

There was also the problem of finding a suitable permanent mate, one who could father his children and be an enjoyable companion. The genetic constitution of the humans was somewhat different from his, but he hoped that it was not so different that they were a separate species. Even if he did have children by one of them, he would not know whether or not his offspring were mules until they grew up.

In the middle of the morning, he was summoned to Shegnif's office. The Grand Vizier did not waste any time on greetings.

"The two Dhulhulikh have escaped. Like birds, they have flown the coop!"

"They must have decided that you would accept my story," Ulysses said. "They knew that the truth would out."

He did not really believe this, but he thought that he would impress Shegnif with it.

"The officer in charge of them opened the door to enter their room, and they flew through the doorway before he could try to grab them. They are much quicker than we. They flew on down the hall, which was wide enough for their wings. They were lucky that the hall was empty, and they went on through a window, which, unfortunately,

Micronite filter.
Mild, smooth taste.
For all the right reasons.
Kent.

America's quality cigarette.
King Size or Deluxe 100's.

was not barred. And now I must explain to the *shauzgrooz* the implications of this escape."

The *shauzgrooz* meant the ruler, king, sultan or chief potentate. Literally, it meant *The Longest Nose*. The present shauzgrooz was Zhigbruwzh IV, and he was two years short of being an adult. Shegnif was, in effect, the ruler, though he could be ousted any time Zhigbruwzh wished to get rid of him. The juvenile was, however, very fond of Shegnif. And he had another reason for not wishing to force the Grand Vizier out. According to Thebi, there had been palace revolutions where the viziers had killed off the ruling family and initiated their own dynasty. Not many of these occurred, since the Neshgai seemed to be more stable and less aggressive than humans. But enough had happened for any ruler to think twice before dismissing his vizier. Especially since Shegnif's nephew was general of the army and also owned many farms, slaves and a number of merchant ships.

"The implications of this escape," Ulysses said, "are that the Dhulhulikh know what I want to do. And they will take it for granted that you will accept my ideas. Which means that they will be attacking before we can put these plans into effect. They will attack whether or not you initiate my proposals, since they will have to assume you are doing so. And the only way to combat this inevitable attack is to accept my ideas."

"Don't be so sure," the Neshgai said. "You may think you've got my nose caught in a crack, but I might decide otherwise. We are an ancient people and the only people with an advanced science and technology. We don't have to rely on a short-nosed stuntling to defeat our enemies."

Ulysses did not interrupt. Shegnif was upset, and also probably scared, by the escape of the two batpeople and its consequences. He knew very well that he needed what Ulysses could give him, but he had to talk big to bolster his own courage and to heal the wound given to the image of the Neshgai as all-powerful. He could talk and brag all he wanted, and then he and Ulysses could discuss what they would do. This was what happened after fifteen minutes when Shegnif finally ran out of breath and images.

There was a long silence. Then Shegnif smiled, lifting up his trunk so Ulysses could get the full benefit of the smile, and he said, "However, it won't hurt to talk about what you could contribute. After all, there is such a thing as being realistic. And you do come from a people far more ancient than the Neshgai, though I wouldn't want you to be saying so to our slaves. Or to any Neshgai, for that matter."

It became evident that Shegnif had been reluctant to make gunpowder because he did not want the humans, slaves or freemen, to know about it.

This meant that the slaves were not happy and had, perhaps, revolted in the past. On the other hand, it could be that they were content enough, but Shegnif knew enough about human nature to know that they would try to get the upper hand if the means were available. It did not matter that they might have few grounds for reasonable complaints.

Ulysses discussed his ideas for the control of the gunpowder. Shegnif approved of secret factories, where only Neshgai would manufacture the powder. Ulysses went along with this because it was vitally necessary to get the powder as soon as possible. Also, the so-called secret would not be kept. The Neshgai powder-makers were bound to do some talking, which the sensitive ears of the slaves would pick up. Or, if this did not happen, Ulysses could spread the word easily. All the humans had to know was that charcoal, sulphur and potassium or sodium nitrate was mixed in certain proportions. And once the "secret" was out, it would never be forgotten. Never? That was the incorrect word. A man who had survived ten million years should not be careless with that concept. It would be a long time, relatively speaking, before the humans would forget.

Ulysses then explained how blimps could be built. This required far more technology and materials than gunpowder. Shegnif frowned and said that he would relax some restrictions. But for Ulysses' own safety, and for reasons of state, he could not be allowed to go everywhere he pleased.

It became evident that Shegnif had not understood, or did not wish to understand, Ulysses' basic idea. Shegnif wanted to use the air fleet against the Vignoom first. In fact, he would like to use the fleet only on the perimeter of The Tree. Thus, the fleet would not be subject to attack from a great number of batpeople, and it could control the buildup of the border enemies.

Ulysses was exasperated by this shortsightedness and timidity. However, the Neshgai were not the only people to suffer from lack of vision, he reminded himself. What he must do now was to get his weapons, aircraft and personnel ready and then worry about their ultimate uses.

Before the conference was finished, they ran into another obstacle. Shegnif did not like the idea that most members of the air force would be humans. He wanted many more Neshgai aboard the blimps.

"But it's a matter of weight," Ulysses said. "For every Neshgai on a craft, you have so much less fuel and bombs. You cut down on the cruising range and the firepower you can deliver."

"That won't matter if the blimps operate near the edge of The Tree. They'll be close to the bases, and they can make more flights to compensate. There's no problem there."

When Ulysses saw Awina the next day, he felt guilty—and also happy. There was no reason why he had to feel guilty. After all, Lusha and Thebi were humans, not furry, cat-eyed, carnivorous-toothed, tailed, crooked-legged creatures. He was free to do as he pleased, and he was becoming very fond of Thebi.

Nevertheless, Awina made him flush with guilt. A moment later, while talking to her, he felt a joy that made his heart beat faster and his breast ache.

It was not what the humans of his time thought of as falling in love. It was not love with any idea of physical mating with her, of course. But he had grown so used to her, so delighted in her companionship, her way of talking and attending to him, that he loved her. Loved her as a sister, he could truthfully say. Well, not exactly a sister. There was more to it than that. Actually, his feeling for her was indefinable as yet. Or, perhaps, he told himself in a flash of frankness, the feeling was better left undefined.

Definitions aside, she made him happier than anybody else he had met since he had awakened. Maybe even before he had awakened.

There was no doubt about *her* feelings. Her eyes opened wide when she saw the two women, and her black lips curled to reveal the sharp teeth. Her tail stiffened out. She slowed her walk, and then she looked at him. She smiled, but she could not keep smiling. And when she got close to him he could read the expression beneath that black mask of velvet fur. She was very angry.

He could understand her reaction, but he did not intend to put up with it for long. She would have to take a realistic attitude. If she did not, she would have to go. He did not want this to happen. He would feel sorrow if he had to send her away. It would be a deep sorrow, but he could endure it, and the sorrow would fade away. More than anyone else, he should know what the passage of time could do.

This did not help him at all.

Awina did not try to conceal her intentions, though she did dampen the tendency to violence that she must have been feeling.

"It is good to be back at your side, my Lord. You will have your handmaid, a *free* person and a worshiper, at your side."

She spoke in Ayrata, doubtless to make sure that the two women understood.

"It is good to have you back with me," he replied gravely.

He winced at the thought of her hurt when he would tell her that she would be sleeping in a separate room from now on. He made a lousy god. A god should be arrogant, above consideration of mere mortals' feelings.

Knowing that he was being a coward, and hating himself for it, he put off telling her. To dull the reproach, he rationalized that he did have more important matters to attend to just now. But he realized that he was only lying to himself.

She did go with him to the conference and the two women were left behind. She was intelligent, and she could later explain to his people what was going on. They would be restless and resentful for some time because there was no place for them in his plans. They did not have the knowledge and skills needed for the next phase in the war against The Tree and its servants. But he would tell them that and also explain that the time would come when they would be very much needed. Once the attack was launched on the Dhulhulikh, the three feline groups would be much more valuable in The Tree than the pachyderms or the humans. They were more agile and more familiar with The Tree.

The days and nights were busy and productive, though not as productive as he wished. The Neshgai looked so elephantine, they seemed above such human traits as pettiness, jealousy, graft, competition for prestige and money and position, backbiting, and just plain stupidity, Unfortunately, they were *not* above such things. It was true that they did not seem to be as active in these traits as their human counterparts. But this was because they were slower. And so events went at the pace of a sick turtle. Or an anemic elephant. He spent half of his time in straightening out administrative squabbles, soothing wounded egos, listening to petitions for advancement or wild schemes for using the blimps, trying to find out what had happened to materials or workers he had ordered.

He complained to Shegnif, who only shrugged his shoulders and waved his trunk about.

"It's the system," he said. "I can't do much about it. I can threaten to cut off a few trunks here and there or even a head. But if the culprits were found, and then brought to trial, you would lose even more time. You'd have to spend too much time as a witness in court to get much done on your projects. Our courts are very slow. As the proverb says, 'A head once cut off can't be put back on.' We Neshgai don't forget that Nesh is, first of all, the god of justice. We can't be too careful to avoid injustices."

Ulysses tried being subtle. He said, "The border scouts report that large numbers of Vignoom and Glassim are gathering on the branches near the edge of The Tree. They should be attacking soon. Are you going to consider the course of possible injustice against them if you should attack them first? Or are you going to let them pick the time and the place?"

Shegnif smiled and said, "You are telling me that if I don't take quick action with the new weapons and craft, we will be hurt badly? Well, you may be right, but I can't do anything about speeding up your projects. Or cutting down the cost, either. And don't argue with me."

There was no one else to appeal to. Any appeal to the ruler, Zhigbruwzh IV, would go through Shegnif, and even if the Vizier passed it on, Zhigbruwzh was not likely to ignore the advice of his Vizier. Especially if the petition issued from an alien.

Ulysses was not sure that Shegnif did not plan to do away with him as soon as the gunpowder, aircraft manufacturing and the navigating techniques were complete and fully understood. After all, he was a human, and he had no reason to be loyal to the Neshgai. It was conceivable that Shegnif could suspect him of being an agent of The Tree. Ulysses could have been sent to spy on the land, stir up the slaves and get the Neshgai to build an air fleet which would be turned against the Neshgai.

Ulysses admitted to himself that, if he were Shegnif, he would be contemplating these possibilities. And he would be tempted to imprison Ulysses as soon as Ulysses' basic work was done.

All Ulysses could do was hope that Shegnif realized he would need Ulysses for a long long time. Surely Shegnif must know that The Tree had to be killed before the Neshgai would be safe from it.

Meanwhile, the production of black gunpowder, bombs

and rocket cases had started. The preliminaries of making sulfuric acid, and then getting enough zinc with which the acid could react to form hydrogen, had been passed. Iron, which also could have been used, seemed to be absent even in minute quantities. It was not altogether absent, of course, since it existed in many rocks. But the materials, labor and time needed to extract it was enormous—prohibitive, as far as Shegnif was concerned. Ulysses had trained a team to look for zinc, and within ten days a man had found it in the form of sphalerite. This sulfide ore was roasted to form the oxide, which was mixed with compressed charcoal and heated to twelve hundred degrees centigrade (or six hundred *grengzhuyn*). The zinc vapor was condensed outside the reaction chamber and then cast into spelter blocks. Using a low temperature process, the sulfide was roasted to the sulfate, later extracted with water. Zinc metal was then obtained by electrolysis, using the vegetable batteries.

The skin of the blimp was formed from the inner husk of the plant which furnished the motors. This was extremely light, strong and flexible; fifty sewn together made a large enough bag to contain the hydrogen.

The main problem was the motor. There was not enough iron to make even one motor nor any bauxite available to make aluminum nor any metals that could be substituted. The only propulsive power was the vegetable muscle-motor used to drive the cars, trucks and boats. Ulysses tried the water in a manner similar to that of the jet mechanism of land engines first but they just would not turn a propellor long enough and fast enough. He experimented with the jet motors of the sea ships, which took in and expelled water in a manner similar to that of the jet mechanism of an octopus. However, they were not effective when expelling air.

A solution to the problem came from Fabum, a human overseer on a motor plantation. He sent in a formal suggestion to Ulysses. The paper was lost somewhere in the administrative jungle that had grown up around the embryo air force. Fabum got tired of waiting for a reply and succeeded in getting permission from his immediate Neshgai superior to make the experiment himself. He enclosed two automobile motors in a gondola and grew the muscle ends of the two motors together. The result was that the energy output was tripled, not just doubled. Four such gondolas, containing eight motors, could turn propellors to drive a blimp at twenty-five miles an hour in still air.

Fabum's boss then went directly to Ulysses (an act which got him several reprimands later on), and he told Ulysses what Fabum had done. Fabum was lucky in that his boss did not try to take all the credit, but there *were* honest and honorable Neshgai.

Of course, the addition of more motors, and thus more fuel, added to the weight. But the trip to the base-city of the Dhulhulikh, Ulysses estimated, would be helped by a tail wind all the way. Getting back was a different matter. If the blimps had to be abandoned and the return made on foot, so be it.

Shegnif, hearing the latest reports, was pleased. He gave Fabum his freedom, which meant that he still, in practice, was a slave. But he could live in better quarters and could make more money, if his employer cared to pay him more. And he did not have to ask permission to leave the immediate area.

The Grand Vizier was not at all worried about the limited range or the speed of the blimps. He had no plans for using them except on the perimeter of The Tree close to the Neshgai borders.

Three weeks later, the first blimp took its maiden voyage. The day was bright, and the wind was only six miles an hour. The flight took an hour with several circles over the palace so that the populace could see it. Then, on the way back to the hangar, the blimp dropped twenty thirty-pound bombs over a target, an old house. Only one bomb made a direct hit, but that was enough to blow it apart. And Ulysses told Shegnif that practice would improve their aim.

Nine more blimps were built while the crews were given their ground training. Ulysses complained again about the excess number of Neshgai offiers and the consequent reduction in range and bomb capacity. Shegnif said that that did not matter.

There were more reports from scouts about the massing of giant ursoids and leopardoids, and the clashes between border patrols and small groups of enemy became more frequent. Ulysses did not understand why they had not made a large-scale raid before now. They certainly had enough personnel to penetrate some distance into the Neshgai territory if they made a surprise attack. Moreover, keeping peace among those naturally hostile groups and feeding them was a job requiring much organization. Since none of the groups seemed capable of the sophistication necessary for this, he suspected the batpeople. There were more

135

of them around, according to the scouts, but not in numbers to alarm.

Three times, a lone winged man appeared over the airfield, just out of arrow range, and observed them. Four times, a bat-man flapped alongside a blimp in flight. Other than a few insulting gestures, they offered no harm.

By then, Ulysses had moved his headquarters from the palace—with Shegnif's permission—to the airfield. This was ten miles outside the city, and he could not afford the travel time back and forth. He used the radio plants to report to Shegnif twice daily, however.

Lusha was gone. Although detailed to Ulysses, she had been promised in marriage to a soldier stationed on the border. Weeping—although she was glad to be married to the man—she took her leave. Even Thebi, who could not have been blamed for being jealous of her, wept and kissed her and said she hoped they would see each other soon. Awina seemed glad that she was getting rid of one woman but she took up her sullen attitude toward Thebi as soon as Lusha was out of sight. Thebi, by now sure of her position, had begun treating Awina as if she were a slave girl. Awina took the indirect insults and off-handed treatment without replying in kind. Apparently, she did not want to endanger her relationship with Ulysses by displaying the violence she normally would have used against an insulter. But she was seething. Ulysses could tell that. So he had reprimanded Thebi, causing her to burst into tears and Awina to smile like a cat that had just eaten a stolen salmon.

Ulysses was working so late into the night and getting up to early, he wanted only to fall into bed when his day's work was done. He permitted no one into his bedroom, and so Awina gloated over this. Thebi did not protest that she was allowed little chance to serve him. She was still a slave, and, moreover, she was not that sure of him. He was an alien, despite his similarity to her people, and he had very strange ways of thinking and acting. But she let Ulysses know in several ways, some subtle and some not so subtle, that she was hurt.

He was getting tired of balancing the one female against the other. He just did not have the time for delicate relationships, and he wished, sometimes, that both would leave him alone. Though he could have sent both packing with a few words, he did not want to hurt them that much. Besides, he liked both of them, though in different ways. Awina was very quick and very intelligent. She was from a preliterate society, but she learned swiftly, and she was able to act as a very efficient secretary. Such duties were beyond Thebi. She was proficient in domestic activities, but anything outside taking care of a man or children did not interest her.

One day he took out all ten of the blimps and put them through some very demanding maneuvers. The wind was a stiff fifteen miles an hour from the seacoast, and the big gasbags moved sluggishly when pushing against the wind. Once, two collided, and they tore the motor gondolas off each other. Immediately, they swung away from each other and were carried away by the wind. Ulysses gave the order over the radio for the gas to be let out to bring the craft to the ground. The crews should then walk to the field, which was about twenty miles away. He would radio orders for cars to be sent out to pick them up.

The blimps turned home then, and they reached the field shortly before sunset. Just before his vessel was hauled into the hangar, he looked out the rear port of the gondola. There, outlined against the red rays near the horizon, was a number of tiny figures. They could have been birds, but their silhouettes made him believe they were bat-men. He put in an alert notice and went to his office.

That night, he was awakened by a screaming outside his door. He leaped out of bed (it was built for a human), and opened the door. Outside, the sentry was trying to separate two struggling screeching forms. They were hand to hand, face to face, with Awina holding a flint knife and Thebi's hand locked around the wrist that held the knife. Awina was shorter and lighter, but she was also much stronger, and only the desperation of Thebi and the sentry's efforts had kept the knife from going into Thebi's belly.

Ulysses shouted for her to drop the knife.

At the same time, there was an explosion outside the building, and the windows blew in, cutting all of them in dozens of places.

Ulysses and the sentry flopped on the ground.

Thebi released her hold and, staring, turned away from Awina.

Awina, ignoring the explosion, and the three that followed it, thrust at the woman.

But Thebi had raised her arm, and the knife sliced across it, gashing it and sending a spurt of blood across Awina's face. The knife continued on an upward direction and stabbed into Thebi's jaw. Its force, however, was much reduced.

Thebi screamed. Ulysses leaped up and chopped across Awina's wrist, knocking the knife to the floor.

Another explosion, much closer, blew in the door at the end of the hall and sent a cloud of smoke into the hall.

Awina had gone to her knees, but she sprang up again as soon as the smoke reached her. Ulysses took the knife, but she shouted at him, "No! Give it back! I won't use it on Thebi! Don't you understand? We're being attacked! I might need that knife!"

Although he was half-deafened by the explosion, he could hear her. Silently, he held out the bloody blade, and she took it by the hilt. A figure dashed through the smoke, crying, "Lord, it's the bat-men!"

It was Wulka, the Wagarondit, covered with black gunpowder smoke and bleeding from a wound on his shoulder.

Ulysses ran out past him into the hangar, which housed his office and living quarters. Two blimps were anchored to the ground by thick plastic cables. A great-winged pygmy swooped out of the darkness in the upper part and a streak shot toward Ulysses. He had dived back, and it may have been this, or bad marksmanship, that caused the tiny poisoned arrow to plunge into the dirt a few inches before his feet. An Alkunquib archer raised his bow, coolly tracked the winged man, and loosed an arrow that went upward through the flier's leg and into his belly. The bat-man plunged into the ground a few feet from Ulysses.

There were several other Dhulhulikh flying around in the upper part of the hangar and a number who had settled down on top of the blimps. These were shooting their poisoned arrows. Apparently, all those inside the hangar had dropped their bombs. Outside, lit intermittently by the electric bulbs and torches, was a swarm of the winged men. They swooped in and out of the illumination, dropping little stone-weighted wooden darts, shooting tiny arrows or dropping small round bombs with lit fuses.

The explosions from the bombs added their momentary illumination to the scene.

There were bodies inside the hangar and outside on the field. Most of these were the defenders: Neshgai, humans and the felines, but Ulysses could see at least a dozen pairs of leathery wings spread out among the corpses and wounded.

He turned and shouted at Awina, "Outside! Through the other door!"

She looked startled and he repeated his order. She ran back into the door of the building. He yelled his command again to the felines shooting at the bat-men above them, and then he shouted, "Get away from the blimps before they catch fire!"

They had been lucky so far. None of the exploded bombs had set off the hydrogen in the great bags. If they had, everybody in the hangar would have died.

Even as he turned, there was a loud roar, and light streamed out from a hangar nearby. A blimp, two blimps probably, since there were two to a hangar, had just gone up in flames. Which meant that the other hangars were bound to catch fire and to ignite the blimps they housed.

He waited until his men had streamed in through the door or else run out through the cavernous front end. Some of them did not make it; poisoned, they fell.

He whirled and pushed the Wufea ahead of him through the door and then through several rooms to the door that opened in the side of the hangar. Once all were outside, he got them into battle order, and they moved out between the two hangars into the open area of the field. Another hangar to the right burst into noise and flame, and, in two minutes, all six buildings were burning fiercely. His entire air fleet was destroyed.

There was nothing to do but to take his people out onto the broad field. They could not go back, and they had to get out of the brightness and into the dark. The Dhul-hulikh had not left, but were flying overhead, seemingly intent on killing all the air force personnel. Ulysses' troops fell on all sides of him, but he had seized a shield dropped by some dead human and held it overhead. A few arrows thudded into its leather-wrapped wooden disk, and heavy stone-tipped wood darts and arrows thunked around him, or struck those around him. No bombs were tossed at them, although these would have been the surest way of killing. He presumed that they had expended them in the initial attack. It was possible, however, that other bat-men with bombs were being called in.

Then they were on the edge of the darkness and under trees. They formed concentric circles and shot out at those bat-men who came low enough to provide reasonably good targets.

Far to the west, where the city was, the clouds reflected bright lights, probably from burning buildings.

There were other dangers besides flying bat-men. An armored car drove up, and a human hopped out and ran up to him. He ordered Ulysses to report to the Neshgai officer in the car. Ulysses did so, and found Bleezhmag, the equivalent of a colonel in the armored car corps, waiting there by the open door. Bleezhmag had a deep gash across his forehead, a light cut across his trunk and a hole in his left arm. His human soldiers had gotten out of the car and were shooting wooden bolts from wooden crossbows.

"I have orders from the Grand Vizier to take you out the danger zone, wherever that is," he said. He leaned out and looked up at the great-winged figures flickering from darkness to the glare of burning gas. "We've been hit twice on the roof by bombs, but aside from temporary deafness, we haven't suffered. Get in!"

"I can't desert my men!" Ulysses said.

"Oh, yes, you can!" Bleezhmag said. He trumpeted impatiently—perhaps a trifle hysterically—through his proboscis.

"It's not just the Dhulhulikh! The other Tree peoples are in on this raid! They're not a horde, if our information is correct, but they are a large body, and they've formed a spearhead which has swept through most of our defenses in this area! They're being held up now, but they won't be kept back long! The Grand Vizier says they're probably intent on getting you! They can't hope to take the city! But they could get you!"

Something nudged the darkness aside and revealed itself as another armored car. Like the first, it looked like a wheeled tortoise. The curved roof was made of three layers of thick densely grained wood over a thick layer of plastic. The sides were double-walled and contained doors and slit-holes. It held a driver, an officer, and six archers. Though there had been no thought of its withstanding explosives when it was built some years before, it had proved capable of shrugging off the small bombs of the bat-men.

Ulysses crouched near the door while the crossbowmen stood outside to cover him. Then he gestured at Awina to run out to him. She did so, almost ending up as a recipient of a poisoned arrow. This missed her by several inches, and then she was by his side. A bowman was lucky enough to hit the bat-man who had flown in to shoot at Awina. His bolt caught the bat-man in his arm, pinning it to his side. The bat-man screamed and dropped his bow and then fluttered down. Another bolt struck deep into his ribs just as his feet touched the ground.

"Get in!" Ulysses said to Awina. He spoke to Bleezhmag. "I will go if you will see that the rest of my people are transported, too."

"Very well," Bleezhmag said.

Ulysses gestured at his men under the tree, and those still on their feet helped the wounded to get across the open area to the cars. Either the bat-men had exhausted their supply of missiles or they were too respectful of the bowmen. They did not try to attack the group while it was unprotected.

The cavalcade moved out onto the road at twenty miles an hour. The headlights were not bright compared to those on the cars of Ulysses' time; they illuminated the road perhaps twenty feet ahead of them. Ulysses asked Bleezhmag why the lights were on. They would only attract the invaders, and they were not really needed, since the drivers knew this road well.

"I have no orders to turn them off," the Neshgai said. He was slumped down in his seat and breathing heavily through his mouth. The blood was still running from his wounds.

Ulysses was standing on the seat beside him, which had held another Neshgai officer, presumably left behind because he was dead or incapacitated. On Ulysses' right was a Neshgai driver. Behind him, in the space in the center, Awina and seven Wufea were crowded together. The archers peered out through the slits into the darkness half-lit by the beams of the vehicles behind them.

"You have no orders?" Ulysses said. "Are you forbidden to turn them off unless you get orders to do so?"

Bleezhmag nodded. Ulysses said, "I am ordering you to turn off the lights. It may be too late now, but do so anyway."

"I am an armored car corpsman, and you are an officer of the air force," the Neshgai said. "You have no authority over me."

"But I have been entrusted to you! Ulysses said. "You are charged with delivering me to the capital. My life is in your hands! By not turning off the lights, you are endangering me! Not to mention my personnel, for whose lives I am responsible!"

"No orders," Bleezhmag said drowsily, and he died.

Ulysses spoke into the transceiver box. "Commander Singing Bear, speaking for Colonel Bleezhmag, who has delegated his authority to me because of his wounds. Turn off the lights!"

A moment later, the cavalcade rolled over the highway in the darkness. The road was whitish enough for them to follow it at a fifteen-mph speed, and Ulysses had hopes that they might get to the capital unattacked.

He pressed the button marked *HQ* in the Neshgai symbol on the side of the box. This would cause pressure on a nerve spot in the vegetable organism, and the frequency band would be shifted.

He got no reply to his repeated demands to be put through to the Grand Vizier or the general of the army. Even when he identified himself, he failed to get a response. He switched back to the frequency used among the cars and told the operator in the car behind him to send requests to HQ. Then he turned in on all the frequencies available to the transceiver, hoping to find out how the defense was coming. He heard a number of conversations, but he was left as confused as those he listened in on. Then he tried to cut in on some of these with the hope that he could get his request relayed to HQ, but he failed.

The Neshgai driver, peering through the slit, said, "Commander! I see something on the field just ahead!"

Ulysses told him to hold his speed and he looked through the slit. He saw a number of pale figures advancing swiftly across the fields, evidently intending to cut the train off. He switched on the lights, and the figures became somewhat clearer. Eyes gleamed redly in the reflection, and the paleness became leopard-spotted bipeds with tails. They held spears and round objects, which must be bombs. How had The Tree people gotten gunpowder?

He spoke into the transceiver. "Enemy on the right! About thirty yards, I'd say! Full speed ahead! Run over them if they get in the way. Archers, fire at will!"

The first of the running leopard-men got to the road. A red glow suddenly appeared, and then a sputter of fire. He had opened a firebox and applied it to the fuse of a bomb. The fire described an arc as the bomb flew toward the lead car. A crossbow twanged, and a bolt shot out of the front right slit. The enemy screamed and fell. There was a thump against the roof, and then an explosion that rocked the car and half-deafened them. But the bomb had bounced off the roof and onto the road by the side of the car. The car kept on going.

Other figures rushed up, some with spears and a few with open fireboxes and bombs. The spearmen tried to thrust their weapons through the slits, and the bombardiers tossed their weapons at the side of the car.

The spearmen fell, pierced by bolts. Bombs struck and bounced off the sides and the roof and blew up on the road, doing more harm to the enemy than to the carmen.

Then the lead car was past them, and the survivors were

attacking the other cars. More than half of the enemy was left dead or wounded. One leopard-man, running desperately, leaped upon the sloping roof of the last car. He placed a bomb on the roof, leaped off, and was shot in the back. The bomb blew the two top layers off and cracked the third. The occupants could not hear for some time, but they were unharmed.

When the cavalcade rolled into the city, they found a few buildings burning and some minor damage. The bat-men had dropped bombs and shot down soldiers and civilians in the streets. A suicide team had flown through the windows of the fourth story of the palace (which had not been barred, though orders had been given two weeks before to do so). They had killed many people with their poisoned arrows but had failed to kill the ruler and the Grand Vizier. And all except two of the team had died.

Ulysses learned this from Shegnif. He said, "Do not kill your two prisoners, Most Excellent. We can torture the secret of the location of their base city out of them."

"Then what?" Shegnif said.

"Then we use a new air fleet, much better than the first, to attack and destroy the base city of the Dhulhulikh. And we attack The Tree itself."

Shegnif was surprised. He said, "You are not at all downcast by what happened tonight?"

"Not at all," Ulysses said. "The enemy really accomplished very little, and they may have done us a service. If the blimps had not been destroyed, I might have had a hard time getting you to authorize the building of better craft. I have in mind much larger craft. My native tongue called them *dirigibles. Directibles*, or *steerables*, would be a good translation. These will require much more material, planning and time, but they will be more than adequate for the mission I plan."

He had thought the Vizier would be angry because of his assumptions, but Shegnif was pleased. He said, "This invasion—which is still going on, by the way, but is being contained—convinces me of one thing. You are right in that the enemy must be hit in the heart. We could fritter away our resources and personnel by just defending our borders. Though I do not see how we can harm The Tree, even if we kill its Eyes, the Dhulhulikh. Perhaps you have a solution?"

Ulysses outlined his plans. Shegnif listened, nodding his great head, feeling his tusks, tapping his forehead with the tendriled ends of his trunks. Then he said, "I'll authorize your plans at once. The Vignoom and the Glassim are being pushed back, and we're rushing more troops up. And we've taken about twenty more wounded bat-men."

"Some can give us information," Ulysses said. "And others can be used in the training of the hawks."

Again, he was very busy from dawn until long past dusk. He did have time to investigate the quarrel between Thebi and Awina. He had not seen the woman after leaving the office to go into the hangar, but she showed up a few days later. Her story was that she had staggered out into the open immediately after Ulysses left, and she had collapsed between the hangars. She awoke on the field by a group of corpses. Her wound had bled a lot but was not deep.

Both females admitted that they had been quarreling about which was the highest in his affections and about whom should be his permanent aid. Thebi had attacked Awina with her nails, and Awina had pulled her knife.

Ulysses decided not to inflict any imprisonment or physical punishment on either. He defined their duties and positions and how they should behave in the future. They must conform to these. Otherwise, both would be sent away for a long time.

Thebi wept, and Awina wailed, but they promised to behave.

One of the first things he did was to call in a large number of hawk trainers. These were free men whose only job was to raise and educate the several types of accipitrine birds for their masters, who liked to go ahawking. Instead of training these fierce birds to go after ducks, pigeons and other feathered prey, they would teach them to attack the bat-men. There were enough Dhulhulikh prisoners who would be expendable after they had recovered from their wounds.

Five months later, Ulysses attended the first showing of the results of the new training. The young ruler, the Grand Vizier and the military brass were there. A sullen-faced bat-man who knew what was coming, was released. He ran down the sloping field, his wings flapping, and took off slowly. He had attained about forty feet, flying against the wind, when he wheeled around and came back over the field. He carried a short spear with a stone tip, and he had been promised that if he could successfully defend himself against two hawks, he would be allowed to fly home.

He probably did not believe the promise. It would be stupid of the Neshgai to permit him to carry the news of this new weapon to his people. If he did kill the two hawks, others would be loosed at him. He had no chance of outrunning them.

But he did as he was told and came back over the field at the specified height so that the attack could be witnessed. As he swept back down, the hoods of the two hawks were pulled off, and their trainers threw them into the air. They circled for a moment and then, crying hoarsely, climbed above the bat-man. He winged away desperately. The two hawks came down like feathered lightning bolts and struck with a noise that the observers could hear. Just before they did, the bat-man had folded his wings and whirled to face them. One struck his head, and this one died from the knife, but would not loosen the talons. The other hit a few seconds later, digging its talons into the belly of the bat-man. Shrieking, the winged man fell and hit the ground with enough force to break his legbones and one wingbone. The surviving hawk continued to tear at his belly.

"We can't carry a trainer for each bird, of course," Ulysses said. "We are training them now so that they will be in individual cages, the doors of which will be opened by a single mechanism. They will be unhooded, and they will fly out and attack the nearest bat-man. And they will keep on attacking."

"Let's hope so," Shegnif said. "I don't put much faith in the efficiency of hawks. There is nothing to keep a number from attacking one bat-man while the other bat-men go by unhindered."

"My trainers are working on that," Ulysses said.

Despite his objections, the Grand Vizier seemed pleased. He made his bows and trunk-touchings to the ruler, who was carried back to the palace in an elaborately carved vehicle. Shegnif walked beside Ulysses for a while, talking, and, once, affectionately touching Ulysses on the nose with the tip of his trunk.

"We are indeed fortunate that the stone god was awakened by a lightning bolt," he said. "Though no doubt it was Nesh who sent the lightning."

He smiled, Ulysses had not yet determined whether or not the Vizier's frequent references to his god were the result of piety or irony.

"Nesh de-stoned you so you could be of service to his people. That is what the priests tell me, and I, even though the Grand Vizier to His Majesty, bow when the lowliest priest informs me of the merest truth.

"And so, I have been delegated to tell you that you are indeed the fortunate one. You are the only alien, the only non-Neshgai, who has ever been invited to read the Book of Tiznak. In fact, very few Neshgai are so honored."

He found out what Shegnif meant early next morning. A priest, clad in hood and robes as gray as his skin, and holding a wand with an X in a broken circle carved at its end, came for him. His name was Zhishbroom. He was young, affable and very polite. But he made it clear that the high priest was summoning, not requesting, Ulysses' presence at the temple.

Ulysses drove out to the western edge of the city and was conducted into a square-walled triple-domed building of stone. Its smallness surprised him. It was a sixty-foot cube and held nothing but a granite statue of Nesh in its center. Nesh looked like a male Neshgai, although his tusks were somewhat longer than average and his snout thicker.

Three priests stood like sentries, each forming the apex of a triangle in the middle of which was the statue.

Zhishbroom led the man past the first priest and stopped. He stooped and pressed on a tiny block of stone, and a block of the granite floor sank before him. He led Ulysses down a steep flight of granite steps lit by the cold light of vegetables. The granite slab moved out and then up behind them, and they were entombed—in a manner of speaking.

He had not suspected that there was another city under the one above ground.

This was about four square miles in area and in four levels. It had not been built by the Neshgai. It did not take long to determine that even without being told so by the priests. Ulysses realized that he was inside some sort of very ancient museum.

"Who built this city?" he said.

"We do not know," the priest replied. "There is evidence that it was once inhabited by a people descended from dogs or some sort of canines. But we do not think that they built this. They found it, and they lived in it without disturbing the objects you see here. And then they disappeared. They may have been killed or have left for some reason. There are people who live with The Tree who resemble these ancient peoples. They may be their descendants.

"In any event, we Neshgai were a small and primitive tribe when we wandered here, some say as refugees from The Tree. We found much here that we could use. The vegetable circuits, batteries and motors, for instance, were grown from seeds found preserved in containers. There were also many objects the purpose of which we have never been able to determine. If we could we might be able to blast The Tree to destroy it. Perhaps this is why The Tree is so intent on destroying us. It wishes to kill us before we find out how to kill it."

He paused and then said, "And then there is the Book of Tiznak."

Ulysses said, "Tiznak?"

"He was the greatest of our priests, an ancient who found out how to read the Book. Follow me. I will take you to the Book, as directed. And to Kuushmurzh, the high priest."

Kuushmurzh was a very old and very wrinkled Neshgai with thick spectacles and shaky hands. He blessed Ulysses without getting up off his huge many-cushioned chair and said he would see him after he had read the Book. That is, he would if Ulysses was able to read the Book.

Ulysses followed the young priest past display after display, all protected by transparent walls of some material. And then he came to a cubicle which was empty except for a plate of some metal fixed to the base of a metal platform. He stopped before it, and said, "That is strange. What was once there?"

"I think *you* were," Zhishbroom said. "At least, that is the legend. The platform was empty when we Neshgai found this place."

Ulysses' heart beat faster, and he felt his skin turning into a mushy and cold liquid. He bent down to stare at the black lettering on the yellow metal. The room was so silent he could hear the blood singing in his ears. The sourceless light was as heavy as the cover on the Tomb of the Ages.

The letters looked as if they might have evolved from the Latin alphabet. Or from the International Phonetic Alphabet (IPA), which was based on a number of alphabets. He studied the letters while the priest stood as patiently as one of his elephant forebears behind him. If he took for granted the similarity of the letters to those of the IPA, then he might be able to figure it out. There were thirty lines, and surely he could decipher some words here and there, no matter how much the language might have changed.

Of course, he told himself, the language might not be a form of English. He had no right to believe that he was still on a portion of the North American continent. He could have been moved to Eurasia or Africa, and this could be de-

147

scended from any one of a thousand languages of his time.

Still, the Arabic numbers should not have changed. And there was nothing like them except for some ones, which could be ells. Maybe the numbers were, for some reason, spelled out.

Čuziz Zine Nea. These were the only capitalized letters. Could they stand for Ulysses Singing Bear? The initial *y* phoneme in Ulysses had become affricated for some reason, perhaps because of a word-final affricate preceding it? Maybe, in some cases, the word-final sound immediately preceding the word-initial sound of the next word influenced it if it were in a certain class. Just as *Zine* may have been *Singing* at one time, and the *s* became voiced when preceded by a voiced sound. The *ing* had become *en,* and then the *n* became a nasalization of the *e,* but during the evolution of the language it had influenced all words which, following it, began with a bilabial or labiodental phoneme. So that, though the final *n* of *Zine* had disappeared, *Bear* (once *Ber,* then *Be*) was *Ne* when it followed any word that had once had a final *m* or *n.*

If he proceeded on this theory . . . he whistled and murmured then, "I think I got it!"

There was some sense in the words. The letters were evolved from the IPA or something like it. The language had been English, but it had changed to something analogous to the structure of the Celtic languages of his time. There were words that he could not translate at all or could only guess at. After all, new words come into every language almost every year, and some become more or less permanent. And there were elisons and intrusions for which to account.

But there it was. TO HERE . . . ULYSSES SINGING BEAR, FAMOUS PETRIFIED MAN, ACCIDENTALLY . . . TO HIM . . . MOLECULAR STASIS DURING SCIENTIFIC EXPERIMENT IN SYRACUSE, NEW YORK, TO OLD NATION OF UNITED STATES OF AMERICA. "PETRIFIED" STATE SINCE . . .

The date was unintelligible. For some reason, the Arabic numbers were not used. But the date had to be the equivalent of 1985 A.D. The date given for the erection of the exhibit was also unreadable.

It did not matter whether it was 6985 A.D. or 50,000 A.D., though it was probable that the earlier date was more correct. In fifty thousand years, the language would have become absolutely unrecognizable.

It did not matter. What did was that he had once sat on this metal, or plastic, platform with the affixed plate and many visitors, perhaps millions, had filed by and read these words (in various forms as the language changed) and gazed at the immobile features with awe. And also with amusement, since humans could not keep from making witticisms even in the presence of death. They would have looked at him with jealousy, too, if they had known that he would be living when they had been dust a hundred thousand times over.

He wondered what had happened to him. Had someone stolen him? Or, more likely, had he and the platform been located somewhere else, and then taken here? Had he been separated from the platform en route? Who knew what had happened? It had taken place so long ago that it would always be a mystery.

He straightened up, and Zhishbroom walked on ahead. They went down many corridors, and at last the Neshgai halted before a blank wall. He spoke one word, and the wall seemed to melt and then become fuzzy, and there was an open doorway. He followed the giant into a small room shaped like the interior of a ball. A silvery reflecting substance coated the interior and, in the middle of the room, suspended on nothing, was a huge silvery disk. Zhishbroom took Ulysses' hand and guided him to a spot before it. The disk hung vertically before him and reflected his image.

But it did not reflect Zhishbroom, who was standing directly behind him.

"I can read nothing in the Book," Zhishbroom said sadly.

He added, "Call out when you are finished reading. The door will open. I will then conduct you to Kuushmurzh, and you can tell him what you read."

Ulysses did not hear the Neshgai walk away. He continued to stare at his reflection, and then it disappeared. Evaporated, rather. Layer after layer of his flesh faded; his bones stood before him; they, too, slid into nothing; only the disk was left.

He stepped forward, thinking that he could not possibly step into the solid material—but did he know that it was solid? —and then he was inside. Or he thought he was. Like Alice through the mirror.

Things appeared around him as if they had been hidden by an invisible fog which had melted with the sun of his coming.

He walked forward and put out his hand and could touch nothing. He went through the great tree before him, passed through darkness, and was out on the other side. A woman, a beautiful brown woman wearing only earrings, a nose ring, finger rings, beads, and painted designs over half of her body, walked through him. She moved swiftly, as if she were in a speeded-up movie.

Things sped by. Somebody increased the speed of the movie even more. Then it slowed down, and he was standing by another gigantic tree in the light of the moon. The full moon was the moon he had known before he became stone. The tree was three times as large as the largest sequoia of California. Its base contained several entrances out of which a "soft" light fell. A youth of about sixteen, wearing ribbons and tassels in his bushy hair and around his ears, fingers, toes and other appendages, came through the well-tended park and entered the tree. Ulysses followed him up the staircase. He did not understand how he could walk up this and yet not be able to touch it. Nor why his hand went through the youth when he tried to touch him.

The youth lived inside the tree with a dozen others. The apartments, or cells, of the tree had a few decorations and belongings. There was a bed of some moss-like material, some tables not more than six inches off the floor, a tiny stove, some pots, pans and tableware. There was a wooden box, painted by some amateur, in a corner. This held food and various liquids. And that was all.

He left the tree and wandered through the park, which began to fade away. He had a sense of the passage of time. Much time. It was still night when things stabilized. The moon was changing. It evidently had an atmosphere and seas but it did not have the complete-planet look that it had in the world in which he had awakened. Trees, much larger than the sequoia-types, grew all over the land, through which he passed like a ghost. These had a Brobdingnagian central trunk and massive branches that radiated outward and sent down verticle shoots to support them and finally bent to plunge into the earth. They were much smaller versions of The Tree that he knew. They formed small towns, and on them grew trees which furnished all the food, except for meat, that the citizens needed.

There were also trees containing experimental laboratories. These housed cats and dogs with much larger braincases than the animals of his time. And there were monkeys which had lost much of their hair and all of their tail and walked upright. And many more animals that had obviously been mutated by geneticists.

The world began to move fast and then he was on the moon with no sense of transition. The brown Earth hung near the horizon; despite the cloud masses he could recognize the eastern end of Asia.

The moonscape was fair and gentle. There were great trees, many bright plants, birds and little animals. To the east was the first intrusion of dawn. And then the sun came up and lit up the western slope of a mountain—once the wall of a crater, he supposed, that had been softened by erosion of wind and water. Or perhaps it had been changed by the god-like powers of the beings that had given the moon an atmosphere and oceans and transmuted the stony floors to a dark rich soil.

The god-like beings must also have given the moon a faster spin, because the sun rose swiftly and, in an estimated twelve hours, had set again. By then he had scudded across the park-like land and seen the trees that grew here and housed men and many different genera and species of sentients. All the nonhuman peoples, except one, seemed to be descended from terrestrial aimals.

The exception was a tall pinkish-skinned biped with kinky hair from the neck up, under the armpits, on the pubic regions, and on the back of his legs. His face was human enough except for the fleshy excrescence, like that of a star-nosed mole, which adorned the tip of his retroussé nose. There were many of these beings, obviously visitors from a planet of some distant star. If they had spaceships, there were none in sight.

Ulysses continued to glide like a phantom over the face of the moon and then he went as invisibly and gently as a breeze into a tree that contained a laboratory. And here he saw humans and nonhumans watching an experiment. There was an immobile figure inside a plastic transparent cubicle. It was the object of many-colored fluctuating rays directed from a device like a laser gun. The gun poured out its energies, which penetrated the walls of the cubicle and splashed over the still figure.

He recognized the statue. It was himself.

Apparently, the scientists were trying to restore the natural motion of his atoms.

He knew what success they would have.

But what was he doing on the moon? Had he been loaned to the scientists there for some reason he would never know? If so, he had been shipped back to Earth, though this may not have occurred until thousands of years later.

As abruptly as he had left, he was back on Earth. Not only space had been traversed. Much time had also passed.

The Earth was desolated. Fiery winds wrapped it. The

polar caps had melted, and earthquakes, exploding volcanoes, and crumbling coastal masses had changed the face of what land was left.

There ws no explanation for what had happened or for what had caused the global holocaust. Possibly, the huge luminous teardrops that tore through the smoke covering the seared earth were the cause. But there was no one to explain. The smoke passed away and the air became clear again except for great dust storms. Little clots of sentients and the animals that had gone underground with them came out. They sowed seeds, and they cultivated little pieces of ground. Some little trees that had been saved underground were planted.

The teardrops appeared again and hovered over the colonies for a while. None took any action, except one. This loosed energy bolts that burned out the little tree containing the forty survivors of *homo sapiens*.

The other sentients, the cat-men, dog-men, leopard-men, bear-men, elephant-men, were not harmed. Apparently, whoever was operating the teardrops—unless these were themselves living entities—wanted to exterminate only *homo sapiens*.

The bat-men were a modified form of *homo sapiens*, and these too had been killed off.

But when the teardrops left, the bat-men came out of hiding.

Neshgai slaves and the Vroomaw were not human. They had descended from mutated monkeys. This explained why they were not bothered by the teardrops.

He continued to drift across the face of the Earth. Time slipped by, or he slipped by time. Each great land mass now had only one tree. The trees had evolved and those on a land-mass met and merged and became one. Each grew and grew. The sentients, one by one, went to live on its surface. The time would come when The Tree would spread across the continent. Only the coastal regions would be free, because salt water inhibited its growth. But The Tree could evolve to overcome this inhibition and would. And then each continental Tree would merge into the other surrendering its individuality through some vegetable mechanism that Ulysses did not understand. It would have one brain, one identity, one body. And it would be the master of the planet. Forever and forever. Amen.

Unless the Neshgai and the stone god could defeat it.

He seemed to step backward out of the disk—a reluctant Alice, he thought.

Afterward, talking to the high priest, he formulated his own theory about the Book of Tiznak. Kuushmurzh had a theological explanation for the strange things that occurred to the readers of the Book. Nesh dictated its contents according to what he thought each reader should find in the Book. But the high priest admitted that his explanation could be wrong. It was not dogma.

Ulysses thought that whoever had made the disk had put into it a recording of the past. This recording probably was not made when the events it depicted occurred. The peculiarity of the Book—one of them—was that it contained what Ulysses could only describe as "resonant points." That is, the individual demands of each Reader brought out in the Book that which interested the Reader. It was the same as picking out a book on a certain historical subject in a library. The Book, working through mental means, detected what the Reader wanted to know and then furnished the information in its fashion.

"That may well be true," the high priest said. He looked with dark blue eyes from under the triple-horned hat at Ulysses. "Your explanation may well fit the facts and yet not conflict at all with the official explanation that Nesh dictated the contents. After all, whoever made the disk did so because Nesh required him to do so."

Ulysses bowed. There was no sense in arguing against this.

"Do you now understand that The Tree is a sentient entity and is our enemy?" Kuushmurzh said.

"The Book told me that that is so."

The high priest smiled and said, "But you do not necessarily believe the Book?"

Ulysses thought it best not to answer. He could have said that much of the Book's contents were true, but that the disk was made by sentients, and any creature of flesh and blood could make mistakes or be in error. But the high priest would only reply that the disk could not be wrong, since Nesh had dictated its contents, and Nesh, the only god, could make neither mistake nor error.

When he returned to the airfield, he had changed his attitude toward Thebi. She was no longer the potential mother of his children. He doubted very much that she or any slave or Vroomaw could conceive by him. Though she looked like a slightly altered form of *homo sapiens*, she probably had a different chromosomal makeup. She would be barren as long as he was her only mate. Enough time had gone by that she had proved that.

Of course, it was possible that she was sterile no matter who her mate was. But Lusha had been with him long enough to conceive, too. Again, it was possible that she, too, was sterile. Or that both women, unknown to him, were secretly using methods of birth control. This did not seem likely, since he had never heard of such among any peoples he had encountered. Fertility was as revered now as in the first paleolithic age of Earth.

During the months that followed his first visit to the temple of Nesh, he found some time to make other visits. Though he was not allowed to read the Book of Tiznak again, he could explore the underground city, or museum, as he thought of it. He found many things the purpose of which he figured out, though many were useless because he did not know how to power them. He did find a device which had not evolved so far from those he knew in his time as to be unrecognizable. He took tissue slides of his skin and of a number of slave women and put them in the matcher. The tissues of the slave women turned scarlet when placed next to his. He could not breed with them.

That was that. He pushed aside the device with a feeling of disappointment. Yet, somewhere in him, was a tickling of elation.

He put the faint good feeling aside. It had to go. If he let it build up into something strong, he would then have to suffer guilt.

But why should he? he told himself. He could not help it that he could not be the father of a new breed of humanity. Nor was it vital that Earth know mankind again. Mankind had almost destroyed the Earth. The flying teardrops had made a point of exterminating *homo sapiens* but had left the other sapient beings alone. Not that they were any less evil potentially. But they had not done anything evil to Earth as of then, and so they had been spared.

Why should he generate his pernicious and destructive breed again?

No reason at all. But he did feel guilty because he was unable to.

He also felt guilty because he preferred Awina to Thebi or any of Thebi's kind.

This explained why he kept Thebi on as his personal servant and then added another human slave. He still called them human, which, in a way, they were. This was a golden-skinned, green-eyed girl called Phanus. She was as bald as any, but her chin was less jutting and her features were very pleasing.

Awina said nothing when Phanus reported to his office. She gave Ulysses a sidelong glance that told him much and made him feel guilty about his treatent of her. To compensate, he put the two women under the immediate supervision of Awina. He might have known that this would make their life, if not a hell, extremely unpleasant at times. But he was too busy with his air force to notice such things for a long time.

The time came, at last, when the first dirigible was finished. The great silvery craft had twelve powerful motors in six nacelles and could carry many men or many bombs or a compromise load of the two. By then, at Ulysses' repeated demands, the quarrel between the navy and the army had been settled. Both had claimed that the aircraft and personnel should come under their jurisdiction. The result was that Ulysses was hampered in getting material, personnel or decisions. Finally, he stormed into the office of the Grand Vizier and demanded that a separate branch be created. Right then and there. Otherwise, there would be so many delays, the enemy would have time to organize another attack. And this would be a full-scale invasion, not a raid.

Shegnif agreed, and made Ulysses the admiral of the fleet, though not head of the air force. He gave this position to his nephew, Graushpaz. Ulysses detested him, but he could do nothing about him. Then his investigation into the cost of the supplies he had been getting, and the inferior quality of much of it, exploded in everybody's face. Shegnif tried to repress the findings of Ulysses' investigators, but Ulysses got the report to the ruler, Zhigbruwzh.

Graushpaz, the nephew, had been selling the air force the inferior goods.

Moreover, a human officer got the courage to come to Ulysses and tell him that the humans in the air force were about to riot because of the bad food they had been getting. Graushpaz had been selling the food to the air force.

Ulysses agreed to plead for the nephew if there would be no more profiteering and delays.

Shegnif agreed, but he did insist that Graushpaz be kept as head of the air force. Otherwise, Graushpaz would have to commit suicide, and he, Shegnif, would be disgraced.

"Everybody knows that he's guilty!" Ulysses said. "Why isn't he disgraced?"

"Everybody knows, true," Shegnif said. "But unless he is publicly disgraced, he does not have to kill himself."

"I won't put up with any more of his crooked deals," Ulysses said. "And I insist that he not come with us when we go after the Dhulhulikh!"

"He has to go with you," Shegnif said. "That is the only way he can redeem himself. He must do something outstanding in war to make up for being caught."

Ulysses gave up on that issue. Later, he smiled wryly about it. The sin was in being caught. The elephantine Neshgai were not too much different than humankind.

He did not smile when Shegnif continued his policy of overloading the dirigibles with Neshgai officers. Despite Ulysses' high standing with the ruler and the high priest, he was not entirely trusted by the Grand Vizier. His attitude was understandable in view of the revolt that had occurred ten days before in a border town. The Vroomaw soldiers had refused to obey orders that they live in the slave barricades. Apparently, they felt that it was a disgrace to be quartered with slaves. When the Neshgai moved in other troops to deal with them, the new troops had sided with the rebels. Neshgai soldiers had been brought in, and there had been a battle. The slaves had taken advantage of this to massacre some of their Neshgai masters. Eventually, the Neshgai had called in more of their ponderous forces and had crushed the revolt.

News of this had spread to the entire human population. There was so much tension, and so many precautions by the Neshgai in the capital, that Ulysses' work was seriously delayed.

Then the situation eased for him when an army of about three hundred bat-men made a raid on the airfield. This time they were detected by the scouts Ulysses had stationed on the edge of The Tree. He had a chance to send up five of his dirigibles with their load of archers, ballista men and hawks. The hawks got their first taste of blood, and the air force found out how much good its training and discipline had done it. They suffered some casualities, but all ships returned. The bat-men, after suffering heavy casualties, flew away.

Ulysses' credit went up even higher. The main effect of the raid, however, was to cause the humans to realize that they must fight on the side of the Neshgai, not against them, for the time being. The bat-men had dropped messages to the effect that they intended to exterminate both Neshgai and their human allies.

It was a cool dawn with a clear sky and a six-mph breeze from the sea when the first of the ten dirigibles rose

156

into the air. The flagship, the *Veezhgwaph* (Blue Spirit), was four hundred and thirty feet long and had a diameter of sixty feet. Its skin was silver, and on its bow a hideous demon was painted in blue. The control gondola was suspended underneath the bow, and three motor nacelles hung from each side. Its hollow interior contained a skeleton made of very lightweight vegetable husks stitched together, the keel, main walkway, catwalks, storage cells and ten gigantic gas ballonets. On its top were four cockpits with archers, catapult men, rocketeers and hawk trainers. Along each side, at the midline, were blisters in which sat catapult and rocket men. Other openings gave access to arrows and bombs to be shot out, and to hawks. The tail structures contained several cockpits and there were openings along the bottom of the dirigible behind which were more projectile men and bird handlers.

There were also bomb hatches and hatches for releasing anchors and grappling hooks.

Ulysses stood on the bridge, the lower deck of the control gondola, behind the helmsman. The radiomen, the navigators, the officers responsible for relaying orders from various parts of the ship, and several archers were also in the gondola. If there were not so many Neshgai, Ulysses thought sourly, they would have had more room on the bridge.

He walked through the crowd to the rear of the gondola and looked out. The other ships were behind him but drawing up swiftly. The last was only a round glitter in the blue, but it would catch up within an hour, and they would then proceed in formation.

The beauty of the great ships of the air, and the idea that they were his creation, made his breast ache. He was very proud of them, even if he knew that they were now more vulnerable than he had originally thought. The batmen could fly above the dirigibles and drop bombs on them. They would not be able to do that, however, until he went down to a lower altitude. The ships were climbing now and would not stop until they reached thirteen thousand feet. The air was too thin here for the bat-men to fly. They would not be able to get close to the dirigibles until these descended over their target.

Their goal was the approximate center of The Tree, if they could believe their informants. Pain was a great destroyer of lies, and the bat-men taken prisoners on the first and the second raids had been subjected to as much pain as their frail bodies could withstand. Two had held out until they died, but the others had finally told what they

157

swore was the truth. Their stories agreed, which still did not mean that they were true.

The bat-men who could still talk were being taken along so that they could identify tree marks and, finally, the base-city.

Below, The Tree was a horizon-spanning tangle, a criss-cross of gray branches and sun flashing off the waterways on their branches here and there, and vivid colors of the trees and bushes which grew on The Tree. Once, a pale pink cloud rose from a dense green jungle. It was an immense flock of birds leaving the vine complex between two mighty branches. The pink cloud passed between a number of trunks and then settled down and was hidden inside another vine coplex.

Ulysses turned in time to see Awina come down the ladder from the upper deck of the gondola. She was beautiful when just resting, as beautiful as a sealpoint Siamese in repose. But when she was moving, she was as pleasing to the eye as the wind would be if it could be seen. Now that Thebi and Phanus were not with them and she was the only one to attend to the Lord's personal needs, she was all grin and purr. He had thought of asking her to stay behind but had decided not to. She knew that their chances for coming back were about twenty to eighty, if that good. She would be hurt if he asked her to stay behind. And there was a good strong possibility that she would brood until she exploded against the two women, since she would blame them.

She wore the goggles which Ulysses had ordered made as part of the air force uniform. They would not be needed very often, if at all, but he liked them. They gave a distinct flair to the men who rode the ships of the sky, and they also gave him a pleasurable nostalgic twinge when he saw them. He had been a World War I aviation buff.

A leather chain with a bright blue symbol in the form of the Maltese cross at its end hung around Awina's neck. A belt with a stone knife was around her waist. That completed her uniform.

She looked at him to make sure that she would not be interrupting him in anything and she said, "My Lord, this is much better than climbing up and down The Tree and riding rafts among the snoligosters and the hipporats!"

He smiled and said, "That is true. But do not forget that we may have to go on foot on the way home."

And consider ourselves lucky to be able to do that, he thought.

158

Awina moved closer until her hip was brushing him and then the side of her shoulder came into contact with his arm. The tip of her tail twitched across the back of his calves now and then. There was too much noise in the gondola for him to hear her purring, and she was not close enough for him to feel it. But he believed that she was purring.

He moved away. He had no time to think about her. Captaining ten ships was a full-time job. The officers and crews had had as much training as he could give them in the little time allowed. But they were not veterans.

So far, things had run smoothly enough. At this altitude, they had a tail wind which was upping their ground speed to fifty miles an hour. This meant that they could not return at this height; they would have been moving backward while their motors strained to go full speed. But now they could reach their target in eight hours instead of the sixteen it would have taken if the air had been still. He would let the motors rest for several hours and be pushed by the wind, so that would bring them to the Dhulhulikh city about two hours before nightfall. That would be enough time for what he had in mind.

The Tree scudded under them like a great gray-and-green cloud. Occasionally, there was a space where the branches did not cross, and he could almost see to the bottom of the abyss. What a colossal being! The world had never known its like. Not in all the four billion years of its existence. Not until about, he estimated, the last twenty thousand years. And here it was: The Tree. It seemed a shame, a tragedy, rather, to destroy such a creature.

Then he caught himself. Who was going to destroy it? How?

Now and then, he saw tiny big-winged figures that had to be Dhulhulikh. They knew that the ships of the stone god and the Neshgai were flying toward their city. Even if he had not seen any, he would have taken it for granted that there were leathery-winged pygmies hidden in the foliage, observing the ten silver needles above them. Nor did they have to send couriers. They would long ago have transmitted messages via the pulse-diaphragms and nerve cables of The Tree itself.

He supposed that they had been aware for a long long time that the ships were destined for their base-city. They had enough spies, and they doubtless had bribed slaves and perhaps even some Neshgai to spy for them. Corruption and treachery seemed to be inherent with sentiency. Humans had not had a monopoly on these.

Awina pressed up against him again, and he lost his sequence of thought.

The hours passed, eased by the demands of commanding the fleet. Below, the scene changed only slightly. There was some variety in the unity, but only in the slightly differing directions the branches took, in the varying configurations of vine-complexes, the lesser or taller heights of the trunks, and an occasional cloud of birds: pink, green, scarlet, purple, orange, yellow, that sped between the trunks and over the branches.

The sun reached its zenith, and Ulysses ordered the speed reduced to the point where there was just enough power to keep the dirigibles from losing head. It was comparatively silent then in the gondola, except for the soft voices of the petty officers talking into the radio boxes, the shuffle of a Neshgai's huge feet or squeak of air through his trunk, a Neshgai stomach rumbling, a cough from a man. There was a steady creaking sound: the movement of the tough husks holding the gondola to the main framework.

The sun went down toward the horizon, and Ulysses ordered their chief Dhulhulikh prisoner brought down. This was Kstuuvh, a scarred little man whose hands were tied behind him and whose wings were threaded together. Some of the fire that his skin had felt was reflected as heat in his eyes.

"We should be in sight of the city," Ulysses said. "Point it out to me."

Kstuuvh snarled, "With my hands tied?"

"Nod when I point to the right place," Ulysses said.

Most of the trunks reached to ten thousand feet, where they seemed to explode in a mushroom of green. About ten miles ahead of them was a trunk that reached almost to thirteen thousand feet. This should hold the city of the Dhulhulikh, somewhere down there on a number of branches and inside the trunk and the branches themselves. From here, nothing could be seen except The Tree itself. The bat-men would, of course, be hiding until the last moment.

Ulysses said, "That great trunk marks the city?"

"I do not know," Kstuuvh said.

Graushpaz placed the fingers of his giant hand around the skinny neck of the bat-man and squeezed. Kstuuvh's face turned blue, his eyes bulged and his tongue shot out.

The Neshgai released his hold. The Dhulhulikh coughed and gagged, and then said, "I do not know."

Ulysses admired him for making another stand, even though he knew what agony would be inflicted on him. He said, "If we don't get it out of you, we have more of your kind who are not so stubborn."

"Use fire on me again", Kstuuvh said.

Ulysses smiled. The bat-men knew by now how flammable the hydrogen was and how many precautions had been taken during the voyage to prevent sparks and fire.

"A needle will do as well," he said. But he paid no more attention to the little man except to have him taken to the upper deck. Too many bat-men, including Kstuuvh, had described this treemark while under torture.

He issued the orders that would place them in bombing formation, in an Indian file. They began to lower, and then the battle-stations order went through the radio boxes of the fleet. The flagship was down to ten thousand feet by the time it had reached the great trunk. It was still out of reach of the bat-men, who could not fly any higher than nine thousand feet and that only without any excess weight.

The *Blue Spirit* went past the mushroom top of the trunk on the starboard side. Some mauve-and-red, huge-winged, small-bodied birds and some thickly furred otter-like creatures stared at the silver goliath as it slid by.

Several miles past the top of the trunk, the flagship made a three hundred and sixty-degree turn on the port side and came past the trunk at nine thousand feet above ground level. It moved at a ground speed of ten miles an hour against the wind, which had dropped to fifteen miles an hour. There was still no sign of the Dhulhulikh below, though there was plenty of evidence of other life. A V-shaped flight of thousands of black-winged, green-bodied, yellow-headed flying mammals rose up toward them, veered and then swooped down into the foliage miles away.

The city was well hidden. The observers on the ships could see nothing but the usual jungle and the waterways.

Yet the Dhulhulikh, under torture, had said that there must be thirty-five thousand living beings there. They had sworn that six thousand and five hundred warriors could swarm up from The Tree to defend the city.

The flagship continued to sink and then, carried toward the trunk by the wind piling against its massive broadside, it moved over a branch five hundred feet below.

Ulysses said, "Bombardiers, fire when ready!"

He glanced at his port. The trunk seemed to be rushing toward them so swiftly that he had to repress a desire to order the ship to turn away. He had made his calculations, and they should be past the trunk by a hundred yards before the wind took them northward.

The bomb hatches had been opened, and the bombardiers, all humans, waited until their sights were on the target.

Ulysses waited. Graushpaz, behind him, shifted. His stomach rumbled, and his proboscis, waving nervously, touched Ulysses' shoulder with its two wet tendrils. Ulysses shuddered.

"Bombs away," the bombardier reported. The ship immediately lifted as the weight fell out. Ulysses looked out of the side port. The dark teardrops were still falling. Some missed the branch and continued on to the one below it. About ten struck. Fire gouted up, and great chunks of wood came flying through the fire and the black smoke. There were sections of the smaller trees that grew on The Tree, and some things that could have been small bodies. But whether they were animals or winged men could not be determined.

The two ships behind them also dropped their load and at once danced upward with relief. Enough of their bombs struck at the same place as the first load to dig huge holes into the branch. But the limb was a long way from being weakened enough to break off. Besides, even if it was severed, it would not fall. There were too many vertical branches growing beneath it. It was possible that it would have remained suspended if all its vertical growths had been taken away. The vine complexes linking it to other branches and to trunks might have held it up. However, the chunks blasted out had opened the way for the riverlet, which now spilled out and over the sides, down the trunk and on to a branch about three hundred feet below it.

Ulysses had known that the entire fire-bomb power of the fleet would be required to sever a branch. He was not after that. He only wished to shake out the hidden Dhulhulikh. Once he knew where they were hidden, he would attack those places.

The big dirigible made a wide circle around the trunk and entered into the pattern just after the final ship of the ten had released its bombs. This time, he gave the orders that dipped the nose of the craft and sent it under the blasted branch. The men in the cockpits on top of the vessel reported that the water from the riverlet was falling down on them. And then the ship had passed under and there was, a moment later, a number of explosions as bombs struck the branch beneath the ship. Some of these were composed of jellied alcohol and burned furiously, sending up a huge cloud of smoke.

There was still no sign of the Dhulhulikh.

Ulysses gave the order to save the bombs for a while. He took the flagship around again, this time flying it even lower, though at a greater distance from the trunk. The wind was much reduced here, and so the airship could maneuver with more safety. But even so the distance between the two branches through which the *Blue Spirit* slid was only two hundred feet. No bombs were released. Ulysses did not want the ship to lift up and possibly rub against the upper branch.

At this point, the air was alive with birds. The explosions and the great droning vessels had scared out all the animal life for miles around. A number of the birds hit the propellors, and blood was splattered over the sides of the ship in the immediate neighborhood. Other birds rammed into the skin of the ship or into the glass of the control gondola ports.

Ulysses was too intent on the steering of the ship to inspect the intensely convoluted and wrinkled surface of The Tree for opening to the city. But as the ship began to turn in a relatively wide space between trunks, he heard Awina gasp.

"There's an opening!" she said.

"Steady as she goes," he told the steersman.

Under the branch ahead was a cavernous hole. It was oval and about a hundred feet across. Shadowed by the branch, its dark interior seemed empty. But Ulysses was sure that there must be many bat-men crowded into it. They would be waiting, until they were sure that the entrance had been detected, and then they would act. Or their commander might decide it would be better to take the offensive.

Graushpaz said, "There's another hole!"

He pointed at a dark oval under a branch in the trunk on their right.

The ship would be passing between the two holes, which meant that it could be attacked from both sides simultaneously.

Ulysses had this information transmitted to the other ships and then ordered them not to follow the flagship but to rise and circle. He was taking a chance by bringing his vessel to a place where the bat-men could get above him. They had bombs now, and it would only take one to blast a hole in the thin skin and another through the hole to turn the *Blue Spirit* into a burning, falling wreck.

He spoke again into the radio box to the rocketeers stationed on the blisters on the sides of the craft and in the cockpits on top. A minute later, as the airship slid by the holes at ten miles per hour, dark objects spurting flame and smoke soared toward the holes from the dirigible. Several struck outside the entrances, but five went into one and three into another. Each had a warhead of ten pounds of plastic explosive and one pound of black gunpowder and a detonating cap of picric acid.

Flames and black smoke belched out of the mouths of the entrances. Bodies came flying out, and then the ship had passed the holes. A moment later, winged men jumped out of the holes, fell, began flapping and then tried to catch up with the dirigible. They continued to stream out incessantly.

At the same time, the Dhulhulikh appeared from holes previously unseen, and the vine complexes yielded hundreds of bat-men.

The second volley of rockets hit the nearest holes again and caught many within them. A dirigible, flying over a gigantic vine complex, dropped time bombs at the junction of the complex and a branch. These tore loose the moorings on one side, causing the tangle to drop to a vertical position. At least a thousand bodies fell from the vines, although most of these began to fly back up. A majority of these were women and children.

Awina pulled at Ulysses' arm and pointed to the starboard at a downward angle. "There!" she said. "There! Under the third branch down! There is an immense hole!"

Ulysses saw it, too, just before the ship's passage took the hole away around the curve of the trunk. This hole was triangular and looked as if it were a hundred yards across. Out of it, in unending files, stepped forty bat-men abreast. They marched in strict parade step, sprang together off the edge of the hole, fell, raised and lowered their wings, checked their fall, and then began climbing upward. They did not attempt to catch the dirigible, as the others had done, but flew upward as if toward a rendezvous.

Probably they were intent on getting as high as they could and would then form to attack.

Ulysses gave the order to put the dirigibles in battle formation at some distance above the height attainable by the

Dhulhulikh. This maneuver took fifteen minutes. The ships had to gain altitude and at the same time make a circle which would bring them all together and facing the opposite way. Then, the flagship half a length in the lead, the fleet proceeded against the cloud of bat-men flying around and around the trunk just below the base of the mushroom-shaped top.

Ulysses intended to attack the city directly afterward, but it would be necessary to deal with the fliers first.

Many of them had bombs. The bat-men had gone to the Wufea village and there learned how to make powder from the Wufea, who had not suspected that the bat-men were now their enemies. Ulysses had learned that in the beginning of the torture of the Dhulhulikh by the Neshgai.

As far as he could tell, the winged men knew nothing about rockets. He hoped that this was true. The dirigibles were very vulnerable to rockets.

Also, it did not seem likely that the Dhulhulikh would have a large supply of bombs. Sulfur surely was not available anywhere in The Tree. They would have to get it from the south coast or the far north. He was hoping that there would not be any bombs left inside the rooms in The Tree. If every bomb available was being carried by the winged defenders, then they would be expended when the carriers were expended. At that moment, the forces of the Dhulhulikh looked inexhaustible. There were sections of the sky which were black with them. Perhaps the estimate of the prisoners that there were sixty-five hundred warriors in the city was true.

The fleet and the massed winged men flew toward each other. The ships were just below the extreme height attainable by the Dhulhulikh, but before the first bat-men reached the ships, the ships rose, and then they were over the bat-men. Ulysses gave the order, and rockets with impact fuses soared out from the hatches in the bottom of the ships. They burst among the clouds of men, and tiny pieces of rock—shrapnel—struck the winged men.

Rocket after rocket flew out, but the ships did not exhaust their supply. They needed some for the landing—if they would be able to land.

Hundreds of bat-men were put out of action by the blasts and the shrapnel. They fell, their wings fluttering, and struck the branches or the vine complexes or dropped into the dark abyss of the lower part of The Tree. Many struck those below them and knocked them out or broke their wings, and these, in turn, fell into others below them.

The ships passed on at full speed and left the hordes behind them. They circled and came back again with the bat-men flapping desperately to get on a level with them. This time, however, they had put much space between the warriors to lessen the effects of the rocket blasts. Despite this, they lost several hundred.

The fleet left them behind, turned around and passed over. Now the rockets were spared, and a few bombs were tossed out from the bottom hatches or catapulted from the side domes. By then, about an hour of sunshine was left. The lower part of The Tree was already in night.

For the third time, the fleet came around, and now the noses of the ships dipped, and they slid down an incline of air. The Dhulhulikh commanders saw that the ships would pass under them. Doubtless, they wondered what madness had struck the invaders, but they intended to take advantage of it. They continued to fly around in descending and then ascending spirals, taking one spiral past the other to avoid collisions, the whole army presenting a seeming confusion of corkscrew formations narrowly missing each other, moving back and forth.

The flagship continued to lower and then, shortly before it reached the first of the defenders, it rose. When it plowed into the front of the mass, it was on an approximate level with the highest of them. None of the bat-men were able to get above it.

But they were even with it, and they closed around it like a net.

Rockets burst among the winged men. Bombs, thrown by catapults, exploded among them. The air was filled with puffs of smoke, charging and falling bodies. A moment later, the flagship released part of its hawks. The birds flashed out from the hatches on every side and threw themselves into the faces of the nearest bat-men.

Four of the ships were with the flagship, and these had loosed a quarter of their hawks. The other five ships had continued descending, and such was the havoc caused by the explosives and the hawks, no Dhulhulikh bothered them.

Their motors going full speed, the five dirigibles passed the trunks in a circling movement and sped more rockets into the holes. Their heaviest concentration was on the huge hole, and a rocket must have struck a supply of bombs to judge from the series of explosions. The edges of the hole were ripped apart, and when the smoke had cleared, a gaping wound was revealed in the side of the trunk.

Ulysses grinned at this and then lost his grin. The last one in line of the five ships had burst into flames!

Suddenly, the ship was falling, its skeleton revealed through the burned away skin, and little bodies were dropping from the gondola and the hatches as the men jumped rather than burn to death.

White with the heat of burning hydrogen, the wreck crashed across a branch three hundred feet below the hole and there burned fiercely. The trees and vegetation growing on the branch caught on fire, and the fire spread along the branch. Through the smoke poured hundreds of females and children, forced out of a previously unseen hole. Many fell into the abyss, perhaps because they were overcome by the smoke.

Graushpaz had turned blue under his gray skin on seeing the holocaust. But it was he who first saw the hole above a branch. All the others had been below it, and this had frustrated Ulysses' intentions of landing troops. He needed a place where he could bring the dirigible down just before a hole and grapple the craft to the branch to discharge troops.

However, the air had to be cleared first.

He radioed orders, and the four survivors lifted and then began to swing around. The other five turned, and presently the two halves were moving toward each other. Ulysses spent a few minutes making sure that they were on courses which would not end in collision, and then he bent his efforts to the defense. His flight was still at a level with the upper echelons of the bat-men. These had restored enough order in their ranks to make formations which now attacked en masse. The hawks had either been killed or chased away, though at the cost of heavy casualties.

Now the second fourth of the birds was released. The hawks caused chaos and broke up the front ranks, but enough bat-men got through to the dirigibles. These were met by arrow fire, since the bombs could not be exploded too close to the ships. The bat-men were not inhibited by this, however, and they lit the fuses of their little bombs and lobbed them at the skin of the ships or the gun domes. Some actually struck the skin of the flagship and blew big holes in it. But none reached the big gas cells inside, and the leakage of hydrogen was so little that there was none in the effective range of the bombs.

The ships of each segment were close enough to each other to provide some crossfire of arrows and bolts. Warriors fell into the depths with arrows sticking from them,

167

and many of these had not yet thrown their bombs. Ulysses saw a bomb explode while in the hands of a Dhulhulikh just hit by a crossbow bolt. The bomb blew him apart and sent two others spinning.

He gave the order to lift and increase speed. The winged men fell below and behind.

"Nesh!" Graushpaz said, and trumpeted. Ulysses turned to see a flaming ship in the other segment. Some bat-man had gotten in with a bomb, and it had set fire to leaking hydrogen or blown a gas cell open.

Slowly, majestically, the vessel fell, breaking in half even as it descended toward The Tree. White and red flames roared from it, and a great plume of black smoke followed it. Men were leaping from it, some of them afire. And many many blackened corpses of winged men fell past it. The ship had been the object of an especially heavy concentration of Dhulhulikh. It was this concentration that had enabled the bat-men to get their bombs to it. But there were so many around it, they died by the hundreds, caught in the blast of heat, skins cooked or their lungs seared.

Those some distance below it were diving away frantically to keep from being caught by the falling wreck. Most would make it, but the air space was so crowded that some could not get past their more fortunate fellows. The former disappeared into the flames and went on down with the vessel, though they may have been ashes before the fire-ravaged skeleton landed crosswise on a branch.

The vegetation growing on the branch burned fiercely. But The Tree itself, though its surface could be damaged by fire, would not burn.

Ulysses reassembled the fleet and put it into a formation that took it down toward the big hole just above a branch. The Dhulhulikh were in disorder, swirling around like gnats over a corpse. They did not seem to be so numerous now. They could have lost a fourth of their strength. That still left about forty-eight hundred, an appalling number against which to pit eight dirigibles.

Again, the ship came over the Dhulhulikh just above their flying range. They shot, not arrows, bombs or rockets, but clouds of smoke which enveloped the winged men. The ships threw a few more bombs from the stern hatches, hoping that the explosions in the midst of the blinding smoke would panic the Dhulhulikh.

The dirigibles turned again and came in lower, again laying down a thick level of smoke. The men in the cockpits on top and the domes on the side reported that a large number of bat-men had flown in out of the smoke and rammed against the ship. A few had struck so hard they had gone through the skin, but these were knocked unconscious or crippled, and the crew seized them, cut their throats, and threw them out through the hatches.

When the ships had left the second and lowest level behind them, they turned again. This time four stayed on the same level to lay another cloud, but the flagship and three others went down under the slowly drifting cloud. The sun was finally setting; in sixty seconds it would be below the horizon.

The *Blue Spirit* plunged into an immense alley of trunks and branches about a thousand feet below the city and several miles south of it. It was so dark there that Ulysses had to turn on the searchlights of the ships. He did not think that the bat-men would see them until too late because they were occupied with the smoke clouds and the other ships. What with the night and the smoke, they would be blind. A few might glimpse the lights, but by the time they realized what they were, they would be too late to take action—he hoped.

He stood behind the helmsman and peered into the white tunnel created by the searchlights. On both sides and above and below were the thousand-feet-wide branches and the mile-wide trunks. The dirigible bored on ahead without the constant rise and fall it had when in air in motion and containing areas of different temperatures. It was headed for a vertical shaft, one free of any extension of The Tree. It was so broad that the dirigible could maneuver in any direction toward its goal, the cavernous entrance just above the branch.

As the ship tilted upward and the branches that had been above fell to both sides, the lights illuminated a swarm of winged people flying into the hole. They seemed to be mostly females and children who had fled when the rockets burst in the holes. Or they could be those who lived in the vine complexes but had decided that it was too dangerous to stay there tonight. Under the cover of darkness, they were going into the hole and thence into the chambers in the trunk and the various branches.

As the lights struck them, some winged on into the hole but the majority wheeled away and into the night.

Ulysses paid no attention to them, though he had ordered that the guncrews and the archers keep a strict watch for warriors with bombs. His attention was concentrated on getting the dirigible to maneuver delicately and directly to a position just before the hole above the branch.

This was a daring move, or, perhaps, as some of the Neshgai had said, "stupid and suicidal."

Slowly, the *Blue Spirit* eased forward. And then, while the nose was still approaching the trunk just above the hole, a rocket streaked from the station on the nose. Its sharp plastic cone-nose drove into the trunk, and then the line attached to it stretched as the dirigible began to back away. Other rockets were fired from bottom hatches, and the lines attached to them were drawn tight. Ulysses had tested the ropes several times under conditions simulated to resemble these, but he still was not sure that the ropes would hold.

Grappling hooks were thrown down and snagged in the wrinkles and the convolutions of the gray bark. Lines were let down, and men and the felines slid down the lines and secured their ends with sharp wooden stakes driven into the bark.

More men and a number of Neshgai followed these down the lines. The loss of their weight caused the ship to rise and put an additional strain on the ropes. But they held. And then the crew had set up winches staked to the bark and were drawing the dirigible down.

Ulysses stepped out of the gondola onto the bark. The others crowded out after him.

At the same time, the men still inside the ship released the hawks. Some flew upward into the smoke, which was thinning out. Though they could not see too well now, they could smell out the enemy they had been trained to attack with claw and beak. Others flew into the hole, evidently having sniffed out the winged people there.

The three dirigibles had gone on by. They would loose their hawks in a minute and then they would anchor on branches nearby. Their task was more difficult than that of the *Blue Spirit* personnel. They would have to climb down the trunk and under the branch to enter the holes there. This would take time and leave them exposed to attack while they were clinging to the side of the trunk. But Ulysses was counting on the darkness, the hawks and the other dirigibles to keep the winged warriors still in the air busy. Moreover, the four ships would be ejecting another smoke cloud.

The entrance was empty except for a few bodies of females and children.

Ulysses put on his wood-and-leather helmet, in the front

of which was a light. It did not furnish much illumination, because its biological battery was weak, but it was better than nothing. Moreover, the combined light of the crew would furnish adequate visibility.

Ulysses placed himself at the head of the column, but Graushpaz touched him on the shoulder. He turned, and the Neshgai said, "I demand my right to redeem myself."

Having expected this, and secretly glad, Ulysses stepped aside. Graushpaz then spoke to the twenty Neshgai officers. It was a short and simple speech.

"I have disgraced myself and so cast disgrace upon you, my fellow officers and my subordinates. You know that. Yet you are not required to redeem yourselves. No one will reproach you if you do not follow me into the nest of the Dhulhulikh. It is likely that we will all die, since we are in the van and will be fighting in narrow caves which the batpeople know well. But the people of our race will hear of what we do today. And Nesh will know of it, and if we acquit ourselves as we should, we shall find homes after death on his tusks."

The officers trumpeted and then arranged themselves behind Graushpaz. They held spears, clubs and stone axes and wore stone knives in their belts. On the left arm of each was a wood-and-leather shield thick enough to withstand any battering from the weapons of the tiny Dhulhulikh.

"Stand back a minute," Ulysses said. "We'll send in a dozen rockets. Then you can go in."

The humans came up then, and the tubemen knelt while their comrades touched off the fuses of the rockets. These sped with a spurt of flame and whoosh of smoke into the great hole. Some must have curved off turning walls, because their explosions were muffled. Ulysses hoped that they caught Dhulhulikh hiding in ambush around the corners. Judging from some of the screams, they had.

The towering Neshgai leader raised his ponderous stone ax, trumpeted shrilly and roared, "For Nesh and our ruler and Shegnif!"

He ran swiftly forward with the twenty giants behind him. Ulysses counted to ten and gave the order for his men to follow him. Behind was Awina and then the Wufea, Wagarondit and Alkunquib. After them came the Vroomaw soldiers. The only ones who did not go into the hole were the bombmen and rocketeers in the cockpits and the side domes. All his party wore quilted armor and faceplates. The Dhulhulikh were forty-pound pygmies, but their tiny arrows carried a deadly poison. One prick, and a six-hundred-pound Neshgai would be dead in ten seconds, a hundred-fifty-pound man in two.

"Follow me!" Ulysses shouted, and walked swiftly into the cavern. It was dark at first, but after the second turn in a tunnel wide enough for two men abreast, he came to the first of the internal chambers. This was lit with hundreds of clusters of some vegetable growths that gave a cold light. The light shone on the bloody and dismembered pieces of females, children and old men. There were also a few bodies the heads of which had been smashed by the stone axes or clubs of the Neshgai.

After this chamber, they entered a large one consisting of a twenty-foot-wide street with four levels of open chambers on each side. Apparently, the chambers were occupied by families. Light was provided by the same vegetable growth, which had spread out vine fashion everywhere. There were more dead and mangled females and children on the street, and some frightened faces peering out of the open doorways of the chambers above.

So far, the evidence indicated that the entire adult male population had swarmed *out* to attack the invaders.

Ulysses made a quick decision. He split his forces into half and left one party at the first turn in the wall. They would hold this if the males tried to reenter while a messenger came after the other half. All the rockets except three were left with the holding party.

If it had not been for the directions of the Dhulhulikh prisoners, they would have been lost. Corridor after corridor, many of them as wide and high as the one they were on, branched out. Looking down these, Ulysses could see other corridors. The trunk—and the branches radiating from it—was honeycombed. There was room for far more than the thirty-five thousand the prisoners had estimated as the population.

They passed chambers where animals were penned up, and others where strange plants grew in the cold light of the vegetable lamps. They saw many more tiny faces of women and children looking from the open doorways. Infrequently, Ulysses halted the party and sent a scout up to inspect the rooms above them. He did not want to be ambushed. Each time, the scout reported that the majority of the rooms were empty.

The party pushed on, and then they came to the section which Ulysses had hoped they would find. There were about forty mangled corpses of Dhulhulikh males here. They had fought bravely but futilely against the giants. Two of these lay dead, their once-gray skins purple. The little archers had sent their arrows under the faceplates into the skin; they must have stood at the feet of the elephantine men and fired upward just before the axes smashed their heads in.

They had been defending a huge chamber which had to be the main center of communication for the Dhulhulikh. Around the walls, on three levels, were at least a hundred huge diaphragms. And there were about fifty more corpses and three more dead Neshgai. The chamber floor was inches deep in blood.

Graushpaz, seeing Ulysses, lifted his trunk and snorted shrilly. He said, "This has been too easy. I do not think I have redeemed myself."

"This is not over yet by a long way," Ulysses said. He stationed guards outside the entrance to the great chamber, and then he approached one of the diaphragms. He reached out and tapped it three times quickly, and the diaphragm vibrated and boomed out three times.

Ulysses had availed himself of the knowledge forced from the bat-men prisoners. Though his time had been so limited while building his ships, he had given up hours of sleep to become proficient in the pulse-code.

Now he tapped on the diaphragm, "This is the stone god in the city of the Dhulhulikh."

He had been told that The Tree was an entity and the Dhulhulikh were its servants. And the Book of Tiznak had told him much the same. But he still could not believe.

"The last of the humans!" the diaphragm vibrated in answer.

Could there be some vast vegetable brain somewhere in this colossal trunk? Or perhaps away off in another trunk, in the deep heart of The Tree itself? Or was there a little pygmy winged man squatting before another diaphragm in a buried chamber? A little man determined to maintain the myth of the thinking Tree?

"Who are you?" Ulysses tapped out.

There was a pause. He looked around. The Neshgai standing in the middle of the dome-shaped chamber were grotesque shadowy figures, their skins purple-bluish in the light. Awina was, as usual, beside him. The white parts of her fur looked icy bluish, and her eyes were so dark they seemed empty holes. The Wagarondit and Alkunquib looked like half-cat, half-burglar surrealist statues. The abacus machines with their squares of upright strings and beads were pale subterranean robots. The bat-men prisoners were hunched together in one corner, their brown skins now black in the light and their faces reflecting the knowledge of their sure death.

Ulysses lifted his hand to signal the men carrying the bombs to come to him. At that moment, the diaphragm vibrated.

"I am Wurutana!"

"The Tree?" Ulysses tapped back.

"The Tree!"

The code for the exclamation mark came through seemingly louder. So the vegetable entity, if it was one, could have emotion, in this case, pride. And why not? It was not possible for sentient life to exist without emotion. Emotion was as natural and as vital for sapiency as intelligence. Those science-fiction stories with unemotional, extraterrestrial sapients were based on an unrealistic premise. A life form needed emotion to survive as much as it needed a thinking mind. No living creature could thrive, or even exist, on logic alone. Not unless it was a protein or vegetable computer and, therefore, not self-conscious.

"I learned about you many thousands of years ago," the diaphragm pulsed.

He wondered how this entity could have any sense of time. Did it sense each year by some subtle internal change responding to the change of seasons? Or did it have some internal clock placed in it by the geneticists who had designed it?

"Those who must die told me about you."

Those who must die. Thus it designated the little forms of mobile life that communicated with it.

"Those who must die can nevertheless kill" Ulysses tapped. He got back the answer he expected.

"They cannot kill me! I am immortal! And invincible!"

"If that is so," Ulysses tapped, "why do you fear me?"

There was another moment of silence. He hoped that the vegetable brain was quivering with shock. It gave him a perverse pleasure to upset the creature, though there was no other profit in it for him.

Finally, the diaphragm boomed, "I do not fear you, one who must die!"

"Then why did you try to have me captured? What had I done to you to warrant your hostility?"

"I wanted to talk to you. You were a strange thing, an anachronism, a species that has been extinct for twenty million years."

174

It was Ulysses' turn to be shocked. So the time was twenty, not ten, million years. Twenty million years!

He told himself that there was no reason to be startled. Twenty million years meant no more than ten.

"How do you know that?" he tapped.

"I was told so by my creators. They put an enormous amount of data into my memory cells."

"Were your creators human?"

The diaphragm did not move for several seconds and then, "Yes."

So this was why, despite its denial, it feared him. Men had created it, and so a man could destroy it. That must be its logic. What it probably did not know was that this man was an ignorant savage in comparison with the creators of The Tree. Still, he was not ineffectual. If he could get the proper metals, he could eventually make an atom bomb. Even The Tree could not stand up to a dozen fission devices.

But what if, as seemed likely, Earth had been stripped of all its metals? Twenty million years of sapient life must have taken everything except traces or deposits left undisturbed because of reasons of economy. There was no iron or copper anywhere. He was certain of that. Man and his successors had long ago plucked all of those out of the earth and squandered them.

However, The Tree must have a center which could be killed, after which the body must die. And it seemed probable that The Tree would have located the Dhulhulikh here to protect that brain. If the brain were in this trunk, then it could be gotten to. It would take an enormous amount of blasting powder and of stone chipping tools, and many many people to do it, but it could be done. And The Tree must know this.

It was also possible that The Tree had placed the Dhulhulikh here as a decoy. The brain could be in a trunk a hundred miles from here. Or in the trunk next door.

He was startled out of his reverie by the booming of the diaphragm.

"There is no reason for us to be enemies! You can live on me with great comfort and security. I can guarantee that none of the sentients who live on me will harm you. Of course, the nonsentients are not under my control any more than fleas on the sentients. But there is no such thing as one hundred percent security for those who must die. Yet the life I can offer them is far better than the life they would have without me."

175

"That may be true," Ulysses replied. "But the peoples who choose to live on you also choose a savage and ignorant and very restricted life. They can know nothing of science or sophisticated art. They can know nothing of progress."

"Progress? What has that ever meant to any sentient life except eventual overpopulation, overkill and the poisoning of earth, air and water? Science has, in the end, meant the abuse of science, the suicide of the race and the near-death of the entire planet before the race killed itself off. This has happened a dozen times at the very least. Why do you think that human beings finally concentrated on biology at the expense of other physical sciences? Why do you think that the tree-cities were originated? Mankind realized that he had to become one with Nature. And he did. For a while. Then his arrogance, or stupidity, or greed, or whatever you call it, got the better of him again. But he was wiped out by the Andromedans, because the Andromedans thought that humanity was a very serious menace to them.

"So other sentients inherited the Earth, the sentients that mankind had created from the lesser beings in his domain. And these began to repeat mankind's mistakes and crimes. Only they were limited in their ability to do harm because mankind had exhausted the stock of most of Earth's minerals.

"I am the only thing that stands between the sentients, those who must die and who are also, as you truthfully said, those who must kill, and the death of life on this planet. I am The Tree, Wurutana. Not the Destroyer, as the Neshgai and Wufea call me, but the Preserver. Without me there would be no life. I keep the sentients in their place, and in so doing I benefit them and benefit all the rest of life, too.

"That is why the Neshgai and you, unless you give in, must die. You would destroy the Earth again if you could. You would not do so intentionally, of course. But you would do it."

The humans had lived in their tree-cities, which were also their reference libraries and their computers. The great vegetables contained cells for storing information and for using this information as the residents required. But then, whether by design or the accident of evolution, the computing vegetable had become a self-conscious intelligent entity. From servant, it had become master. From vegetable, a god.

Ulysses could not deny that most of what it said was
176

true. But he did not believe that it was inevitable that every form of sentient life would become a destroyer of life. Intelligence had to be something besides just a vehicle for advancing the interests of greed.

He tapped, "Call off your servants, the Dhulhulikh, and we will discuss our aims. Perhaps we can arrive at a peaceful understanding. We can then live side by side. There is no reason for us to war against each other."

"Men have always been destroyers!"

Ulysses spoke to Wulka. "Put those bombs by this diaphragm. We'll start work here."

The bombs were stacked against the big disk and abacuses were piled against them. Several fuses were lit, and the entire party retreated from the great room to the next. When the explosion had ceased reverberating through the room, and the smoke had cleared away, they went back into the disk room. The diaphragm was gone. In the center of the area where it had stood was a round whitish fiber about three inches across. This had to be the nerve cable.

"Start digging around it," Ulysses said. "Let's see if it leads downward."

He had taken the precaution of stationing some men with rockets outside the doorway. Since there had been no reaction to the blasting of the diaphragm, it seemed likely that this chamber did not have the defenses that the chambers of the Wuggrud had. Perhaps The Tree had not thought it necessary to grow them here, where there was such a strong force of Dhulhulikh.

He was wrong.

The moment that the chipping at the medium-hard wood around the nerve fiber began, reaction came. Perhaps The Tree had been stunned by the blast and had only just recovered. Perhaps . . . who knew what had caused the delay? Whatever it was, The Tree was fully recovered. The spray of water from a thousand hitherto unseen holes in the walls was enough to knock even the elephantine Neshgai off their feet. Ulysses felt as if a number of clubs swung by giants had hit him. He was hurled sideways and then rolled over and over to fetch up against a pile of squirming kicking bodies at the doorway.

Or at what had been the doorway. There was a thick semi-transparent membrane over it now. It had dropped down from what had been a solid wall.

The water was up to their knees within a minute. They had managed to extricate themselves and to stand up, though it was a fight to maintain their upright positions.

Fortunately, the water rapidly rising around them kept sprays from striking their legs. Nevertheless, standing up, or down on the floor, they would soon drown.

At that moment, the membrane bulged and then fell inward over them. The men on the other side had blown it from the doorway with bombs.

Ulysses pushed aside the heavy glassy-feeling skin, rose from the water, now up to his waist, and then was carried forward as it rushed out through the doorway. He was caught in another tangle of bodies, but the men on the other side pulled them out one by one and helped them to their feet.

Awina, looking like a sick wet cat, got his hand and yelled at him above the roar of the spraying water. "The other exit's closed! By something like a honeycomb!"

He walked toward the other doorway, which was filled up with a mass of pale-yellow, heavily flowing stuff inside which was a whitish, semi-rigid, somewhat flexible stuff in the form of open boxes joined together.

Before he reached the other end of the room, he was smashed into by several sprays from different directions. He was hurled forward, knocked back, turned around, and then battered off his feet. He rolled over and over, banged into Awina's wet and soft body, was carried along, struck the quilted back of Graushpaz, and then was buried under four or five Wufea.

The floor trembled under him. Even with the yells, and the thrashings around in the water already up to their knees, and the roar of escaping water from the tiny apertures in the walls, he could feel the floor shake.

And then the water was running out of the chamber, and he was crawling over a slippery mess of fragmented honeycomb into the corridor.

The respite was brief. Water was hosing out of the walls of the corridor and out of the walls of the open cubicles of the levels along the corridor. Shrieking, winged women and children were hurled from their rooms into the corridor and then washed away. Some fell on the invaders, knocking them down.

The rocket men lost their bazookas and missiles and the bombmen let loose of their bombs. Nobody kept hold of their weapons. They needed their hands to scramble, to shove away other bodies, to protect themselves against the sprays.

Ulysses got down on his hands and knees after being bowled over six times. The water was almost up to his nose, but it kept the sprays from being effective at that level. However, he had crawled along for perhaps fifty yards when he had to stand up. The water had risen too high to crawl. A moment later, it was up to his chest.

By then the corridors were jammed with tangled bodies, Dhulhulikh fighting for survival and corpses floating along, face-down or up, their leathery wings outspread.

The Tree's weapons were effective, but they were not specific. To drown the enemy, it would also drown its allies.

Ulysses hoped The Tree would drop no more membranes or honeycombs. If it did, they were done for. Their explosives were lost somewhere in the water.

He looked around for Awina and, for a moment, thought she was lost or drowned. Then he saw her hanging onto the belt of Graushpaz. The huge Neshgai was wading through the water, which was up to his waist, his arms crossed to protect his face from the buffeting of the sprays. He rocked back and forth but he did not go down, as some of his fellows had. Ulysses could see only six other Neshgai, and only about twelve of his own people and ten humans seemed to be on their feet.

Then he began swimming, stopping to hammer at the little bat-women if they got in his way. He went faster then, since there seemed to be a slight dip to the floor, causing the water to flow outward to the great entrance.

He passed Awina and Graushpaz, and he shouted at her to swim after him. She released her grip and came after him.

The nightmare in the corridors came to an end a minute later. He rammed into the first narrow curving hall, was carried away and around the corner and into the next curve. Abruptly, the water level fell, and he swam out onto the branch and, a few seconds later, was beached like a fish. The water still flowed around him and moved him on gently, but he could rise to his feet.

Hands helped him then. The men from the dirigible had left their stations. He shouted at them to get back to the ship, but they ignored him. They left him to help others being swept out.

Awina was lifted to her feet, and she staggered to him. "My Lord, what shall we do next?"

Graushpaz waded out and stood to one side. Five other Neshgai came out within two minutes. The sixth failed to show.

Ulysses looked upward into the night. The remnants of a large smoke cloud was drifting by.

The sky was clear, and the moon was just coming up. He could not see it because the trunk blocked his view, but he could see the paling of the sky. Way up, a needle shape moved across the blackness and the stars.

He shouted at Bifak, the human who had commanded the ship while the invasion of the trunk was taking place. "Where are the Dhulhulikh warriors?"

"Many apparently rammed into each other in the smoke and fell. And then the hawks got many, and many flew into each other trying to get away from them."

That might account for heavy losses among the bat-men but it would not account for their total disappearance. Where had they gone? And why had they gone?

By then, the water from the big hole had become a trickle. The lights from the dirigible showed a logjam of bodies inside the hole and a detritus of corpses, mostly Dhulhulikh, strewn out from the hole. Bifak said there had been many more bodies, but these had been washed away with the first outflux of waters or else dragged away and thrown over the edge of the branch by the crewmen.

There must be thousands of other corpses inside, Ulysses thought.

He shouted at the survivors. They must get into the *Blue Spirit* immediately and prepare to take off. They could do no more here. Some day, they would return with a much larger fleet and with the men and the materials to blast down through the center of the trunk to the brain of The Tree.

In the gondola, he told the officers to start the lift-off procedures. He ordered the radio operator to check with the other ships and clarify the situation in the air.

One ship had been bombed and caught fire during the invasion of the trunk. It had fallen into the abyss and was probably half-buried in the swamp at the roots of The Tree. The two other dirigibles that had landed were getting ready to lift off also. They had lost all landing parties, the personnel of which had drowned inside the trunk or had been washed out of the holes and fallen to death.

Ulysses looked at the hole in the trunk while the crewmen got ready to cut the lines that held the vessel to the branch. It should be possible to make a substance which could be applied to the walls of the chambers inside the trunk. This would have to be quick-drying and strong enough to resist the spray of water. Perhaps some sort of epoxy glue. And the blasting would proceed from above and below with shuttles of airships bringing in tons of explosives. Maybe that laser-type device in the underground museum beneath the Temple of Nesh could be powered. If so, it might be able to drill holes through the wood, and the blasting would go much more swiftly.

He could get to the brain if he could find it. But if the brain was not in this trunk, then he might as well forget about finding it.

Yet, what about poisoning the entire Tree? Some powerful poison, tons and tons of it, placed in the roots, so that the mighty water circulation system of The Tree would draw the poison into it?

The Tree knew what it was doing when it had tried to capture and then to kill him. He was a man and so a threat to it.

"Ready to sever the lines, sir," the lift-off officer reported.

"Sever the lines!"

There was a twanging noise, and the ship abruptly lifted. It rose swiftly toward the branch five hundred feet overhead and then began to turn as the starboard motors tilted to the horizontal and their propellors began whirling. The ship turned slowly and moved out. The four ships in the air had begun moving down to cover the others. Their searchlights probed the night, falling on the vast gray-black wrinkles and fissures of the trunk and the vegetation-covered surfaces of the branches.

Ulysses stood behind the helmsman and looked over his shoulder into the night. "I wonder where they are," he muttered.

Awina said, "What?"

"The Dhulhulikh. Even if over half were killed, they still have a powerful force. They . . ."

His question was answered. Out of the mountain-sized mushroom-shaped top of the trunk above them fell a horde of batwinged men. They dropped out with wings folded, hundreds at a time, and did not open their wings until they had attained a great speed. They abruptly filled the space between the trunk top and the dirigibles; they looked like a locust plague, so numerous were they.

They had been waiting until all the ships on the branches were leaving and the other ships would have come down to cover them. They were making one final all-out attack to destroy the entire fleet.

Only later did it occur to Ulysses that the winged men should not have been able to hide within the leaves of

181

the mushroom-shaped top. This was thirteen thousand feet high, four thousand feet higher than a bat-man could fly. But the explanation of the impossible was easy. The Dhulhulikh had climbed up the trunk. With their wings flapping to half-lift their forty-five pound bodies, the bat-men had swarmed up the rough side of the trunk at a pace that no other sentient, and very few monkeys, could have equaled.

Briefly, Ulysses wondered if this plan had originated in the brain of the Dhulhulikh commander or if it had come from the vegetable brain housed in the trunk. And he wondered why the ships on the branches had not been attacked when they were in their most vulnerable position and crewed with so few.

Later on, he realized that even if they could have flown above the Blue Spirit, they could have dropped bombs on it. They had no bombs left. Even in the beginning, not more than one bat-man in fifty had had a bomb. There had not been enough time to make and transport a great number from the north. Many had been expended in the first attacks, and the others had been lost, with their carriers, when the smoke clouds were dropped and the hawks released. The Dhulhulikh commander, or The Tree, realizing this, had hidden the winged men in the immense trunk top while the smoke cloud was thick enough. The commander had bet that the ships too high to be reached would come down to protect the three on the branches, and he had won that bet.

The difficulty in defending the dirigibles rising up from the branches was the lack of personnel. Most of the crew and the soldiers had been killed inside The Tree. And so, though the three men in the cockpits and in the side domes and the archers behind the openings fought well, they were overwhelmed. Within a few minutes, the three ships were covered with little winged forms, like bugs newly crawled out of a vast egg.

To get the ship up faster, Ulysses had tilted the motor gondolas so that the propellors pointed upward. The ship rose swiftly toward the height at which the winged men could no longer fly. But that would do no good if they ripped open the big gas cells inside the fuselage. The ship would just fall to a height where they could fly again.

The four ships above them, fully crewed and armed with a good many bombs, rockets and arrows yet, had resisted more successfully. The explosives had shattered the first few ranks and, at the same time, the three craft were expelling the last of their smoke clouds. The bat-men kept on coming, but the airships were now going at thirty-five mph and when the attackers did reach the ships, they either bounced off the skin or hit it so hard they went through. Those who penetrated the skin tore off their wings or broke their fragile bones. Within a few minutes, the Dhulhulikh were lost in another cloud. They had also lost their chance to get the four upper ships.

The three lower ones, however, were heavy with the winged men. These, after killing the bomb and rocket crews and archers, swarmed through the openings into the interior. Here, for a time, they did not know what to do or where to go, since the captains of the ships had turned off all the interior lights as soon as they realized their situation. And, though weighted down, the ships slowly continued to rise, aided by the upward-tilted motors.

The Dhulhulikh, after blundering around on the catwalks and girders, and sometimes falling, finally located the main walkway and then the hatch to the control deck. This had been locked, but while some bat-men used tools they had picked up to batter at the hatch, others knocked out more holes in the skin. They let themselves out and dropped down, flapping, and then tried for the gondola. Those who had come out behind the gondola did not make it, because the ship was going too fast. Those who let themselves out of a hole in the nose were able to attach themselves to the gondola. They beat in vain at the plastic transparent ports with their stone knives. Then Ulysses ordered the ports raised, and the winged men were stabbed and fell off into the night.

The hatch to the gondola gave way with a screech. Yelling, the little bat-men poured down the ladder and were skewered, sometimes two in a row, by crossbolts. Graushpaz then ordered the bowmen to step aside, and he and another Neshgai advanced up the ladder, their great stone axes swinging. The pygmies were crushed beneath the heavy stones. Graushpaz, the light shining from the top of his helmet, went ponderously up the ladder and onto the main walkway. The other Neshgai followed him.

Ulysses, even on the lower deck of the gondola, could hear the screams of the bat-men and the trumpetings of the Neshgai. And then, on his right, the darkness became an eye-searing flame as a dirigible exploded. Fire wrapped it around within two seconds, and the airship began to fall at once. A few figures leaped from it, mostly humans and one large Neshgai figure from the control gondola. The

183

majority of the winged men aboard had been caught inside the fuselage. Nobody would ever know what had happened. Perhaps the Dhulhulikh had set off a rocket or lit a match too close to a hydrogen leak. Or, more likely, the captain, realizing his ship was doomed, had set fire to it, incinerating several hundred Dhulhulikh along with himself and his crew.

Ulysses had groaned when he saw the ship burst into flames. Now he yelled, because the other ship was headed toward the falling craft. If it did not quickly turn, it would ram broadside into the other or be caught on its nose by the burning craft.

"Turn, you fool!" he yelled. "Turn!"

But the airship proceeded in a stately manner toward a fiery collision.

A moment later, hundreds of bodies left it. They poured out of the cockpits, the domes and the holes that had been torn in the skin by bat-men who had struck it. They fell with wings half-folded and then, out of harm's way, spread their wings out.

As the Dhulhulikh left, and the weight passed, the ship lifted and quickly was above the flaming wreck. Ulysses smiled, realizing that the captain had deliberately set his ship on a collision course. He and his crew would all be killed anyway by the Dhulhulikh, so he had tried to ram the other ship. But he had not really wished to do so. He must have been hoping for just what did happen. The terrified bat-men had deserted the ship and so allowed him to escape.

The *Blue Spirit*, however, was in grave danger. It was so burdened down that it could rise no higher. And the Neshgai, though they might be waging a homeric battle, would inevitably be overcome by sheer numbers. They had been able to keep fighting so far only because the pygmies were not carrying bows and poisoned arrows. Within a few minutes, the survivors would be charging down the ladder again.

Ulysses said, to the helmsman, "Tie the wheel down. But keep the motors turned vertically. And then fall in with the others."

The helmsman did not ask why he should leave his post. But he was aware that every man was needed.

Ulysses, standing on the upper deck, his feet soaked in the blood of Dhulhulikh, counted his "men." He had three Wufea, two Wagarondit and one Alkunquib. One of the Wufea was Awina, but she would be a deadly fighter against

184

the tiny bat-men. These were all that were left of the two hundred who had set out with him to enter The Tree on its northern side. And he had six Vroomaw "humans."

"We have one chance," he said. "Kill or drive out every Dhulhulikh. Follow me!"

He went up the steps with a flint-tipped club in one hand and the other on the guide rail of the ladder to keep from slipping in the blood. He wore his full armor still, and the light on top of his helmet was on. But this was for emergency only, because he had turned the lights back on when the Neshgai charged into the fuselage.

No one opposed him at first. The Dhulhulikh were too concentrated on the Neshgai even to see him. They swarmed about the sole Neshgai on his feet, hopping on the main walkway before and in back of him and fluttering down from girders to lash out at the giant as they went by. The way was strewn with mangled corpses, and on both sides torn and crushed bodies lay on the skin.

Ulysses ran as swiftly as he dared, stepping over the bodies, until he got to the fight. He smashed in three skulls and broke the bones of two pairs of wings before the little men even knew that help had come for Graushpaz. The Neshgai, trumpeting, summoned new strength to smash out anew. His quilted armor and plastic faceplate were splashed with blood, some of which was his own. His trunk had been deeply gashed near the tip, and two-thirds of a short spear stuck out of his back. Some bat-man had dived down from a catwalk near the top of the ship and driven the spear through the armor and halfway into his body.

There were about forty Dhulhulikh still able to fight. They came down on the ten newcomers with maniacal fury, losing many but stabbing all ten. A Wufea, two Wagarondit and three Vroomaw were dead within sixty seconds. But Graushpaz, relieved of the full onslaught, cracked three heads with one sweep of his ax, reached out and grabbed a wingtip with one bloody hand and tore the wing off, sending the shrieking little man off the catwalk. He wheeled, and trumpeting wildly, charged those around the newcomers. His flailing ax crushed two more and he plucked a winged man off Ulysses' back and squeezed once, crushing the windpipe.

Suddenly, the survivors had run off toward the holes in the skin. They had had enough. But before they reached the holes, they stopped. And then they turned around with a wild exultant cry. Fresh Dhulhulikh were coming in through the holes.

185

Graushpaz screamed, "Dump the bodies off! Get the ship up where they can't reach us!"

He brushed by them on the walkway, almost knocking them off. He bent over, groaning with the pain of the spear in his back, and rolled the great bodies of his friends off the walkway. The dirigible's skin broke wherever the corpses fell through. More air whistled through the breaks but that did not matter. Air was whistling through a hundred holes.

Ulysses shouted at the others to throw the rest of the bodies off. They lifted up their dead comrades and dropped them over the rail, and then began on the bat-men. The reinforcements had continued to come in through the holes, but these were not the overwhelming number he had expected. There were about fifty. Added to those who had been here, sixty in all. Enough, however, to kill the thirteen survivors a dozen times over.

He ran down the walkway until he was past the hatch that led to the control gondola. He went to his right on a walkway to a defense station, and here he looked for a bomb. He planned on lighting the fuse and standing by a gas cell. The bat-men would see what he meant; they would understand his gestures. Either they got off or he threw the bomb against the cell, and they would all die instantly. Perhaps they were fanatical enough to let him do it, but he had only this one chance. Either way, if he threw the bomb, or if he refused to throw it at the last second, he and his men were doomed. But the bat-men just might be frightened enough to take off.

There were no bombs or rockets. They had all been expended.

That was just as well. Otherwise, some bat-man would have taken one, lit it, and all the attackers would have flown away before the dirigible went up in flames.

Ulysses whirled around and ran back on the walkway until he came to a girder. He leaped upon this and climbed up it until he stood on the framework at the base of a towering gas cell. He shouted until every one's head was turned toward him, and he slashed the cloth bag with his switchblade knife.

The rent was a tiny one. Hydrogen shrilled out of it and blew over his head. He stepped back and then pulled a box of matches out of his pocket. He helt it up so all could see what he had, and he made motions of striking it. He hoped that the bat-men knew what matches were. Otherwise, his gesture was meaningless.

186

There was a horrified cry from the winged men and his own people alike.

He yelled, "Dhulhulikh, leave this ship at once! Or I kill all of us! Now! You will burn like moths in a cooking fire!"

There was a crash. Graushpaz had fallen over the guard rail of the walkway and toppled onto the skin below. His body crashed through the paper-thin shell and was gone. He had paid his debt; he knew he had only a few minutes of life; he had jumped to give the ship more lift.

The people on the main walkway and the Dhulhulikh on the girders, struts and catwalks on the starboard side were frozen. They had not moved even when Graushpaz had let himself fall over the rail. They stared at his hands, at the match box and the match.

The Dhulhulikh commander wore a scarlet leather helmet, emblem of a rank equivalent to a colonel. He was crouched on a catwalk, a short thin spear in one hand, the other holding onto the guard rail, his face twisted. He was in an agony of indecision.

Then Awina stooped slowly and straightened up with a club in her hand. She threw it and it spun toward the commander and struck him in the face. He fell without a sound.

The others looked at each other. Their leader was dead, and the next in command had to make up his mind whether they should all die in a holocaust in the next few seconds or retreat. By refusing to leave they would ensure that the prime enemy would die also. But . . .

Ulysses could appreciate what they were going through. Their life was so short. Even if miserable, it was the only one they would have. And if they ran away, they could fight again. That cliché was as true and as persuasive as twenty million years ago.

Holding the match box in his left hand, Ulysses applied the tip of the match to the side of the box.

"One little flame!" he shouted. "That's all it takes! And we all burn to death!"

A Dhulhulikh wearing a greenish helmet, indicating a rank equivalent to a major, shouted back in a thin piping voice, "Then we all die!"

He waved the slender spear and said, "Attack them!"

Without waiting to see if he was being followed, he launched himself from the girder, wings flapping, at Awina. But the air was thinner here, and he did not glide at quite the correct angle. He struck the rail full in the middle and

Awina hit him over the head with her tomahawk. Fast on his heels came about twenty more, some of whom made the same error as their commander and slammed into the railing. The others were met with the weapons of the remaining twelve defenders, who stood back to back, six facing one way and six the other.

Ulysses, seeing that the rest of the Dhulhulikh had dropped quietly out of the holes in which they had come, put the match box in the pocket of his kilt and ran to help his people. He got there in time to pick up a spear and with it run a bat-man through the back. The survivors of the last attack, four Dhulhulikh, fluttered away and dived out through holes in the skin.

They were all so tired that they could barely move, and one Wufea slumped down and died. But Ulysses insisted that three repair the leak in the gas cell and the others come with him to the gondola. There would be no sleep for him until he got the *Blue Spirit* back to the land of the Neshgai.

As it turned out, he got several nights' sleep. The dirigible took fifteen hours to fight against the headwind while it slowly lost altitude. The crew looked for leaks and found four tiny ones but could not locate the others. By the time the airship had left The Tree, it was cruising in the lower levels of the great plant. This helped the speed in one way because there was no wind there. But the demands on the steersman were great. He had to sail between trunks and branches, under branches, between vine complex and branch, sometimes narrowly squeaking through. Ten miles past the last of The Tree, the dirigible settled down on the grassy plains and collapsed.

The survivors crawled out from under the great bulk with their supplies, after which Ulysses set fire to the ship to make sure that it did not fall into hostile hands. Not that he had seen any bat-men, but he was taking no chances. If there was one thing he did not want, that was the Dhulhulikh learning how to make dirigibles of their own.

They set out across the plains toward the mountains, on the other side of which was the country of the Neshgai. The other airships had gone on ahead long ago. Their motors, working against the wind, had tired swiftly, and the ships had to get back before the vegetable-muscle motors died of exhaustion.

Two days later, they saw the great cigar shape of a dirigible coming after them. As promised over the radio, the ship had returned for them after the motors had been rested.

Once the ship was in sight of the people on the ground, its radio went into action. Kafbi, a Vroomaw officer, spoke to Ulysses.

"We were lucky to get away, my Lord. The whole country is knee-deep in blood. While we were gone, the slaves and the Vroomaw rose against the Neshgai. All is chaos. The Neshgai hold some parts of the land and the rebels other parts. The other ships were attacked and destroyed on the field by the Neshgai, but we drove them off. Then we came after you. The slaves and the Vroomaw look to you to lead them to victory. They say that you are the god of the humans, and that you have been destined from time immemorial to free them and to rid the world of the elephant-headed monsters."

The Tree would hear of this soon enough, if it had not already heard. It would rally the Dhulhulikh and summon the hordes that lived on it and strike while the Neshgai and the humans were at each others' throats. If only the humans had put off their uprising until their greatest enemy had been conquered . . . but sentients did not follow cold logic, not very often, anyway. They lived in little opaque cells of time.

"The ruler and the high priest were killed," Kafbi said. "Shegnif, the Grand Vizier, now rules. His forces are holed up in the palace complex, and, so far, we have failed to take it."

Ulysses sighed. Twenty million years of bloodshed, pain and horror were behind him. And it looked as if more would be ahead of him if he were to live that long.

So be it.

He stood on the great plain with Awina by his side, her tail flicking across the calf of his right leg as she nervously waited for the airship to maneuver. Awina said, "My Lord, after we have conqured the Neshgai, what do we do?"

He patted her furry shoulder and said, "I like your optimism. *After* we have conquered, not *if*, right? I wonder what I would have done without you."

For a few seconds, he felt cold in the pit of his stomach. There had been so many times when she could have been killed, and he would have had to do without her.

He said, "There is no reason why the slaves and the Vroomaw have to decimate themselves in order to slaughter all the elephant-heads. I think that it would be far better for everybody if we had a truce and arranged for a new society, one in which Neshgai are neither masters nor slaves but equals with the humans. We need them as much as they need us in the battle against The Tree. We must think about compromise, Awina. It is not weakness to seek for compromise. Strength is in compromise and in alliance."

"The slaves and the Vroomaw want revenge," she said. "They have suffered for hundreds of years under their masters. Now they want to pay them back."

"I understand that," he said. "But the sufferers can forget the past, if they're offered a good future."

"They can?" she said.

"They have. In my time old enemies forgot the past wounds and indignities and even became friends."

"My Lord," she said, swaying so that her hip brushed against his, her tail lashing across his calf, and her eyes looking sidewise at him, "you will be talking of making a compromise with The Tree next! With our ancient enemy, the Destroyer!"

Who knows? he thought. *If the mind of flesh can meet with another mind of flesh, why not with a vegetable mind? Who knows?*

A.E.VAN VOGT

WINNER OF
THE HUGO AWARD
AND THE
NEBULA AWARD
FOR BEST
SCIENCE FICTION
NOVEL OF
THE YEAR

045922	Babel 17 Delaney 95c
062190	Big Time Leiber 95c
106229	City Simak 95c
166413	Dragon Masters Vance The Last Castle Vance 95c
167023	Dream Master Zelazny 95c
172619	Dune Herbert $1.25
196824	Einstein Intersection Delany 95c
249011	Four for Tomorrow Zelazny 95c
478008	Left Hand of Darkness LeGuin 95c
727826	Rite of Passage Panshin 95c
806927	This Immortal Zelazny 95c

Available wherever paperbacks are sold or use this coupon.